Praise for Ke

Death i.
a Phryne Fisher Mystery

"Told with Greenwood's typical aplomb, the story moves smoothly through several twists, lots of fabulous fashion, and interesting dollops of history. Enjoyable beach reading."
—*Canberra Weekly Magazine*

"Arch, witty, enchanting."
—*The Weekend Australian*

"A rich mixture of historical detail, local colour, careful plotting, and throwaway wit, as well as Phryne's excellent taste in clothes, alcohol, food, and men."
—*The Sydney Morning Herald*

"Fans of the sassy Miss Fisher will delight in her latest adventure... New readers who like a mix of crime and history will also be hooked."
—*The Courier-Mail*

"Entertaining and clever, *Death in Daylesford* is a charming and satisfying read."
—*Book'd Out*

"A quintessential Australian story... There is no doubt Phryne is back at her best. *Death in Daylesford* is a perfect addition to the series."
—*The Book Muse*

Praise for the Other Phryne Fisher Mysteries

"[T]he incomparable Phryne Fisher...beautiful, wealthy, sophisticated, but, above all, daring and intelligent..."

—*Library Journal*

"Anyone who hasn't discovered Phryne Fisher by now should start making up for lost time."

—*Booklist*

"Greenwood's stories are brief, but she holds her own, writing well-thought-out plots starring the intelligent, sexy, liberated, and wealthy Phryne."

—*Library Journal*

"Those who like their heroines resourceful and their mystery plots leavened with humor will read this with pleasure."

—*Publishers Weekly*

"Phryne's fans get everything they could possibly want from the long-running and ever more popular series: a fast-talking, tough heroine; an engaging cast of supporting players; a couple of really nifty mysteries; and plenty of fun."

—*Booklist*

★"A most charming, sexy, independent, and candid heroine; clever, literate dialog; and closely woven plotting will win immediate fans for this debut series."

—*Library Journal*, Starred Review

"An unforgettable character, with a heart as big as her pocketbook, a fine disregard for convention, and an insatiable appetite for life."

—*Denver Post*

"The engaging cast of familiar supporting characters—including Phryne's maid, Dot, and her Chinese lover, Lin Chung—will delight longtime fans."

—*Publishers Weekly*

"Those who long to revel in a glamorous if imperfect past will be satisfied."

—*Publishers Weekly*

"As usual, Greenwood populates the novel with an assortment of offbeat characters…and Phryne has plenty of opportunities to unleash her acid tongue and apply her razor-sharp wit."

—*Booklist*

"Phryne handsomely demonstrates once more that even a compulsion to explore every mystery that comes her way needn't interfere with her appetite for life."

—*Kirkus Reviews*

"The real star is Phryne with her Jazz Age fashions, devil-may-care attitude, and dry narrative wit."

—*Booklist*

"With Phryne Fisher, the indefatigable Greenwood has invented the character-you-fall-in-love-with genre."

—*The Australian*

"As always, the star of the show isn't the crime; it's Phryne herself. She's outspoken, bawdy, streetwise, elegant, and absolutely impossible not to love."

—*Booklist*

"Australian author Greenwood will delight fans of Miss Phryne Fisher, who indulges in 'Sherlockery' for Melbourne's citizenry when she's not indulging her passion for 'food, sleep, intellectual puzzles, clothes, and beautiful young men.'"

—*Publishers Weekly*

"It's *Underbelly* meets Miss Marple."

—*Emporium*

"Fisher is a sexy, sassy, and singularly modish character. Her 1920s Melbourne is racy, liberal, and a city where crime occurs on its shadowy, largely unlit streets."

—*Canberra Times*

"Impressive as she may be, Phryne Fisher, her activities, and her world are never cloying, thanks to Greenwood's witty, slightly tongue-in-cheek prose. As usual, it's a delightfully frothy, indulgent escape with an underlying bite."

—*Otago Daily Times*

Praise for the Corinna Chapman Mysteries

"Gentle, funny, and filled with eccentric characters. This mystery is a thoroughly entertaining read."

—*Woman's Day*

"There's plenty to sink your teeth into."

—*The Saturday Age*

★"Put on the coffee pot, whip up a batch of muffins (yes, recipes are included), and enjoy this thoroughly original tale. Strongly recommended for fans of offbeat mysteries."

—*Library Journal*, Starred Review

★"Lose all thought of New Year's diets, you who enter Australian author Greenwood's delectable Corinna Chapman cozies."

—*Publishers Weekly*, Starred Review

"Readers will find themselves charmed by the oddball characters and obligatory recipes."

—*Kirkus Reviews*

"A rich confection that nicely balances humor, villainy, and a puzzle."

—*Publishers Weekly*

"To the usual delightfully quirky characters, lovingly detailed descriptions of food and surprising mystery, Greenwood adds several appended medieval recipes."

—*Kirkus Reviews*

Also by Kerry Greenwood

The Phryne Fisher Mysteries

Cocaine Blues
Flying Too High
Murder on the Ballarat Train
Death at Victoria Dock
The Green Mill Murder
Blood and Circuses
Ruddy Gore
Urn Burial
Raisins and Almonds
Death Before Wicket
Away with the Fairies
Murder in Montparnasse
The Castlemaine Murders
Queen of the Flowers
Death by Water
Murder in the Dark
Murder on a Midsummer Night
Dead Man's Chest

Unnatural Habits
Murder and Mendelssohn
Death in Daylesford
A Question of Death: An Illustrated Phryne Fisher Treasury
The Lady with the Gun Asks the Questions
(*A Question of Death* revised and updated)

Corinna Chapman Mysteries

Earthly Delights
Heavenly Pleasures
Devil's Food
Trick or Treat
Forbidden Fruit
Cooking the Books
The Spotted Dog

MURDER in WILLIAMSTOWN

The NEW
PHRYNE FISHER
Mystery

KERRY GREENWOOD

Poisoned Pen
PRESS

Published by Poisoned Pen Press, an imprint of Sourcebooks
P.O. Box 4410, Naperville, Illinois 60567-4410
(630) 961-3900
sourcebooks.com

Originally published in 2022 in Australia by Allen & Unwin.

Cataloging-in-Publication Data is on file with the Library of Congress.

Printed and bound in the United States of America.
VP 10 9 8 7 6 5 4 3 2 1

To my beloved Belladonna

Prologue

Little Bourke Street was silent. A few yellow lamplit windows showed where midnight oil was being burned in the interests of commerce, but the street was generally as black as a coal pit. Uniformed police flitted into position like wraiths in the darkness. Above the sloping pagoda-like roofs of Chinatown a waxing moon shone down upon them. Then came the sound of a wooden crate being dropped inside a warehouse, and a muffled exclamation in an Oriental tongue. In the brick alley, the uniforms exchanged looks. Detective Sergeant Fraser blew his whistle. The door burst inwards under the blows of a sledgehammer, and the police moved in. Fraser, standing outside in the alley, heard the frightened screams and grinned. He did not follow his men inside. The contraband would be there; he had no doubt of it. There was no need to sully his hands with the actual search.

The moon disappeared behind a cloud, and still he waited. What was taking them so long? They knew where to look: the stuff would be in the silk bales. They must have found it by now, surely. He cursed under his breath. If you want a job done properly, he grumbled to himself, then do it yourself. He raised his truncheon and entered the warehouse. Stabbing beams of torch-light crisscrossed in the darkness.

'Well?' he demanded. 'What are you all waiting for? Christmas?'

There was a breathless pause, and then an electric light was switched on. The warehouse smelled overpoweringly of raw silk and heathen cooking. His men stared at him, unmoving. And standing in the rear, the detective sergeant saw a sight that thrilled his racing senses. This must be the criminal mastermind! The Fu Manchu of Little Bourke Street! The man, dressed in some foreign silk nightrobe in light blue, with a dark blue cap on his head, was speaking in a low, soothing voice to his three pigtailed cronies. They looked terrified, as well they might; but Fraser was perplexed to realise that their leader looked affronted rather than frightened.

'Hey, you! Chop Suey! You speak English?'

'Rather better than you do, Officer.'

To Fraser's further astonishment, the man not only spoke English; he spoke it with a posh accent. And he was young for a criminal mastermind. Probably no more than thirty, if that.

Having calmed his associates, the robed man folded his arms in his sleeves and glared at Fraser. 'Perhaps you can explain the reason for this unwelcome intrusion?'

'Are these your premises?' Fraser barked, attempting to seize the upper hand, which he seemed unaccountably to have lost.

'They are,' the man agreed.

'Well, what do you have to say for yourself, Chop Suey? Looks like you've got yourself in a spot of bother.'

'My name is not Chop Suey,' the man replied with a hint of distaste. 'It is Lin Chung. And I think you'll find, Officer, that *you* are in a great deal of trouble.'

Chapter One

The Honourable Phryne Fisher sat at her Bechstein grand piano, a frown marring her Dutch-doll features.

Around her, all was as it should be. Green, purple, and white walls formed the backdrop to her piano, its ebony polished to a high sheen. A sage-green sofa and two matching lounge chairs were arranged in a semicircle nearby. A tea table stood ready to bear champagne and canapés at a moment's notice. A generous wood-panelled fireplace held court beneath its capacious chimney. The floor was covered in a new sculptured carpet (supplied by the Lin family) in blue, grey, and crimson. Vases of red roses stood here and there in shapely *arts décoratifs* vases in improbable shades of blue, green, and purple, filling the parlour with their fragrance. From outside the window, a warm afternoon sun shed its radiant beams on her score: a copy of Cole Porter's 'Let's Misbehave,' which she had purchased in a music shop the previous week. She considered the sentiments apposite. It might well be that good girls went to heaven, but they had a dull enough time of it on earth.

She moved smoothly through the opening chords—G7, F9, G7, Cmaj7, C, and Gaug5—and the furrows on her brow deepened.

She paused, her fingers resting on the ivory keys. The fifth was by no means as augmented as it ought to be. The D sharp was as blunt as a butterknife, without the common courtesy to backslide to D natural; it had instead vanished into the tiny crack between the keys. And the bass notes seemed oddly unsure of themselves. For the present, there was nothing doing with the piano.

She closed the lid gently then rose from the stool and moved to recline on the sofa.

Mr. Butler appeared without the necessity for Phryne to ring, and enquired if madam would be wanting anything.

'A gin and tonic, if you would, Mr. B.'

Mr. B inclined his head very slightly, and melted away into the corridor, to be replaced by Dot, dressed in her customary shades of brown and with an expression of similarly glum hue.

Phryne waved her companion to a vacant chair. 'Dot, you look as if you've lost a winning lottery ticket in the wash. What's wrong?'

Dot blinked, sat herself down on the chair's edge, and placed her hands in her lap. She opened her mouth to speak, closed it again, and clasped her hands together. 'It's nothing, Miss,' she murmured.

Dorothy Williams had been Phryne's lady's maid, companion, and assistant since Phryne's arrival in Melbourne a year before. And what a year it had been! Dot had been kidnapped, terrorised, and driven much too fast in her employer's Hispano-Suiza. She did not regard herself as courageous, but she had bravely endured all these perils for the sake of Miss Fisher. She looked at her now with devotion. Phryne wore a stunningly beautiful emerald silk dress embroidered with a spray of multicoloured orchids, and Dot's downcast demeanour brightened momentarily at the sight before lapsing once again into gloom.

Phryne fixed her with a look of unusual severity. 'Come on, Dot, out with it. Something has upset you.'

Dot gazed at her employer solemnly. She reached into her reticule, drew out a piece of plain cardboard, and handed it to Phryne without comment. The uppermost side was blank. Phryne turned it over to find a single word in block letters clearly cut from a newspaper had been glued onto the card with mucilage. Phryne sniffed at the offending object. The glue was not quite dry, indicating that it had been assembled that very day. The message was brief and to the point. *REPENT!*

'Where did you find this, Dot?'

'It was left in the letterbox today. I went to check the mail because I'm expecting a letter from my aunt. And…' Dot gave an unhappy sigh and gestured to the card. Then she sat up. 'Though it wasn't addressed, Miss, so perhaps it was meant for a different house?' She looked at her employer hopefully.

Phryne laughed lightly. 'I'm sure it wasn't. It is no doubt directed at me and my immoral habits. But never mind, Dot. Sticks and stones, you know.' She leaned forward and patted Dot's hand in what she hoped was a soothing manner. 'If someone wants me to repent, with an exclamation mark thrown into the bargain, then they'll just have to wait along with everybody else, for I have no intention of doing so.' She put the card on the tea table, took the gin and tonic Mr. B had deposited there wordlessly, and reclined once more. 'If any more of them arrive, you just give them straight to me. If they become a nuisance, we can always ask Hugh Collins to look into it, now that he's been made a detective sergeant.'

'Oh, Miss, please don't tell Hugh!'

Phryne tilted her head. 'Why on earth not, Dot?'

Dot gave another heavy sigh. 'I think…' Her voice dropped to a whisper. 'I think Hugh might be going cold on the whole idea.'

Phryne looked at her in astonishment. 'He doesn't want to be a detective sergeant?'

'Not that, Miss.' Dot blushed with what looked like excruciating embarrassment. 'The marriage.'

'I remember the two of you had agreed that he should wait for a promotion before you married, Dot, but that was months ago now. Has something changed in the meantime?'

'Well, Miss, at first he was talking about setting a date later this year. But lately...' The corners of her mouth turned downwards. 'Lately I've hardly seen him. Just last week we had tickets to the theatre, but at the last moment he said he was busy with work and couldn't come.' Her brown eyes gleamed with a moistening dolour. 'I'm wondering if perhaps I'm not good enough for him, now that he's a detective sergeant.'

'Dot, look at me,' Phryne commanded. Her companion raised her head to meet her employer's green gaze with her glistening brown. 'You are quite certainly good enough for Hugh Collins,' she said firmly. 'You must dismiss any thought to the contrary immediately.'

'Yes, Miss,' Dot replied obediently.

Phryne took a thoughtful sip from her glass. 'But now that you mention it, Hugh has been making himself scarce lately. You haven't argued, have you?' An unwelcome thought suddenly struck Phryne between the eyes. 'Dot, is he still insisting that you should give up working for me after your marriage?'

Dot nodded, but far from encouraging further waterworks, her face was now registering resolute determination, with a side serving of mulish obstinacy. 'He tried, Miss, but I've told him that I'm going to keep on with you. At least until...' Dot coloured, as she generally did when corporeal matters obtruded into the conversation.

'Even when you are expecting, Dot, there's no reason for you to give up working if you don't want to,' Phryne said briskly. 'You are my right-hand woman. Hugh will have to learn to live with it. And I'm sure he will respect you more for sticking to your guns.'

'That's what I thought, Miss. Or rather, that's what I hoped, because I will be—sticking to my guns, I mean.'

Phryne nodded approvingly. 'Good for you, Dot! Now, don't you worry any more about Hugh. He's an honest and transparent young man, and I think you can safely assume that he is telling you the unvarnished truth when he says he's busy with work. Anything else in the letterbox?'

'Just this.'

It was a postcard from Phryne's friend and fellow pilot Bunji Ross, who, it seemed, had flown her biplane to Bendigo. Phryne read the scrawled message with a smile.

Dear Phryne,

Jolly little place they have here. Not so little, actually. A spiffing ride up, though I ran into some rough weather around the hills. For a good minute I couldn't see anything except rain, and rather too much of that. Did you know they have their own Chinatown here? Might be worth a visit, considering your interest. Anyway, pip-pip. Come for a spin with me some time?

Love,
Bunji

She turned the card over. The picture showed what was presumably the main street of Bendigo. A gigantic municipal edifice frowned in the centre, surrounded by gently rolling hills. Motor cars meandered along streets, and over all loomed a threatening sky. As a selling point for their township it seemed somewhat outré, but they were clearly very pleased with it. Phryne had never been to Bendigo, and it might well repay a visit.

'And there was this,' Dot continued, proffering a thick, creamy envelope that exuded expensive good taste. 'I haven't opened it, Miss, because it's for Ruth and Jane.'

Phryne took it from her and saw that *Misses Ruth and Jane Fisher, 221B The Esplanade, St Kilda* was inscribed on the front in matchless black copperplate calligraphy. She turned it over, and revealed the sender to be Mrs. M. Reynolds of 47 Banool Avenue, Kew. 'I have a strong suspicion this is a party invitation, Dot—I can feel the crinkled edge of a card inside. It looks as though Ruth and Jane have been accepted into high society.' She grinned at her companion. 'Well, that is a turn-up, is it not? Whether they will want to sally forth into said society is another question, but it is pleasing to know they will have the choice.' Phryne was exceedingly proud of her adoptive daughters, and the dazzling transformation they had undergone since she had extricated them from lives of dismal poverty and domestic servitude.

'Just as you say, Miss.'

At that moment, the girls in question could be heard approaching the front door. They appeared to be arguing at a steady *mezzo-forte*, which was unusual enough to cause Phryne to raise an eyebrow, relations between the girls being generally harmonious. The door opened, and was slammed shut with unnecessary force.

'Ruth? Jane?' she called. 'Come and say hello, if you would.'

The parlour door opened with commendable tranquillity, and the girls stood on the carpet before her. Phryne regarded their immaculate school uniforms: box-pleated navy skirts, navy jackets, the finest silk stockings money could buy, gleaming black leather shoes, and straw boater hats with silk ribbons around the brim. Not for the first time, Phryne wondered how many more children with miraculous talents laboured unseen and unappreciated in the slums. There was no doubt the girls had blossomed like rare orchids at Presbyterian Ladies' College.

'So how was school today, ladies? And what bone of contention has caused you to imperil the very fabric of my front portal?'

'Sorry, Miss Phryne.' Ruth was generally more forward in speech, and she took up the running at once. 'But it's our school! They're sending us to the Blind Institute!'

Phryne regarded her daughters with some surprise. 'So far as I am aware, you both possess excellent eyesight.'

Jane, standing a little to the rear, proceeded to expound further. 'It's the Good Works program, Miss Phryne. Ruth and I are being sent to the school for the blind. I think it will be most illuminating, if that isn't a contradiction, but Ruth doesn't agree.'

'Neither of us can read braille,' Ruth grumbled. 'I just don't see how we can be of any use there.'

'You really won't know until you go, Ruth,' Phryne interposed.

'And it's only for four days over two weeks,' Jane added.

'Then it will soon be over,' Phryne said consolingly. She patted the sofa. 'Now, come sit down, girls—something came for you in the post.'

The girls sat, and Phryne held out the envelope.

Jane opened it, and then she and Ruth stared at the contents in mystified silence.

'So?' Phryne prompted.

'It's a party invitation. To Frances Reynolds' sixteenth birthday.' Ruth and Jane exchanged a meaningful look. 'It's in two weeks' time.'

'And who is Frances Reynolds?' Phryne enquired. 'Am I right in thinking that she is one of the fashionable girls at school?'

'Yes, she is,' Jane answered. 'But I'm not sure we want anything to do with her. Ruthie? What do you think?'

Ruth coloured. 'Miss Phryne, she was the girl who bullied

Claire! She pretended to like her and then insulted her in front of all her friends!' She shook her head. 'If Claire hadn't felt so isolated at school, she might never have got herself embroiled with Tom.'

Claire's entanglement with Tom—a schoolmate of Tinker, the third of Phryne's adopted children—had led to her accidental death, the mystery of which had been unravelled by Phryne's charges.

'I see,' said Phryne. 'So you consider this Frances to bear some responsibility for Claire's death. Have you made your feelings known to her?'

'Oh, yes,' Ruth answered. 'I told her off. I called her a bully and a coward.'

Jane looked at her sister in surprise. 'I didn't know that, Ruth. That was very fine of you. Well done!' Jane frowned. 'It seems odd that she would then invite us to her party.'

'I know,' said Ruth, puzzlement writ large on her face. 'Frances's sixteenth is the party of the season. I never dreamed we'd be invited—and I'm not sure we should go. What do you think, Miss Phryne?'

'Well, you must decide for yourselves what to do, but it seems to me that the invitation is an extension of an olive branch—perhaps even an admission that you were right, Ruth, and she was wrong.'

The girls looked at each other and nodded. 'All right,' Ruth conceded. 'We'll think it over.'

With that, the girls rose and exited the room in the direction of the kitchen, where Mrs. Butler would have a jug of fresh lemonade and scones and jam ready for them.

'Well, Dot,' Phryne said, taking up the card urging her to repent, 'the letterbox was certainly full of surprises today.'

———

Dot returned to her room and prayed for Miss Phryne. Early in her employment, Dot had been so troubled by Phryne's amorous adventures that she had taken herself off to a distant church and confessed that she was labouring in a House of Sin. The anonymous priest had thereupon leaped to the conclusion that Dot was working in a brothel, and asked for further scandalising particulars. On receiving Dot's exposition—she had taken care not to reveal Phryne's name, as she had sworn never to reveal her employer's secrets—the priest had assured her that her employer was clearly a remarkable woman, and doubtless a vessel for Divine Grace regardless of her sins; that the latter were certainly not Dot's responsibility; and that Dot should pray for the salvation of Phryne's soul. Dot, whose conscience had been eased by the exchange, had set about this task assiduously.

Phryne, meanwhile, lay on the bed in her luxurious bedroom and considered the anonymous missive again. *REPENT!* She wondered who could possibly be responsible. Her neighbours? It seemed unlikely. She had lived on The Esplanade for nearly a year and she barely knew them. They seemed to be shy, retiring folks who tended their small gardens and politely discouraged intimacy. They had exhibited no interest whatsoever in Phryne and her household.

She lay back on her pillow and accepted some caresses from Ember, who rubbed his furry black head against her hand and purred like a small, well-satisfied locomotive.

While she had been quick to allay her companion's concerns, she would nonetheless be on the alert for any subsequent activity on the part of the unknown correspondent. She recalled Hugh Collins's account of a crime which had begun with anonymous letters and ended up in full-blown assault.

'I couldn't get the sergeant to take it seriously!' he had complained, his pink features alight with outrage. 'It turned out it was a lonely bloke who was too terrified of the girl down the street to ask her out. So he started leaving notes for her in the letterbox.'

'And she reported it to the police?'

'Yes, Miss. She didn't know who it was, but she was scared. I wanted to investigate, but the sergeant reckoned leaving notes wasn't a crime and I shouldn't waste my time on it. Then one day the fellow attacked the poor girl outside her house!'

'Was she all right?' Phryne asked, aghast.

'She fought back, Miss, you'll be pleased to hear, and her cries attracted some passers-by, who were able to detain him until we arrived. He was fined ten quid and given a stern warning to bring his toothbrush if he ever tried it again.' Hugh had shaken his head in frustration. 'If we'd only warned him off earlier, it could have nipped the whole thing in the bud.'

Phryne was only too aware that the police force as a rule took an indulgent view of lovesick young men and their unwanted attentions. Hugh's outrage was all the more commendable. Hugh at least realised that these matters could escalate if allowed to proceed unchecked. Still, a single message was probably nothing to worry about... But even as she had the thought, she felt a distinct pricking in her thumbs. Phryne had learned to trust her thumbs. She stared down at them, and decided that what they really needed to hold was a cocktail. Preferably a sidecar. She rang the bell for Mr. Butler.

In accepting her cocktail she had a sudden inspiration. 'Mr. B, have you received any impertinent anonymous messages lately?'

Mr. Butler's eyebrows rose. 'Yes, Miss. It so happens that there was one in the letterbox yesterday. I didn't want to trouble you with it.'

'And do you have it still?'

The butler inclined his head. 'I kept it, in case it might be needed as evidence.'

Phryne sipped from the glass and narrowed her eyes. 'Do please bring it to me, Mr. B.'

Mr. Butler withdrew, and returned promptly with his gleaming salver, which he presented with eyes slightly averted, as if offering her a deceased rodent.

Phryne accepted the card. *WHORE OF BABYLON* indeed! 'Thank you, Mr. B. You did rightly.'

'Have there been other similar communications, Miss?'

Phryne gave him a bright smile. 'I'm afraid so. But I'm hoping the correspondence will prove fleeting.'

'Very good, Miss. I will inform you if there are any further such offerings.'

He withdrew once more, leaving Phryne to move from sidecar into slumber.

Chapter Two

Frank Hammond was leaning back in his chair and staring out the window across the bay, smirking complacently, when a knock sounded on the door.

'Come in,' he called.

The door opened to reveal the expected visitor.

'Mr. Brown—good of you to come.'

'Well, Hammond, I have your envelope.'

Hammond took it from him and waved his guest into a chair. A quick glance through the envelope's contents produced a pleased smile. Not a new note among them. Ten one-pound notes, all well worn with constant commerce. He nodded at his visitor. Jet-black hair, regular eyebrows, smooth features. A big player, or so he imagined. Serious tickets on himself. 'Yes, that's quite satisfactory,' Hammond declared. 'And when will the next consignment be arriving?'

Mr. Brown gave a brief, sardonic grin. 'Not yet. Our clients—or some of their adherents, at least—have been quite troublesome. They have made a report to the police.'

'I see. And what have you done about that?'

Mr. Brown gave an unblinking stare. 'I have turned it to our mutual advantage.'

'Oh? Do explain.'

'I made an anonymous telephone call to a certain detective sergeant of quite exceptional stupidity. I suggested that he should raid certain premises in Little Bourke Street.'

'And did he?'

Brown smiled. 'Oh, yes. It was a most satisfactory fiasco. Nothing of substance was found; goods were damaged; the proprietor was furious; and the whole affair will be forgotten in a fortnight.'

'Just one of those embarrassing police blunders we keep hearing about?'

'Exactly. So we only need to wait a little longer.'

'Well done, Mr. Brown.' Hammond gave the briefest of grins. 'I'm sure we'll meet again.'

'I expect so.'

Mr. Brown departed, and Hammond stared out the window again, musing on the possibilities. If the customer base was causing trouble, they might also feel inclined to take action against Brown. In which case the goods might well be available afterwards, if a man were quick off the mark and spoke to the right people.

He rose, put on his overcoat, and decided to go in search of Wing, with whom—unbeknown to Mr. Brown—he, Hammond, already had a secret understanding. It was time this relationship were pursued more closely...

Chapter Three

Next morning, Phryne awoke early. She opened the window and inhaled the salt and seaweed odours of St Kilda beach. It was a bright day, and the still waters of the bay looked agreeably pleasant. She wrapped her yellow silk robe about her and proceeded down the stairs. The girls were up and about, and Phryne was surprised to see they were not dressed in their usual uniforms. Both wore white blouses with slate-grey skirts, dark blue jackets, stockings, school shoes, and their school hats.

'No school today?' she enquired.

Ruth shook her head. 'We're off to the Blind Institute.'

'Oh, I hadn't realised they meant for you to start immediately. Well, would you like a lift?'

There was taut silence. Jane's view of Phryne's driving was akin to Dot's: a ride in the Hispano-Suiza was an experience to be endured rather than enjoyed. But Ruth dearly loved it, and waved at everyone she passed. 'Very well,' Jane conceded with a quick smile. 'You shall have your ride in Jehu's chariot, Ruthie.'

'For she driveth furiously!' Ruth exclaimed, clapping her hands. Clearly the Second Book of Kings was currently featuring in the school's Bible study.

Phryne returned to her room to get dressed, casting a glance out the window as she did. It looked a pleasant enough day. And since she was up and about, she might go seeking adventures on her own behalf.

Dot knocked briefly, entered with a cup of coffee on a silver tray, and withdrew discreetly. Someone, probably Mr. Butler, had made the coffee thick enough to stand a spoon in, recognising that the lady of the house was unaccustomed to such an early hour. Phryne imbibed it gratefully. Under the influence of industrial-strength caffeine, she felt equal to any task the day might propose. After three cups, you could probably contemplate at least some of the Labours of Herakles.

Dressed in dark blue trousers, a white silk blouse, and a light magenta coat, Phryne returned downstairs. Without, the throaty exclamation of the Hispano-Suiza announced that Mr. Butler had cranked the mighty engine into uproarious life.

'Come on, girls.'

———

Phryne drove along the wide boulevard of St Kilda Road sedately enough. Ruth's face was flushed with excitement, and she waved to several pedestrians with her gloved hand as if she were royalty. Jane's hands were folded in her lap, and she looked down at the leather upholstery on which she was seated in tense contemplation. Phryne pulled up in front of the tall, wrought-iron gates of the Blind Institute precisely at nine.

'Here we are. I'll pick you up at three-thirty. Have fun!'

'Thank you, Miss,' the girls chorused.

Jane and Ruth alighted to an enraptured audience of purple-clad schoolboys gadarening their way into Wesley College next door. Phryne waved to the schoolboys and accelerated away.

Now, whither should she proceed? She had no desire to return home as yet. She pulled over to the side of the road in front of an enormous row of hydrangeas and gazed north. At the end of the straight road she could see the half-built acropolis that was to be the Shrine of Remembrance. Phryne had mixed feelings about this. The less she thought about the Great War, the happier she would be. But Sir John Monash had insisted upon it, and in deference to his wishes, Phryne had contributed ten pounds to his public subscription.

She set off towards it, inclining her head as she drove past its mock-Hellenic pillars. The general was not visible today among the toiling labourers; but since he was in charge of the construction, there was an excellent chance that, once built, it would stay built. He had been a distinguished civil engineer until the war, but he had volunteered for the army. Phryne was extremely glad that he had. He and Allenby between them had managed to devise methods of waging war, and winning battles, without slaughtering half their own men in the process. She drove onwards and into the city centre. She turned right up the slope of Collins Street, changing gears as she passed Madame Partlett's boutique. If the girls decided to accept their party invitation, she would take them to Madame for new dresses.

She was momentarily tempted by the prospect of the Windsor, a couple of blocks away on Spring Street, but it was far too early for lunch. And breakfast, though lavish, was only for residents. Turning instead onto Russell Street, she considered the university; she had a friend there, after all. She smiled, remembering how she had helped to recover the *Hours of Juana the Mad*, a prayer book belonging to the university which had gone missing in mysterious circumstances. The culprit had been Jeoffrey Bisset, lecturer in classics and English. His motives for the book's removal had been purely altruistic, and thus Phryne had kept his secret. Perhaps she should drop by on the off chance he was about. She remembered, though, that Jeoffrey had complacently let on that his lectures were mostly in the afternoon. Apparently students—and staff—in classical studies liked their beauty sleep, and preferred to start their working day first thing in the afternoon.

She swung down Lonsdale Street to Elizabeth Street, eventually leaving the car in Royal Parade, next to University High School, whose scholars ogled it through the cyclone wire fence with some considerable fascination.

The cloisters at the University of Melbourne might have done justice to Westminster Abbey, save for two things. First, they were built of yellow sandstone rather than the darker hues of that place of serial coronations; and second, the hallowed portals hereabouts lacked the deep indentations caused by a thousand years of devout footsteps. But jolly impressive cloisters they were nevertheless, and Phryne admired them anew. Scholars in academic gowns passed her, and looked with interest at the elegant young woman wearing somewhat shocking blue trousers with her white silk blouse and light magenta coat. She smiled broadly at everyone, following the general principle that she had every right to be anywhere she wished. Thus far it seemed to be working.

The English Department was still where she remembered it, and she presented herself at the front desk, where a middle-aged secretary with her hair in a severe bun seated behind her Underwood typewriter gave her a sharp look. 'May I help you?' she enquired.

'I'm looking for Jeoffrey Bisset, if he's around.'

As if on cue, the man himself emerged through a nearby doorway. On seeing Phryne, his face lit up. 'It's all right, Marjorie—this is the Honourable Phryne Fisher. Lady detective and all that. Very definitely One of Us.' He held up a sheaf of handwritten notes. 'Look, Phryne, I have to deliver a lecture on the Lake Poets this morning as a favour to a colleague who's come down with something. If you'd like to come, I could take you to Naughtons for lunch afterwards.'

Phryne nodded graciously. 'By all means, let us do that.'

———

The lecture theatre smelled of well-aged wood and metaphysical boredom. Phryne ascended the wide stairs and took a seat, ignoring the astonished looks from the undergraduates. She was no particular fan of Wordsworth, but the opportunity to see Mr. Bisset in action was too good to pass up. She recalled the undeniable attraction she had felt for the man during his madcap escapade. As Jeoffrey proceeded through his notes, Phryne watched the students with an indulgent eye. Some, especially the young women, dutifully filled their notebooks with Jeoffrey's pearls of wisdom. Several of the younger men seemed to be dozing. One began to snore, and had his elbow jogged by his colleague.

'A few pages in to Wordsworth's *Prelude,*' Jeoffrey was saying, 'you begin to realise that the man expected an awful lot from the humble adjective. And to be honest, I do find the whole thing a bit of an effort. And yet—yes, Mr. Jacobs? You have a question?'

A long-haired youth with spectacles who had been sitting to Phryne's left rose unsteadily to his feet and began to orate. 'Mr. Bisset, do you have any comment to make on how these passionate young poets began all afire with revolutionary zeal, and then—with the single exception of Lord Byron—turned their coats? Wordsworth finished his life as the postmaster of Westmoreland, writing pompous reactionary nonsense. Would you care to express an opinion on this?'

The boy sat down abruptly and an awed hush fell over the

assembly. This was apparently strong stuff in an English lecture. All eyes turned to Jeoffrey Bisset, who folded his arms and smiled.

'I am glad you asked that, Mr. Jacobs. Lord Byron was always the odd fellow out, you know. If the others had stayed pro-France, then he would have thrown in with the Tories. Although I would suggest that Byron's heroic struggles for Greece do place him above criticism. Wordsworth, Shelley, Southey, and Coleridge? The *ancien régime* was Europe's disgrace. Everyone welcomed their downfall until it dawned on them that Napoleonic France was a great deal worse than anything the Bourbons could have dreamed up. We thought the Great War was bad—well, the war with France lasted twenty-two years, with millions dead and whole countries devastated. Bad as the Tories were, there was simply no alternative. And several times during that titanic struggle, England stood alone against the monstrous genius who held all Europe in his iron grip.'

Jeoffrey paused. 'When you are all struggling through Wordsworth's *Prelude*, I would like you to remember that he might well have been a pompous old fool for most of his long life; but he also wrote this.' Jeoffrey paused for effect, then began to recite from memory, his voice rising in pitch to fill the cavernous theatre.

> *'It is not to be thought of that the flood*
> *Of British freedom, which, to the open sea*
> *Of the world's praise, from dark antiquity*
> *Hath flowed, "with pomp of waters, unwithstood,"*
> *Roused though it be full often to a mood*
> *Which spurns the check of salutary bands,*
> *That this most famous Stream in bogs and sands*
> *Should perish; and to evil and to good*
> *Be lost for ever. In our halls is hung*
> *Armoury of the invincible knights of old:*

We must be free or die, who speak the tongue
That Shakespeare spoke: the faith and morals hold
Which Milton held.—In everything we are sprung
Of Earth's first blood, have titles manifold.'

There was another tremendous moment of silence. Then, one by one, the students began to applaud. Even Jacobs joined in, and Phryne herself did too, until the sound became a wall of thunder. Jeoffrey Bisset gave a slow, satisfied nod.

The remainder of the lecture was anticlimactic, but the atmosphere in the theatre had lost its air of torpor. Students scribbled notes furiously, Jeoffrey pointed out intriguing nuances the students had not discovered for themselves, and thus the time passed. When the clock on the wall struck twelve, Jeoffrey gathered up his notes, and the students filed out. Phryne walked down the stairs to Jeoffrey, still standing behind the podium.

'Well, Phryne? What did you think?'

Phryne grinned at him. 'That was superb, Jeoffrey.'

'Why, thank you. And now, may I offer you lunch?'

'No, Jeoffrey—I will offer *you* lunch. You deserve it. I will never look at Wordsworth in quite the same way again.'

'My colleague may not forgive me, but I don't care. There's no point pretending Wordsworth's collected works are anything but a Sisyphean struggle. But he really did have his moments.'

'I take it you know the young rabblerouser Jacobs?'

Jeoffrey led the way through the cloisters. 'Oh, yes. He's in my Latin class. He's a fine young man, really. An excellent scholar. I can forgive the Bolshevik opinions of anyone who can write proper Latin poetry. Mind you, it's a bit too Catullus for my liking.'

'You don't admire Catullus?'

Jeoffrey pulled a face, as if tasting a sour lemon. 'Not really, no. An awful little schoolboy at heart, you know. I rather sympathise with poor Clodia. I doubt she deserved the terrible things he wrote about her.'

And this, Phryne considered, was a most creditable view of that much-wronged woman.

Jeoffrey led Phryne through some rather excellent gardens. There were limes, elms, planes, and a number of others which all spoke more of Europe than the Antipodes. 'They've heard about planting local trees but thought better of it,' he explained. 'Eucalypts are better suited to the Australian climate, but there's just one problem with them.'

'What's that?' Phryne asked.

Jeoffrey grinned. 'When they feel like dropping the odd branch to conserve water, they'll drop it anywhere—including on your roof, if it happens to be underneath. So the English trees aren't such a silly idea after all, as long as they remember to keep them watered. Now this, on our left, is the conservatorium. It's called Melba Hall, after Dame Nellie. It's not at all bad, as a concert hall. And the classrooms are in there as well.'

'Is it a good music school?' It would want to be, Phryne thought, regarding the square, stone building with disfavour; as architecture went, it lacked a great many things.

'Actually, it is. I was a cathedral singer, you know, so I can tell good music from bad. They recently had their first blind graduate, George Findlay. He lectures at the Blind Institute now.' Before Phryne could note the coincidence of having come from depositing her daughters there that very morning, he waved his hand towards Royal Parade, which they were approaching, and said, 'Naughtons is just across the way. They do a very decent steak.'

They paused, while a red rattler tram trundled down the middle of the road and ground to a halt, decanting a variety of folk, most of whom headed into the university grounds.

The tram trundled northwards, and they completed the crossing.

'Well, here we are.'

Naughtons turned out to be a rather superior establishment in white-faced stone. An agreeable miasma of beer and roasted meat wafted out to greet them as Jeoffrey escorted Phryne through the door marked *Ladies Lounge* in gold serif.

As Jeoffrey went to fetch their drinks, a smart waitress in black and white shepherded Phryne to a polished dark wood table, and she sat and looked about her. At the next table, two young men were paying court to a sweet-looking girl. The men wore grey suits, clean shoes, garish ties, and unconvincing adulthood, and gulped at odd moments from tankards of beer. The girl was apparently paying close attention to their every utterance, while her lemon squash remained before her, untouched. She caught Phryne's eye for an instant and winked.

Phryne smiled inwardly. The girl was presentable-looking, though dressed demurely enough to pass muster at a vicarage tea party. Female undergraduates were still in the minority, and this did offer them scarcity value. Phryne put the boys' ages at around nineteen. The girl was probably seventeen. You weren't supposed to sell liquor to anyone under the age of twenty-one, but Phryne could see the general sense in the police turning a myopic eye. The undergraduates would be Naughtons' prime source of custom. As long as they behaved themselves...well.

'I hope you like beer?' Jeoffrey sat himself down and placed a full glass on a coaster near Phryne's right hand. His own glass had already experienced an ebbing of the tide.

'Indeed.' In pursuit of romance she had imbibed far more venomous drinks than Victoria Bitter.

They ordered steaks, as seemed to be the custom, and chatted of this and that as they ate—until Jeoffrey set down his fork and gave her a nervous look. 'Phryne, I wondered if I could persuade you to have dinner at my house sometime?'

In seeking him out, Phryne had been rather hoping such an offer might be made. Yes, she had Lin Chung, of course. But Lin was a busy man these days. His wife, Camellia, was expecting, and Lin was hardly the sort of man to delegate care of his beloved wife to his domestic staff. And as head of the family firm he had many responsibilities.

'By all means, Jeoffrey. When were you thinking?'

Jeoffrey lowered his voice. 'Well, how about tomorrow night?'

Phryne raised an eyebrow. 'Midweek?'

'Well, I have a full dance card most days, but I've managed to keep Thursdays free this term, which means that on Wednesday nights I can, er, stay up late.'

Phryne, who rarely had a pressing need to rise early and was not averse to late nights, replied, 'Tomorrow would be splendid, then.'

Jeoffrey reached into his wallet and handed Phryne a plain card on which was inscribed: *Jeoffrey Bisset, 27 Lark Lane, Williamstown W16, Tel. AW 873.* 'Would six thirty suit you?'

'Certainly.' Phryne stowed the card in her purse.

She refused his polite offer to view the *Book of Hours* again and returned to the Hispano-Suiza, which had by now accumulated its customary audience of rapt schoolboys. She waved at them as she drove away up Royal Parade.

She returned home along the waterfront of Port Melbourne, which never ceased to charm her. The bay wore a different colour every time she saw it, and today under skies turned cloudy it was gunmetal grey. Two or three yachts patrolled offshore in the breeze, and she smiled to herself. It had been a good day so far. Pausing at an intersection, she checked her wristwatch and, seeing it was now twenty minutes to three, realised there would not be time to return home. She turned left onto Fitzroy Street and headed for St Kilda Road.

Chapter Four

'Well, Fraser? I have read this...report of yours.' The Commissioner waved a dismissive hand at a sheaf of notes and grimaced, rather as if he had discovered a family of rodents nesting in his morning newspaper. 'Do you have any further comments to make, now we're alone together?'

The Commissioner wasn't happy. He was sitting behind his own desk, and he hadn't even asked Fraser to be seated. The latter made a movement towards the chair opposite, but caught the Commissioner's frosty glare and remained standing. The Commissioner was rumoured to possess a keen sense of humour. Of this there was not the slightest vestige in the pink, perspiring face. His piercing eye looked like it could open the most obdurate of oysters by sheer willpower alone.

Fraser twisted his hat between his fingers. 'Well, sir, I was acting on information received.'

'I see. And does your informant have a name?' The Commissioner flicked through the typewritten sheets before him and raised his eyebrows. 'No, I see he doesn't. So on the basis of an anonymous tip-off, you called in half-a-dozen uniforms, on overtime pay, and raided a warehouse in Little Bourke Street belonging to a completely innocent man.'

'But sir—'

The Commissioner raised a large hand to forestall further speech. 'No excuses, Fraser! You're suspended for a week. Without pay. Now get out of here.'

Chapter Five

When Phryne had driven off, Jane and Ruth followed the curving pathway towards the tall red-brick building which announced itself as the Royal Victorian Institute for the Blind. No one was about, and the girls exchanged a look of apprehension. 'I hope this is the right place,' Ruth whispered, taking her sister's hand.

'It must be,' Jane said. 'There can't be two Blind Institutes on St Kilda Road.'

She pushed open the building's heavy front door. In the foyer stood a tall woman of thirty-odd years, dressed in grey with her hair pulled back in a tight bun. 'You must be Ruth and Jane from Presbyterian Ladies' College,' she said. 'I'm Miss Thomas, one of the music teachers here. Mr. Stanus Hedger, our director, is expecting you. He said I'm to take you to see him.'

She led them along a passageway which smelled strongly of wood polish, phenyle disinfectant, and what appeared to be perfumed wax. Jane, whose sense of smell was very sensitive, detected overtones of perfumes. Was this hair oil? Frowning portraits of worthies lining both walls looked down on these interlopers.

Halfway along the corridor, Miss Thomas stopped and

knocked on a closed door. 'Mr. Hedger? Our visitors from the ladies' college are here.'

'Come in, come in,' came a voice from beyond.

Miss Thomas turned to Ruth and Jane and, as if sensing their nervousness, assured them, 'He's very kind really.'

She opened the door and the girls filed in. Mr. Hedger rose from behind his enormous wooden desk. He was tall, Jane noted, and slender. What hair he had (there was not a great quantity of it) was brown, as were his eyes.

'Welcome, ladies. Your school has given me excellent reports of you both and it's a pleasure to have you here. Now, which one of you is Jane?'

Jane raised a tentative hand.

'Ah, I believe you're a whiz with maths and science? You'll be able to help out there. We keep the boys and girls apart, of course, except at mealtimes, so you'll be working with the girls' classes. And Ruth, they tell me your passion is cooking—would you be willing to help cook lunches for the students?'

'Of course, sir,' Ruth replied.

Hedger gave them both a steady look. 'Now, please remember that while our students won't be able to see you, they can hear you, so I don't want any reports of either of you talking out of turn.' His gaze turned hawk-like for a terrifying moment. 'But I'm sure I can rely on your discretion. Now, Miss Thomas has volunteered to supervise you, so I'll be leaving you in her capable hands.' He gestured to where Miss Thomas stood waiting by the door, then gave a nod to indicate that they were dismissed.

As the girls followed Miss Thomas along the corridor, sounds of music emerged from behind locked doors. From one room came the sounds of a piano accompanying beautiful female voices blending in harmony. From another the wailing of saxophones could be discerned. At the end of the seemingly interminable passageway, Miss Thomas stopped, turned to the girls with a smile, then opened the door. An agreeable smell of baking scones filled their nostrils, and for the first time since their arrival, Ruth relaxed slightly.

The dining room was big enough for at least eighty people. Wooden tables and long benches were arrayed in four long lines. A large shuttered window in the back wall was open, and the scent of eggs and bacon hung heavily in the atmosphere. Beyond the window was a kitchen, currently tenanted by a tall, slender young woman in a mob cap and apron. She took no notice of the visitors, and busied herself with hessian bags of what appeared to be oranges and apples.

Miss Thomas took them to one of the small wooden tables and told them that she would be back shortly.

Jane and Ruth sat opposite each other on the long, low benches and exchanged a look.

'Mr. Hedger's a bit overpowering, isn't he?' Ruth suggested.

'He looked positively fierce when he warned us against talking about the students,' Jane agreed.

Miss Thomas slipped onto the bench beside Ruth. 'You mustn't mind Mr. Hedger's abrupt manner,' she said. 'He's a kind man, really—just very protective of the Institute. Now, I have written out your schedules for today, but the first lesson of the day is always music for those that can, and manual for those who can't, so I've asked the cook to serve us tea and scones to begin with—something to sustain you before you start. Strange places can be a bit intimidating, can't they?'

Jane smiled gratefully. 'That was very thoughtful of you, Miss Thomas. This building is rather oppressive, isn't it?' She was thinking of the cavernous ceilings and the portraits glaring down from the walls of the long corridor. Then, not wishing to sound critical, she asked, 'What sort of manual do the non-musicians do?'

'We make things here, and sell them to the public,' Miss Thomas explained. 'Wicker baskets, for example. The boys and girls are so clever. I'm sure I couldn't make a basket someone would buy, and I have two working eyes. They do it all by touch.'

'The music sounded wonderful,' put in Ruth. 'But I was surprised by the jazz.'

'That's our saxophone quintet. They get hired out for parties, you know, and they bring in a lot of money. But they're all adults, from the Institute.' Seeing the girls' blank look, Miss Thomas explained, 'The Institute is actually separate from the school. It's on the east side of the building. Mr. Hedger is in charge of both. We look after the blind all their lives, here—although many of the adults live in their own homes and merely come here to work, or for music practice. It's a wonderful place now.'

The plain young woman they had earlier spied in the kitchen appeared carrying a wicker tray with a teapot, three cups, a small blue milk jug, and a wooden sugar bowl. She served them quickly, smiled briefly, bobbed a perfunctory curtsy, and tiptoed back to her kitchen without having spoken a word.

Their tea was strong, black, and fiercely aromatic. But the scones were feather-light, and slathered with generous quantities of butter and strawberry jam. Suddenly famished, the girls proceeded to devour all the scones between them, while Miss Thomas sipped at her tea and smiled indulgently. Only when they had finished did their supervisor lay two handwritten sheets on the wooden table. Jane scanned the one given to her.

Second period: senior mathematics
Third period: intermediate mathematics
Fourth period: music theory

Ruth, meanwhile, discovered that she was going to be in the kitchen all day. 'I'm sorry about that, Ruth, but I'll do my best to think of some suitable classrooms for you when you return on Thursday. Are either of you musical?'

Both girls shook their heads. They sang in the main school choir, as did all the students, but neither had shown any great aptitude for it.

Miss Thomas shrugged. 'It doesn't matter. All the music scores are braille, in any case, so unless you can read it they won't be any use to you. So will you be all right in the kitchen for today, Ruth?'

'Oh, yes.'

'Good. Now, the teachers probably won't let you take any classes yourself, Jane, but you'll be able to help the girls out with their work. And there was one other thing you might help with, if you're willing…'

'I do want to be useful while I'm here,' Jane assured her.

Miss Thomas looked pleased. 'Well, I was thinking that, seeing as you are good with numbers, you might spend some time with Mr. Blake, our bookkeeper. He does his best, of course, but…'

The girls waited while Miss Thomas wrestled with what was presumably her conscience. Then she leaned forward and, lowering her voice, said, 'I probably shouldn't be telling you this, but I think—I fear—that there's something amiss there. Before I became a music teacher I used to work as a bookkeeper myself. I rather enjoyed it, I have to say, and I offered to help Mr. Blake out myself. But Mr. Hedger is very loyal to all his staff, and he said I should just let the poor bloke get on with his job.'

'I presume by "something amiss" you mean embezzlement,' Jane said matter-of-factly.

Ruth gasped, even though she was used to her sister's plain speaking.

'Oh!' Miss Thomas looked startled. 'I didn't mean to suggest anything so serious as that. It's just that I read the last annual report, and I can't help thinking that we're spending more than we should be. It wouldn't surprise me at all if the poor man's got the accounts in a muddle. And since you're so clever with numbers, Jane, I thought he might welcome your assistance.' There was an awkward pause before she continued, 'The thing is, I wouldn't want Mr. Hedger to know, since he's already asked me not to interfere with Mr. Blake's work.'

'You don't have to tell Mr. Hedger, do you?' Jane said. 'You're the one in charge of drawing up our schedules.'

Miss Thomas nodded. 'You're right—I am. Well, that's what I'll do. So on Thursday, Jane, you can go to the office. I'll tell Mr. Blake myself.' She ran her hands down her angular sides and sighed. 'We're always short of money. Mr. Sutherland—he's our chairman—has to go cap in hand to every council in the metropolis because the government cannot make their minds up to do anything to help us. It's a scandal. But it would be a bigger scandal if it turned out we were wasting money through sheer inattention to detail.' She rose to her feet. 'Well, the first period will be ending soon. I'll show you to your classroom, Jane. Ruth, you can stay here with Hester.'

———

Ruth entered a kitchen smelling of egg and bacon and porridge—which argued a moderately generous provision for the inmates—and introduced herself to the cook. In her own domain, the formerly silent young woman was far more expansive, and Ruth found her to be a kindred spirit. Hester was full of praise for Mr. Hedger, who, she said, had decreed that at mealtimes every table was to be decorated with vases of flowers. '"They may not be able to see them," he said, "but they can smell them. I don't want our charges thinking they're just an inconvenience. I want them to feel as if they are valued guests!"

That was what he said. And we grow all our own flowers here in the gardens. We have stocks in summer, and they are wonderfully fragrant. This week we have salvias. The blue flowers don't smell, but the leaves are wonderfully fragrant.'

Ruth agreed that this was a fine initiative on the director's part.

They set about making piles of sandwiches that were a mixture of salad and cheese, corned beef and pickle, and egg with mustard. Again, this was Mr. Hedger's idea.

'I wasn't here before his time,' Hester told Ruth, 'but my predecessor told me that the food here used to be horrible. And the blind weren't even allowed knives and forks, you know. Just spoons, so there was no chance they would cut themselves. Mr. Hedger put a stop to all that.'

Laying out all the cutlery and plates—cheap china, but with no chips or cracks showing—took until half past twelve. Just as Ruth and Hester set out the last of the vases, a deep bell resounded through the building. 'And now we get to rest,' Hester told her. 'The teachers will supervise lunch. Come along. We can go back to the kitchen now. And may I say, Ruth, you have worked like a Trojan today. Well done!'

———

Jane found that the senior mathematics class was quite small: only thirteen students instead of the thirty-something she was used to in her own classes. The girls' uniforms looked a bit drab—grey dresses to the knee and calf-length woollen stockings—but the fabric seemed decent enough. The only decoration was white butterfly collars worn over the dresses.

Mr. Walker, the teacher, was a gaunt man who paced the room like a restless tiger in a zoo. He had an irritation on the side of his face which he scratched constantly, and he looked sidelong at the girls with what Jane first decided was a predatory manner. After twenty minutes or so, she revised her diagnosis. The man was clearly in discomfort—probably eczema—and would not have been able to teach the sighted, who would have noted his contortions. So he was permitted to teach mathematics to those who could not see his continual fretting. He had introduced Jane to the class in a kindly enough voice. 'Please feel free to ask Miss Jane if you need assistance,' he had said. 'She does not read braille, but she is an accomplished mathematician.'

The lesson was algebra, at which Jane excelled, and Mr. Walker had provided Jane with a copy of the textbook in plain English, so she was able to follow. At first, no one sought her help, but on scanning the room, she noted three of the girls were struggling with their work. She consulted with Mr. Walker, who permitted her to teach the three girls at the back of the room, pitching her voice low enough so as not to disturb the other students.

'In the first example, you should remove z,' she explained, 'and you will be left with a simple two-variable equation.' As the girls set to work, it occurred to Jane to wonder whether her school's Good Works program really did benefit the Institute. Without the ability to read braille, Jane was not able to provide much assistance to her classes. Ruth would be more help in the kitchen, she supposed, but presumably they would manage without her, since their four days of volunteering would hardly make a difference. So what were they doing here? The only conclusion she could reach was that Mr. Hedger wanted the work of the Institute—and his charges, for that matter—to be visible to the world of the sighted. Then, perhaps, it might be that much easier to persuade the government to provide appropriate funding. She would wait till lunchtime and ask Ruth what she thought.

———

Lunch was something of a revelation. Ruth stood in the kitchen doorway watching as the students flocked in, leading each other by the arm and touching the walls at intervals. The noise of excitable conversation rose to a clamour, until Mr. Hedger entered the room and held up a little bell, which he tinkled. Conversation ceased at once, and Mr. Hedger intoned the briefest of graces, flicked his restless eyes around the tables, nodded with what was probably satisfaction, and stumped out of the room, leaving the door fully open behind him.

Behind Ruth, Hester whispered, 'Doors here must be either fully shut or fully open. Usually they're open, you see.' Ruth saw at once. When you relied largely on touch, a half-open door was a hazard.

Jane entered the room, and Ruth went over to join her at one of the wooden tables.

'So how was your morning, Janey?' Ruth asked, selecting an egg sandwich.

'Not what I was expecting. I've been wondering why we're here, to be frank.' Jane bit into a corned beef sandwich. 'I'm not sure how much use I can be, unless Miss Thomas is right about the problem in the office. You?'

'Well, I've been useful, I'd say. I've never made lunch for so many people!'

There were a good sixty-odd students in the hall, all talking volubly as they ate.

Hester brought one of the students forward. 'Girls, this is Jennifer Barnes. May she sit with you?'

'Of course!' Ruth exclaimed. 'I'm Ruth, and to my left is my sister, Jane.'

Jennifer sat herself down without much difficulty. The girl looked plain enough in her school uniform, but there was a neat elegance about all her movements.

When she was settled, Jane looked at her enquiringly.

'Jane? I believe you are looking at me with a question on your lips?' Jennifer asked in a low, melodious contralto, her sightless eyes turned to Jane.

'Why, yes I am.' Jane regarded the girl with frank curiosity. 'I gather that you asked Hester to bring you over, and I was wondering if you had a special reason for wanting to meet us. But I am curious as to how you knew I was looking at you.'

'It is quite simple.' Jennifer folded her hands together. 'Humans can sense when someone is looking at us. It's a sixth sense.'

'I see,' Jane answered. 'Though as far as I'm aware, there is no science behind that.'

'There is a good deal science does not understand,' the girl responded.

'I won't argue with that,' Ruth broke in. 'So tell me: why did you ask to meet us?'

The girl gave a brief, dazzling smile. 'I know you are the daughters of the famous Miss Fisher, that's why.'

'I'm surprised you've heard of her,' Ruth exclaimed, then put her hand over her mouth. 'Oh, I'm sorry. That was a rude assumption, wasn't it?'

Jennifer inclined her head, but she didn't appear to have taken offence. 'Perhaps, but I know it was said without malice. Many of us here take a keen interest in the world outside, and Miss Fisher is a renowned warrior for justice.' She paused. 'So you are Miss Fisher's adopted daughters, is that right? And you live with her in her home? What's that like?'

'Well, it's on The Esplanade, by the beach.'

'Is it very grand?' their interlocutor wanted to know.

Jane stepped in and sketched out the architectural plan: three up, three down, spacious kitchen, parlour, servants' quarters, three bathrooms, and a shed at the back for Tinker.

'Is Tinker your dog?'

Ruth laughed. 'Oh no. He's from Queenscliff. Miss Phryne adopted him too. I think he feels rather outnumbered by all the women in the house, so he prefers the shed. He doesn't mind having to share with Molly.'

The sightless eyes opened wide. 'Is Molly adopted too?'

It was Jane's turn to laugh. 'No, Molly is the dog!'

'She was our dog originally,' Ruth explained, 'but she loves Tinker best. We don't mind. And we still have Ember, our black kitten.'

'It must be wonderful to have pets,' Jennifer said dreamily. 'We're not allowed to here. But one day I'll have a house of my own. And I shall have a cat and a dog, and a piano... Do you have a piano?'

'We do, but it's out of tune at the moment. Miss Phryne was complaining about it last night.'

Jennifer's lips parted for a moment. 'Do you know we tune pianos here? It's one of the services we offer. I would be happy to attend to it, if you'd like.'

'We can certainly mention it to Miss Phryne,' Ruth said.

They continued eating and chatting until a bell sounded. Jennifer rose uncertainly and extended an arm. 'Would you mind?'

Ruth took her arm and guided her towards the corridor, where they encountered Miss Thomas. 'Thank you, Ruth. I will take Jennifer from here.'

Ruth returned to the table to find Jane consulting her schedule. 'I have intermediate mathematics and then music theory,' she said. 'I'll come back here to collect you after fourth period.' And she hurried off, leaving Ruth to help Hester clear up.

———

Jane was able to help a few girls with their mathematics in third period, but she doubted she would have much to offer a class in music theory. There was little enough she could do on the subject in an ordinary classroom, let alone one where the students read in braille. But she could hand out music scores and generally assist Mr. Findlay, whom Jennifer had told her was a superb pianist.

Mr. Findlay in person was a small, neat individual. His sightless eyes were opaque, but he was—well, *dapper* was the word, Jane thought. Dapper from his shiny black shoes to his beautifully tailored dark blue suit. He was young, not much more than twenty, and he exuded an air of self-contained confidence. 'Now, Miss Fisher, our music director—Mr. Palmer—wishes me to teach key signatures this afternoon. Are you familiar with them?'

'I know C, G, and F major,' Jane said uncertainly. 'And perhaps one or two of the others.'

The teacher smiled wryly. 'I see. Well, I'm sure you're a quick study. After today, you will know them all, I expect.' He waved towards a wooden cabinet behind him. 'In that cupboard you will find the textbooks for today's lesson. They're titled *Key Signatures* and should be labelled in English as well as braille. Mr. Palmer tells me that he put them there last night. Would you be so kind as to lay them out on the desks?'

Jane did so.

Presently the students filed in, Jennifer Barnes among them, and took what Jane assumed were their accustomed seats.

'Miss Barnes, I would be obliged if you would take over the piano,' Mr. Findlay said, turning in the direction of the girl's desk.

Jennifer made her way without assistance to the piano stool, lifted the lid of the instrument, and sat expectantly.

Mr. Findlay said, 'C major, if you please.'

Jennifer obediently riffed through an octave in the middle of the keyboard. 'Now, ladies, you all know this one. No sharps or flats. Just C, D, E, and so on up to the next C. Now, can anyone tell me the major scale with a single sharp in it?'

A hand went up. 'G major, Mr. Findlay,' proffered a small girl with a long pigtail down the back of her grey uniform jacket.

At once Jennifer played a higher octave.

'Correct, Miss Watson!' He rubbed his hands together. 'And which note is sharpened?'

'The F, sir,' the girl answered.

'Correct. Now, we call this the dominant. G is the dominant of C. Up a fifth, you add a sharp. At the tritone, you know. Now, what is the dominant of G?'

Another voice piped up. 'Is it D major, Mr. Findlay?'

'Indeed it is, Miss Broad. Well done. And what notes are sharpened now?'

Again the piano rippled out an octave.

'F sharp and C sharp?'

'Yes! You have it! And how do we get there?'

'Up a fifth again, sir?'

'Just so! Now, Miss Barnes, please play the next dominant above that.'

Jane leaned against the side wall, entranced. Not only was Mr. Findlay's enthusiasm infectious, she had never heard music theory expounded so clearly. It was all logical, mathematical, and clear.

'And now, we shall return to C major again. The subdominant of C major is what, ladies?'

Jane guessed it would be down a fifth to F major, and so it was. And the subdominant of F was B flat major, and so on.

'Now,' said the teacher, 'I believe you are ready for the first exercise. Please open your textbooks to page seven.'

The girls each put their fingers to page seven and began to read.

Ruth, meanwhile, had joined Hester at the sink and then the sideboard, and between them they washed, dried, and put away the multitudinous cups and plates. When all was finished at last, it was only quarter to three, so there was still some time left. Hester waved Ruth to a chair then made a pot of tea for them both and produced two slices of fruitcake to go with it.

'You have well and truly earned this, Ruth,' she said.

The cake was splendid: rich, sweet, and filled with raisins, currants, lemon peel, and preserved cherries. Ruth approved, and despite her resolve to eat it slowly discovered to her surprise that she had eaten her entire slab before she had even marked its passing.

'Do you like working here?' Ruth asked, as they sipped their tea.

Hester nodded. 'Oh, yes. I worked in a hospital before this, and I couldn't stand it. I would hear the patients crying and whimpering, and it made me so sorry. And the boss was not at all a pleasant woman. Not like Mr. Hedger.'

No sooner had she got the words out than a sudden commotion broke out in the corridor. The voice was Mr. Hedger's, and his bellow of outrage might have woken the dead from their graves.

'Get out of here!' he roared. 'I'll do what I want to do. I'll stand over dead bodies to get what I want. It's got nothing to do with you. I run this place, not you.'

Ruth looked at Hester wide-eyed, then stepped lightly across to the door and peered through it. Halfway down the long passageway, Mr. Hedger's office door was flung open and Ruth saw two men in shirtsleeves exit in haste.

Ruth resumed her seat.

'Mr. Hedger just evicted some visitors from his office,' she said breathlessly. 'What on earth could that have been about?'

Hester just grinned. 'That would be the Brushmakers' Union. They're complaining about conditions in the workshop here.'

'What do you think?' Ruth enquired.

Hester's dark eyes regarded Ruth with considerable earnestness. 'I'm from a strong union family. At my home, I mean. I hope that doesn't shock you, Ruth.'

Ruth shook her head. 'Not at all. Miss Phryne is friends with some union men. And she says that without unions the workers always get done down.'

Hester clapped her hands together. 'Well, I am pleased to hear that. But I have to say Mr. Hedger is right. I heard the union complaining about the lack of lighting in the workshop, which is just silly, really, when you come to think of it. Normally, I'd back the union, but I think they should let this go.'

At three thirty the deep bell resounded, and Ruth rose. 'I'm not sure where Miss Thomas will put me on Thursday, but if I don't see you again, it was lovely to meet you.'

———

Jane found Ruth waiting for her in the corridor, and they had just started for the door when Jane realised she had left her satchel in the music room. 'Wait for me in the foyer, Ruthie,' she said. 'I won't be long.'

She found Mr. Findlay still at his desk in the music room. Sensing her presence, he looked towards the door. 'Who's that?' he asked, sounding a trifle peevish.

'It's Jane Fisher, Mr. Findlay.'

'What do you want, Miss Fisher? Everyone has gone for the day.'

'I think I left my satchel in here. May I help you, since I'm here?'

He shook his head. 'No, thank you, Jane. I know the way.'

Jane watched as Mr. Findlay packed up his briefcase quickly

and efficiently, then made his way directly to the door. He waved vaguely at Jane and was gone. She looked around the deserted classroom, spied her satchel at the back, and went to fetch it. Then, seeing that the door to the adjoining storeroom was ajar, she walked over to close it properly, but before she reached it, the door began to close by itself.

'Who's there?' she demanded.

There was no response except for the turning of a key in the lock on the other side of the door.

'Hello?' Jane gripped the doorknob and turned it, but the door would not move.

'Hello?' she said again. There was no reply. Feeling a strange frisson of fear—she had the unaccountable feeling that a ghost had just locked itself in the storeroom—she hurried away.

Chapter Six

'Did you get away without being seen?'

'I think so.' The young woman dropped a large canvas bag onto the floor. 'I told the housekeeper I was taking my clothes to the laundry.'

'There, you've done it now! We can be together at last!'

'Yes! I'm so glad! But…what are we going to do about money?'

The other gave her a quick smile. 'It's all right. You know who I dance for, don't you? You can come and join the troupe. He pays us very well.'

'He doesn't want'—the young woman squirmed uncomfortably—'anything extra?'

'He's never laid a finger on me.'

'Well, I'm surprised. You're so beautiful! I wish I were as beautiful as you. And he's never said anything improper? Or made advances?'

'You're too modest, Peony. You're very beautiful. Anyway, I don't think he's interested. Some men aren't, you know.'

Peony looked around nervously. 'My father will send out men to look for me. Are we safe here?'

'Don't worry, they won't find you. The landlady doesn't ask

questions. As long as we pay the rent every week, she doesn't care what we do.'

Fingers joined in the lamplight. 'And the other people here?'

'They're all musicians or dancers like us. I've told them about you, and they won't give us away.'

There was a long silence. Then Peony whispered, 'I love you.'

'I love you too.'

Chapter Seven

Phryne arrived at the Blind Institute as the Wesley College clock was approaching three twenty. The clock itself was quite small, and nestled inside a modest portico supported by four ionic columns. She pulled to a stop outside the Institute, and watched as a man in a grubby fawn dustcoat opened the gates, stepped through, shut them behind him then stormed towards her. Had he possessed a flaming sword he would have been flourishing it. 'You can't park here!' he growled at her.

'Why ever not?' With the motor still running, Phryne leaned her elbow on the open window frame and said, 'Anyway, as you can see, I'm not actually parking here. I am merely waiting for my daughters, who will be here any minute.'

'That's as may be, but you can't stop here.'

Phryne looked at the man more closely. He had a soiled hat to match the raincoat. He glared at her out of icy blue eyes, while his nose was large, red, and appeared to be leaking into his unspeakable brown moustache.

'It's all right, Charlie. Leave her be.'

To her surprise, Phryne saw a tall, balding man in early middle age approaching. Charlie looked over his shoulder, nodded once, and removed himself back through the gates, which he left open this time.

'It's Miss Fisher, isn't it?' said the newcomer, affably. 'Don't worry about Charlie.' He rested his hand on the bonnet of the Hispano-Suiza. 'He's the head gardener, and he's a bit protective of our grounds—and our inmates, too.' He extended an authoritative hand, which Phryne shook. Even through her glove she felt the tension in the man. He was like an over-wound violin, she decided. 'I'm Stan Hedger. And you'll be after Miss Ruth and Miss Jane, I expect. They'll be out in a minute.'

Indeed, as he spoke Ruth and Jane appeared on the winding path leading from the Institute to the gate. They bade Mr. Hedger goodbye then tumbled into the back seat of the Hispano-Suiza. 'How was your day?' Phryne enquired, reversing the machine away from the gates.

'It was all right,' Ruth said, as Phryne gunned the engine and they roared off towards St Kilda Junction. 'I spent the day helping in the kitchen and only saw Jane at lunchtime. We met a girl called Jennifer who'd like to tune your piano. Apparently, it's one of the things they do there, to raise money for themselves.'

'Really? I didn't know that. Well, I'm willing to give it a go. I'll ring them up and arrange it. Jennifer, did you say?'

'Yes, Miss Phryne. Jennifer Barnes. And Jane says she found something mysterious.'

'Oh? Do tell, Jane.'

Unlike Ruth, who was sitting back in her seat and giving every appearance of enjoying the ride, Jane looked distinctly unsettled as the car sped along Barkly Street. Her hands were clasped tightly together. 'I went back to get my satchel, which I'd left in one of the music rooms, and the door to the storeroom closed by itself. I tried the handle, but it had been locked from the inside. But the teacher, Mr. Findlay, who was just leaving when I got there, was quite definite that everyone else had left.'

'I see,' said Phryne, though she didn't. 'Well, I'm sure there's no reason to suspect dark deeds at the Blind Institute.'

'Actually, there is a reason,' Jane said. 'Miss Thomas—our supervisor—thinks there's something wrong with the bookkeeping, and that they're spending more money than they should be.'

'And she's asked for your help?'

'I've agreed to have a look at the books, Miss Phryne. I'm not much use in the classroom.'

'All right. Let me know if you uncover anything of interest, won't you?' Phryne let the matter rest for now, though she resolved to make her own enquiries. 'And have you made up your minds about Frances Reynolds' party? They'll be expecting an RSVP.'

There was a brief silence in which Phryne could sense the girls exchanging glances behind her. At length it appeared a decision had been reached.

'Yes, we have,' Ruth announced. 'We're going.'

'Good for you! On Saturday morning I'll take you to Madame Partlett for some new party dresses.'

This seemed to produce an air of satisfaction from the back seat. Phryne smiled to herself, thinking of her adoptive daughters and their unexpected acceptance into what passed for Melbourne's high society. Did their school friends know that the girls had only lately been removed from the slums? Phryne had never asked them, but she doubted it. As the adoptive daughters of a famous detective—who happened to be an aristocrat possessed of seemingly unlimited wealth—a goodly measure of status was assured them. And just to be certain, Phryne made sure that the girls' school uniforms remained spotless through frequent costume changes. Ruth and Jane had four changes of attire available to them, and the sharp eyes of their classmates would not have overlooked such details.

Yet Phryne's patronage alone would not ensure their popularity; Jane's complete indifference to public opinion would also have been noted, along with her brilliant brain. She would not lack for friends at an exclusive girls' school devoted to learning, self-reliance, and independence. And Ruth? Phryne considered that Ruth's public chastisement of Frances Reynolds had probably swayed opinion very much in her favour. And good for her!

The girls were decanted at The Esplanade, then Phryne took herself off to visit her sister Eliza. If anyone knew about matters philanthropic, it would be Eliza and her beloved Alice.

Eliza and Alice lived in a bluestone and brick single-storey house on Beaconsfield Parade, furnished with tall, intimidating bookcases, stuffed to the rafters with improving literature of the Fabian variety. Having ushered their uninvited—but always welcome—guest inside, Eliza retired to the small kitchen and prepared a pot of tea. Alice invited Phryne to sit at a tea table and, with a framed photograph of George Bernard Shaw looking impressively avuncular listening in, enquired after Dot, Jane, Ruth, and Tinker.

'Just thriving, all of them,' Phryne responded. 'In fact, the girls have been sent by their school to the Blind Institute to help out for a few days. Do you know much about it?'

Alice dimpled, and folded her hands in her lap. 'That is most commendable, Phryne. I am glad to hear it. Presbyterian Ladies' College may well be a bastion of wealth and privilege, but I do approve of the school's wish to encourage their students to take a lively interest in social issues. Ah, thank you, Eliza dear.'

Eliza placed a silver teapot, three china cups, a small Japanese-looking milk jug, and a sugar bowl on the table before them, then disappeared into the recesses of the library. Phryne tasted the tea (black, without sugar) and nodded. She did not generally drink tea, but her sister did not keep coffee in the house.

As Phryne put down the cup, Eliza reappeared, carrying a thick booklet. She sat down in her padded armchair and flipped through the pages. 'This is last year's annual report. They seem to be doing well enough, no thanks whatever to the state or federal governments.' She frowned.

Seeing Phryne's questioning look, Alice explained, 'Both like it to be known they're in favour of helping the Institute, but so far as giving any actual funds—well!'

'At least the municipalities have stood up for these poor souls!' Eliza picked up a local newspaper from the magazine rack and shook it. 'The City of Williamstown has just voted four hundred pounds to the Institute—and this on top of twelve hundred pounds they gave seven years ago.'

Alice nodded. 'It is possible that the future of Fabian socialism in these Antipodean lands might well lie in the municipal councils rather than the more elevated levels of democracy.'

'I see,' said Phryne. 'Eliza, since you have the annual report there with you, can you see any suggestion of excessive expenditure there?'

Eliza flipped through the pages. 'Here's the financial statement.' She looked at her sister. 'Phryne, are you suggesting...'

'I'm not suggesting anything, Eliza. But Jane did hear murmurings about expenditure, and since she has volunteered—or, rather, been asked—to help out in the office on Thursday, I was wondering if there was anything in particular she should be looking out for.'

Eliza handed the booklet to Alice. 'You're better with figures than I, Alice dear. Does anything here strike you as odd?'

There was a long silence during which Phryne considered a picture above Alice's head of a tweed-clad Beatrice and Sidney

Webb, the high priest and priestess of Fabian Socialism. Alice and Eliza were dressed in tweeds identical to those in the photograph, she noted.

The corners of Alice's mouth curved downwards into a frown, and she handed the booklet to Phryne, tapping a column of figures. 'I don't like the look of this, Phryne. Look at this against last year's expenditure.'

Phryne looked as directed. 'It does seem to have grown,' she agreed. 'By around two hundred pounds, it appears. But perhaps there is a reasonable explanation.'

'Are you going to investigate, Phryne?' Eliza asked.

Phryne gave her sister a demure smile. 'I'd like to. But I have no *locus standi*, and without that you're just peering through the bars on the wrong side of the gates in the rain. Unless the Institute's chairman or director asks me to investigate, my hands are tied.'

'But Jane is in a position to?'

'And I'm sure she will. In the meantime, do you know about their piano-tuning service? It's the first I've heard of it.'

'Oh, please do call on them, Phryne, if your instrument needs it,' Eliza urged. 'They have ever so many piano tuners there. And they need the work, of course. Tuning pianos is something you can do without sight. The dignity of labour is important for them.'

'And,' Alice added, 'if you can solve the mystery of their last year's balance sheet, that would be an even more effective form of philanthropy.'

Phryne took her leave shortly afterwards and motored back to The Esplanade, parked the Hispano-Suiza in the garage, and repaired to the study. It was a small anteroom with a bay window next to the parlour. Within there was a plain desk, with notepaper, envelopes, penny stamps, an ink bottle (black), and a selection of fountain pens. It appeared Ruth and Jane had made use of these, as prominent among them was a sealed and stamped envelope addressed to Mrs. Reynolds. The girls had wasted no time with their formal acceptance. Phryne approved their efficiency but felt no desire to replicate it. She considered most correspondence to be vexatious and foolish. (Although that of Bunji Ross was a hoot. If Bunji ever stayed in one place long enough for a reliable return address, Phryne would certainly write back.) Phryne's purpose for visiting the study was to make use of the telephone extension there. She picked up the receiver, rang the Blind Institute and enquired about their piano-tuning services, saying a Miss Barnes had been particularly recommended.

Yes, Friday afternoon at four o'clock would be most convenient.

Phryne replaced the receiver and considered it for a moment, wondering whether she should call Lin Chung, but she refrained. If Lin wanted her company he would call her. He was no doubt busy with affairs domestic and professional, and she, meanwhile, had Jeoffrey's dinner invitation. She smiled as she left the room to inform Mrs. B that tonight she would be dining *en famille*. Tomorrow night, she was anticipating something rather more debauched…

Chapter Eight

Phryne slept in the next morning. She had been dimly aware of a general susurrus of movement and adolescent giggles from without as Ruth and Jane prepared for school, but she turned on her pillow, and buried her head in it. Thunderous purring in her ear announced the arrival of Ember, who smelled of fish. He burrowed under the blankets and nestled next to Phryne's back, and soon she was fast asleep once more.

Dot's voice woke her some hours later. 'Miss? It's eleven o'clock. I brought you some coffee.'

Phryne sat up, stretched, and surveyed her silk nightgown, which seemed to have acquired substantial holes in its fabric during her slumbers. She gave Ember a sharp look, but the cat blinked solemnly at her and resumed his repose on her pillow. Feeling that trying to outstare a cat was a futile endeavour, she turned her attention to the cup of Hellenic pick-me-up. As she was perusing the day beyond the window, noting its bright and sunny mien, Dot spoke up.

'Miss, I was wondering if I could go and visit my mother today,' Dot ventured. 'She's caught a chill, and I'd like to go and help her out.'

'By all means, Dot,' said Phryne absently, thinking on her own plans for the day. Jeoffrey's home in Williamstown that evening... She was not well acquainted with Williamstown, but she recalled Eliza saying that the local council had granted four hundred pounds to the Blind Institute. A place that was home to handsome scholars and civic-minded councillors must have something going for it. Why not go earlier and see what that something was?

She sat up straighter. 'I'm going to Williamstown today, Dot, and I might not be back until tomorrow.'

'If you're sure that's wise, Miss.' Dot's own reluctance to cross the Maribyrnong River was founded largely on the reflection that every time her employer went westwards, trouble followed her. But there was more to it than that. Dot had grown up in the back streets of Collingwood, and one of the lessons she had learned at the parental knee was that those who lived out west were Trouble with a capital T. Phryne suspected that sectarianism lay at the back of this. The inner west was militantly Protestant in flavour.

'It's all right, Dot; I have good reason to believe they're not all savages there. Give my regards to your mother.'

The more the strong coffee revived her, the more Phryne's interest in her own scheme for the day grew. Summoning Mr. Butler, she made a few enquiries. Mr. B, it turned out, had a brochure on Williamstown, and Phryne discovered that he and Mrs. B were wont to go there on their days off.

'There's a fine ferry, Miss. She's called the *Rosny*, and she sails from Port Melbourne.'

She could, of course, simply drive the car, but—perhaps some of Dot's caution was rubbing off on her—she felt reluctant to do so into unknown territory. Besides, it was unlikely Jeoffrey possessed a lock-up garage, and the car was irreplaceable. The train was also an option. But given the bright and shining day, why not take the ferry? She could spend some hours sightseeing in this foreign land before her dinner and sharpen her appetites. In the plural.

In no particular hurry, Phryne rose, ate, bathed, and dressed herself in comfortable grey trousers, a plum-coloured blouse, her patent leather walking shoes, an overcoat and a straw sunhat. It was early afternoon when she called Bert and Cec and asked for a lift to the port.

They arrived within five minutes. 'Afternoon, Comrade Phryne,' said Bert out of the left side of his mouth. The other half of Bert's thick lips were wrapped around his inevitable cigarette: a roll-up of such ancientry it might have emerged from an Egyptian pyramid.

Cec bestowed on her a taciturn smile and opened the rear door of their battered taxi. 'If ya don't mind my askin',' he said, as Phryne climbed into the padded leather back seat, 'what brings you to the port today?'

'I'm off to Williamstown,' she explained, 'and I thought it would be fun to take the steamer.'

Bert engaged the clutch and the motor roared into life. 'What, the *Rosny*? Yeah, well, it's a pleasant enough trip, I s'pose. Train'd be quicker, but.'

'I'm not in a hurry. I want to look around. What can you tell me about Williamstown?'

'Willi? We don't get out that way much. Lots of cargo goes through Willi.' He shrugged. 'Don't know what else to tell ya.'

'Well, what sort of people are they there?'

'Blokes say they're a bit, well...they keep themselves to themselves there. See, it's a peninsula. They've got the bay on three sides and they don't mix that much with outsiders like us.'

'Too right,' Cec volunteered. 'Lots of rich folks live there, but.'

Bert nodded. 'Yair, that's true enough. But they ain't really your actual boor-jwah. For real class warfare, you need to 'ave the rich segregated from the urban proletariat. Ya don't get that in Willi. Everyone lives on top of each other. An' there's no high fences to separate folk from their neighbours. Not like out east, where the bloated capitalists live behind big hedges locked away from the common people.'

'I see.' Phryne considered this as the cab rumbled past Victoria Dock. Some of the most loathsome individuals she had ever had the misfortune to meet did indeed live in the eastern suburbs. Who knew what iniquities were shielded behind the thick walls and vast hedges there? Phryne had seen more than enough of them.

Port Melbourne was its customary bustling self. Stevedores in open-necked shirts ferried back and forth like myrmidons, carrying bags of wheat over their shoulder onto cargo ships. Their faces looked grim and weather-beaten, as well they might, given the scandalous conditions of the Beeby award under which they currently laboured. The port smelled of engine oil and weary patience. Phryne was about to suggest that Bert drop her at the street corner next to the pier, but Bert clearly had other ideas, as he began to drive down the pier itself, steering an erratic path between wharf labourers and their burdens. He stuck his head out the window and cupped one hand to his mouth.

'Oy! Glass-arms! Give a man some elbow room, will ya?'

A tall, forbidding figure with a grubby clipboard in his left hand gave him a frosty stare. Then the craggy features relaxed into something approaching a smile.

'All right, Comrade Bert. Easy as ya go.'

The man dubbed Glass-arms waved his clipboard at his sweaty entourage, who made room for Bert's cab. 'Cheers, mate,' he called through the window.

Bert pulled up outside the ticket office and pointed to a steamer of substantial dimension which was bobbing gently in the oily deeps next to the jetty. 'That's the *Rosny*, Miss. Tickets in there.' He pointed towards an office.

Phryne handed him five shillings and alighted, noting with amusement that Bert really did have a way with people.

The ticket office lacked something by way of interior decoration, but the youth behind the counter was comely enough. 'That'll be a shilling, Miss,' he announced. This seemed a little over the odds, Phryne thought, but she paid it anyway. 'Better hurry,' the young man added. 'We're casting off any minute.'

The foghorn sounded as they slipped anchor. The stentorian noise brought to mind the sound a hippopotamus might make if its foot became stuck in a mud pool. The coal-tar tang of the steamer wafted around them as the ferry slid out into the sparkling bay. Phryne's nose twitched at the fug of perspiration and cigarette smoke which was the predominant sensation in the main compartment, so she moved out to stand on the deck, leaning against the sturdy brass railing, and felt the breeze catch at the chin strap attached to her hat. Phryne's fellow passengers appeared similarly braced by the salt spray and warm sunlight on their faces. There were around fifty of them, she estimated. Some were family groups, but the majority seemed to be courting couples. There was a definite sensation of romance in the air, which spoke well of the erotic potential of Williamstown, she thought.

Phryne gazed towards a distant hill to the south, beyond the maritime suburbs. That was undoubtedly Arthur's Seat. It did not look very much like the Edinburgh original, but it was certainly a hill of respectable proportions: perhaps a thousand feet above the bay. There appeared to be a wooden lookout tower on the summit, presumably to keep an eye out for invading Russians. She wondered about the Mornington Peninsula. Perhaps she might take Dot there in due course. Polite hints had been dropped to that effect by her companion, and it was well worth thinking about. Phryne suspected that Dot was really hankering for a quiet holiday without mysterious dead bodies, exploding grenades, wayward cabers, and attempted poisonings. Perhaps her wish might be granted. Though adventures did seem to follow her around like a pod of dolphins.

One of the trippers—an excitable-looking young woman in a floral print dress—pointed ahead of the *Rosny*'s prow. 'This must be Williamstown now. It looks—'

The foghorn intervened before she could finish her sentence. What Williamstown looked like, Phryne thought, was a small version of Port Melbourne: all grime, warehouses, and the ubiquitous march of wharfies carrying cargo to and from holds. Dominating the dockside was an impressive bluestone tower.

The young woman nudged her companion, a gormless youth with his hands in his pockets and a vacant smile. 'It's for the time-ball, George,' she said. 'They don't use it anymore because of the telegraph, but it says in the guidebook I was reading that there was a copper ball inside, and at one o'clock every afternoon the ball fell into its cradle, and that told all the ships' captains what time it was.'

Her young man studied it critically. 'It looks like it ought to be a lighthouse, though.'

'It was that too.'

Being first in the queue to disembark, Phryne watched as the gangway was extended onto the jetty. She stepped ashore, and found she had to pause for a moment to regain her land legs. The remainder of the passengers streamed past her. Some walked straight onto the train platform, and others began a leisurely saunter down towards what was presumably Williamstown proper. Phryne decided to follow the example of the former. She fronted the ticket office, where a man in a light blue uniform and peaked cap was dispensing tickets. 'Single to Williamstown Beach, please,' she said, when her turn came.

'That'll be a penny halfpenny, Miss.'

Phryne accepted the small stub of cardboard and parked herself in a wooden seat which appeared to have been designed for sufferers from scoliosis. A smallish horde of children dressed for the beach and their attendant parents gathered around her. The children were chattering excitedly. Trousers had already been rolled up. Wide-brimmed straw hats predominated, and white dresses for the girls. The train jerked on its tracks and began to rumble westwards through a thicket of trees and shrubs. The line was sunken below the level of the adjoining streets, and eaves and gables were all that could be seen of the houses.

As the train chugged its way out of the station, Phryne gazed out on the railway yards visible through the north-facing window. It appeared that this was where the trains were built and repaired. Hammers rang, sparks flew, paintbrushes and rollers were wielded with vim and vigour. Sundry other workers milled about before an impressive-looking furnace which dripped molten metal. Out the southern window, sun-dappled waters lapping against basalt rocks made a contrasting maritime prospect. Yachts skimmed, seagulls dived and squawked, and heavy industry was nowhere in sight.

Two stops later she alighted at Williamstown Beach station, a simple two-platformed affair in red brick. Her ticket was collected by a guard, who gestured to a ramp. 'Straight down to the left or right for the beach, Miss,' he informed her. 'It's about a furlong.'

'Thank you.' Phryne waited for the overexcited children to stampede past, with their parents hastening behind carrying baskets and hampers, then followed in their wake.

A waft of salt-laden air blew in her face as she reached the shore. The beach itself was nothing to write home about. Exposed rocks predominated, although there were certainly stretches of yellowish ochre sand. Most of the available strand and all of the nearby water was crammed with children. Swimming was not permitted, it seemed, so while parents minded the luggage and discarded shoes, their offspring frolicked and cavorted in the shallows.

Phryne wondered briefly whether or not to join the paddling throng, but decided instead upon a vast thicket of pine trees which lined the foreshore, presumably planted to stop the winter winds battering the local houses. The path through the pine trees was narrow, and the sea breeze whispered in the pine needles like an insistent ghost. She passed through a narrow gate into the botanical gardens and found herself confronted by an imperious statue. It depicted a man in a frockcoat sporting a truly Assyrian beard. He was gazing hawkishly into the middle distance, and to Phryne's eye he looked rather youthful to have merited a statue of himself.

'Alfred Thomas Clark,' Phryne read aloud from a nearby plaque. 'Member for Williamstown.' The statue had been erected by his grateful constituents, it seemed.

'He died aboard a ship to London, aged forty-two,' said a gruff voice behind her. 'But he was a fine man, and a credit to this city.'

Phryne turned and found herself confronted by an elderly man holding a magnificent roan horse by the cheek strap. The man was dressed all in brown, from trousers to waistcoat to shirt and boots and hat—to match his horse, presumably.

He gazed for a moment at the restless face of the late Alfred Clark. 'He was a good man,' he repeated, with something approaching reverence. 'A great philanthropist.'

'He seems to have been greatly cherished,' Phryne commented. 'Look at those eyes!' This, she thought, was a man who would spend sleepless nights worrying about the state of the world, and what more he could do to amend it.

The brown-clad man turned to her, seeming to appreciate her interest in the statue.

'I'm the curator of these gardens,' he said. 'Bill Crowe.' He removed his hat and inclined his head briefly.

'I'm Phryne Fisher,' said Phryne. 'I am pleased to make the acquaintance of Mr. Clark. And yours too, Mr. Crowe.'

But Crowe was no longer looking at her. He was staring in speechless fury at two boys riding bicycles across the lawn. Finally he found his voice. 'Oi! You two stop that right now!' he bellowed.

He strode forward, still holding the horse's cheek strap. The horse whinnied and pulled free, then bolted away. His horse forgotten, Crowe sped off down the gravel path towards the boys, who stared up at him in horror and turned their front wheels around in a panic. Crowe was surprisingly fast for a man of his age, but fear lent speed to his prey. Their feet were a blur on the pedals and they were soon out of sight. Crowe stopped in his tracks, drew a deep breath, and stood, legs apart, like an avenging angel, glaring at the lawn that had been disturbed by the bicycle tyres. A young couple sitting nearby stared up at him, frozen into immobility in what had clearly been a loving embrace.

Having caught his breath, the park's guardian looked around to see Phryne leading his absconding helpmate by the cheek strap, whispering endearments into a nervously pricked equine ear. She returned the horse to her master, who approached her with an air of contrition. 'Hey, now, Rosebud,' he cooed. 'You all right, my dear?' Rosebud nuzzled his shoulder and shifted on her hooves. Crowe doffed his hat to Phryne once more. 'That was extremely kind of you, Miss Fisher. You've quite a way with horses.'

'I think she's picked up a flint,' Phryne observed.

Bill Crowe inspected the trembling horse, and found the off hind foot was bleeding from a jagged cut in the frog.

'It's them blasted kids, I'll wager,' Crowe commented. 'They'll feel the back of my hand next time I see them. Probably they had a soft drink bottle and smashed it.'

'Let's have a look, shall we?' suggested Phryne.

Performing her own inspection of the hoof, Phryne quickly

discovered the offending fragment. 'This looks like a broken pipe.' She handed about two-thirds of a clay pipe to the gardener, who received the fragment as though it were an unexploded bomb and sniffed the tarry black interior of the broken bowl.

'I very much doubt it was our bicycle riders after all,' he said, eyes narrowed. 'That ain't tobacco, Miss.'

'No, it isn't,' agreed Phryne, who had caught a whiff of vinegar. 'That's opium. And I really didn't expect to find it here.'

'Nor I,' said Bill Crowe grimly. 'Well, it's against the law, for a start—not that I approve of that stupid law.'

'The law is indeed an ass,' Phryne agreed. Opium had been outlawed in 1905 in Australia, and as a result the Commonwealth had been deprived of a lucrative source of customs duties. The price had been driven up, and addicts impoverished and driven to crime and prostitution in consequence.

'I'm glad you see it the same as I do, Miss. But much as I pity 'em who need the stuff, I won't have 'em smoking it here—not if it means leaving hazards on my grounds.' He glanced at the pipe in Phryne's hand. 'You gonna take that to the cops, Miss?'

'Do you advise me to?' Phryne enquired, with a meaning look.

'I think you'd better, Miss.' Then, divining her look correctly, he added, 'The local cops are on the straight.'

Phryne gave him a dazzling smile. 'Then I shall proceed to the local police station forthwith. Thank you, Mr. Crowe. I'm delighted to have met you. And you too, Rosebud.' She gave Rosebud an affectionate stroke down her long nose, then set off through the gardens.

As she walked, she admired the gardener's horticultural endeavours. The lush, well-groomed grass was crisscrossed with gravel paths. From the statue due north was a double line of palm trees flanking the main pathway. There were thickets of exotic shrubs and abundant flowers—daffodils, jonquils, and irises prominent among them—and a resplendent golden elm among the proliferation of Moreton Bay figs. There was even a lily-bedecked lake and a granite drinking fountain. Lounging on the lawn were courting couples eating picnics. It seemed that Mr. Crowe's protective instincts did not extend to Keeping Off The Grass, provided only that the grass were treated with a proper respect.

Phryne wound her way clockwise around the gardens and reached an impressive set of wrought-iron gates. A young woman with a sprightly straw hat was sallying through them and Phryne hailed her. 'Hello? Can you tell me the way to the police station?'

The woman's mouth made an O of surprise. 'Golly! I hope you haven't been robbed?'

'Not at all,' Phryne assured her. 'I just have something minor to report.'

The woman pointed vaguely northwards with her gloved hand. 'Number ten Thompson Street. You can't miss it.'

'Thank you.'

And pipe in hand, Phryne set off in search of constabulary assistance.

———

The police station was an unpretentious affair nestling beside the courthouse, which did not appear to be in session. Phryne opened the shining navy-blue front door and was confronted by a plain anteroom with a wooden bench along one side, American oilcloth on the floor, and a raised wooden counter, behind which stood a tall youth in a blue uniform.

'Hello,' Phryne announced, and set the broken clay pipe on the desk. 'I thought you might be interested to know that I found this just now in the botanical gardens. The curator's horse sustained an injury because of it. I merely wished to inform you that you may have a local problem with opium smokers.'

The policeman was young, freshly scrubbed to a becoming pinkness, with ears sticking out the sides of his close-cropped, angular head. At being addressed so forthrightly by a self-possessed and fashionable woman, he gaped, removed his helmet, and scratched his head. 'Oh, right, Miss. Could you wait here a moment? I think the sergeant will want to see this.'

The young man carried the broken pipe through a glass-fronted door behind the counter. The door silently proclaimed that members of the public were Not Admitted.

'By all means,' Phryne said to the constable's departing back.

Moments later, a dull rumbling voice erupted from behind the glass doors.

'Bloody hell, Taxi! What are you sayin'? What's all this about?'

Muffled conversation trickled out under the door, and the bull-like roar subsided. 'All right, I'll talk to the sheila.'

The door ground open and an enormous, red-faced creature with sergeant's stripes emerged through it. He was well over six feet tall and had several axe handles across the massive shoulders. His brick-red countenance glared at Phryne, then at the pipe she had brought him, and finally at the business card Phryne had placed before her on the counter. His lower lip wobbled like an ill-set blancmange. 'Frinny Fisher, is it? Private investigator? And where did you find this object?'

'In the botanical gardens, Sergeant, as I have already told your constable. Mr. Crowe, the garden's curator, advised me to bring the pipe here, seeing that it indubitably reeks of opium and his horse Rosebud was injured by this very same object.'

'Billy Crowe sent you, eh?' The sergeant's demeanour softened somewhat. 'Well, 'e's all right. Well then, Miss Fisher, thanks for bringin' this in. If I want you, I can ring this number?' He peered again at her card. 'Hang on, what's this Honourable bit about?'

Phryne beamed at him. 'It means my father is a baron. But not a very good one.'

The sergeant's watery blue eyes opened wider, and he laughed, a sound that called to mind a water buffalo breaking wind. 'All right, Honourable Miss.' He held up the pipe. 'Thank you again.'

Phryne left the station, wondering why the sergeant had called the young constable Taxi. Perhaps it was the ears, she speculated. When a taxi was on stand-by, the cabbie sometimes left both doors open in the back. Not a very charitable nickname, but compared with what sergeants sometimes called their gormless underlings, Constable Taxi was getting off fairly lightly, Phryne supposed.

It was approaching five o'clock now. With an hour and a half to go before her dinner rendezvous, Phryne decided upon a brief snack. The town centre was straight ahead, and she meandered towards it. Williamstown proper, she found when standing in its midst, was a most superior-looking locale, the street lined with two-storey stone buildings boasting shops on the ground floor and dwellings above. On the left was an array of all the usual conveniences: fruiterers, grocers, bootmakers and the like. There were several hotels, tenanted with beer-drinking gentlemen in shirtsleeves and waistcoats. On the right was a verdant park, a jetty, and a surprising number of yachts: some at anchor, and some gently gliding over the bay. The park had its inevitable cannon, pointing entirely the wrong way to repel boarders. In the park, shifty-eyed vendors proffered goods that had no doubt fallen from the backs of lorries.

Spying a teashop nestling between a bootmaker and a milliner, Phryne made her way hence. Like most of the shops on the waterfront, it was a narrow-fronted affair, barely five yards across. Inside was arranged a long row of round wooden tables which might comfortably seat no more than three people. A brisk waitress in black and white was taking orders. What had attracted Phryne to it was the oblong sign painted on the window announcing Italian ice cream.

The waitress looked up, took in Phryne's expensive garments, and offered a smile. She indicated a vacant table. 'Afternoon tea, Miss? We have Devonshire teas.'

'Just coffee and ice cream, please,' Phryne responded. She seated herself on a wooden chair appearing to have been built entirely for speed rather than comfort. The waitress bustled away into the distance, and Phryne took her eyes from the overdone red wallpaper and considered instead the opium pipe she had deposited into the care of the brick-red sergeant. It seemed to her curiously out of place in Bill Crowe's beautiful gardens. But it was probably nothing, she thought, as the waitress returned with a laden tray. And certainly nothing to do with her.

Phryne's espresso was passably good, giving her to suspect that there was indeed an Italian presence in the kitchen. The ice cream was delivered in a plain white china bowl, unadorned and unashamed of itself. It had no reason to be. After tasting one small spoonful Phryne closed her eyes for a moment and sighed. It was magnificent. She ate the rest of the delectable vanilla-flavoured confection slowly, savouring every morsel. Definitely Italians in the kitchen.

Just after six o'clock she paid the bill, leaving a two-shilling tip for the waitress, and strolled over the road to the park. Dusk was falling, and the streets were beginning to empty. The purveyors of doubtful goods packed up their suitcases, children gathered their toys and belongings and scampered homewards, and Phryne consulted the map she had sketched of her destination. From Nelson Place she should head back towards Williamstown Pier station and the railways yards there. It appeared that Lark Lane was near the waterfront.

She set off, walking past warehouses and boatyards, mostly silent and shuttered for the night. One in particular struck her as singular. It was a three-storey building of sullen red brick. Fragments of mortar were falling unregarded to the footpath. It looked utterly deserted. A chipped signboard announced that Haggerty Pty Ltd were an impt/expt company, but neither impting nor expting had occurred there for some time. Yet despite its abandoned air, Phryne could hear soft thumps coming from within. As she tilted her head to listen she was startled by a blood-chilling scream, abruptly cut off.

Without pausing to think better of it, Phryne hammered on the door with her gloved fist. 'Open up! Police!' she shouted.

There was no response from within, though she thought she detected a muted whimper. She turned her attention to the lock on the door. Could she pick it, perhaps? But if she did, what then? There were no lights showing through the shuttered windows, which might mean a blind chase around an unfamiliar interior, possibly in the company of people violently opposed to uninvited guests. Deciding that discretion was the better part of valour, she instead set off at a run for the police station.

A sudden blast of cold wind blew in the elm branches above her head, and this was followed by a sudden squall of rain against which her sunhat proved poor protection. A cat rushed past her, head down, and disappeared into a dark hedge. Lucky cat, to have refuge so near.

The police station was dark and empty when she arrived. She pounded on the door in frustration, then heaved a deep sigh. What now? She could call City South police station, which she knew was manned around the clock, but what would she tell them? That she'd heard someone scream inside a deserted warehouse? It sounded a little thin, but as a concerned citizen she felt bound to report the incident. She would use Jeoffrey's phone.

She wrapped her coat tight around herself and headed eastwards towards Lark Lane as the rain came down by the bucketload.

———

'No, no. Look, Peony, you've learned Nanchuan, haven't you? The movements aren't so very different. Like this!'

Peony watched her lover's graceful movements. 'You're right—it is like Nanchuan.'

She felt her body go into its familiar routine and fluttered her eyelashes, enjoying the worshipful gaze of her beloved. 'But…jazz?'

'It's complicated, I know. But this music is very popular in Shanghai these days. And he wants to impress his friends and business associates.'

'I see.' Peony continued to dance, and closed her eyes with delight as the other's hands took hers.

Chapter Nine

'Phryne? What's wrong? You look all done in!'

By the time Phryne reached Jeoffrey's front door she was wet through. As his front door opened, she all but fell into his arms. Warm yellow light blossomed behind his tall, welcoming figure. She gave him a rueful grin. 'I'm sorry, Jeoffrey, but I've had a bit of a shock, that's all.'

'Here, come in. And please, take off your coat. I wasn't expecting rain tonight.'

'Neither was I.' Phryne shed the coat, handed the sopping garment to her host, and followed him down a bluestone corridor. Jeoffrey paused and waved a long, pleasingly sculpted arm clad in crisp shirtsleeves. 'Bathroom at the end, if you want. And—oh, my. You really are wet through!'

Phryne gave a rueful laugh. 'I really am. If you have anything suitable I could change into, that would be wonderful.'

Jeoffrey disappeared for a moment and re-emerged carrying a pair of flannel pyjamas. Phryne stared. There were flop-eared rabbits in blue waistcoats chasing each other around the sleeves and up and down the front. They looked like happy bunnies, but it was not exactly what she'd meant by suitable.

They both began to laugh.

'A Christmas present from my mother,' Jeoffrey confessed. 'But they're warm. Or there's my dressing-gown, if you like.'

The dressing-gown proved to be a dismal tartan in coarse wool, frayed at the edges and collar. 'Perhaps not,' Phryne said, deciding the pyjamas were the lesser of the two evils.

'Fair enough. I've got the fire going in the dining room. But perhaps you'd like a hot bath first?'

'That would be lovely, Jeoffrey.' Phryne accepted the pyjamas and betook herself to the bathroom, thinking to herself that Jeoffrey had probably never imagined getting her out of her clothes would be as easy as this.

The bathroom was spartan compared to what she was used to, but it was admirably clean. The bath—gleaming white—was immensely welcome. Jeoffrey even had a small jar of perfumed bath salts. She lifted the lid and sniffed. Attar of roses, no less. She inserted the plug, turned on the hot tap and sprinkled a liberal handful of crystals into the water. She disrobed, hung her wet clothes over the towel rail, inserted herself into the aromatic suds, and mused on what she had learned so far from her surroundings. Bachelor establishment, no doubt about it; there was no real impression of a female touch around the premises. But it was no bachelor squalor either. Jeoffrey Bisset grew more promising by the moment.

There were three large fluffy white towels hanging on hooks, so when Phryne felt circulation had been sufficiently restored to her chilled limbs she dried herself and dressed in Jeoffrey's pyjamas. Which fitted her surprisingly well.

Now here was a mystery. These pyjamas would not have fitted Jeoffrey since he was twelve. So…a present for his childhood self, and dutifully retained by him ever since? Maybe.

She emerged and listened for culinary sounds elsewhere in the house. She stood in the hallway and looked down the passage. The kitchen was first on her right. She popped her head in the door, and inhaled a most pleasing herbal aroma. But no Jeoffrey. The next door seemed more promising, not to mention ajar. There was the clink of silver and glass, both of which sounded exceptionally inviting. She opened the door wide and posed theatrically on the threshold.

Jeoffrey looked up at her in frank admiration. 'Phryne, you look wonderful, even in those pyjamas. But we must do something about your wet clothes. Believe it or not, I have a patent drying cabinet in my laundry, designed by a friend from the engineering department. Shall I deposit your wet things in it?'

'I'd be most grateful if you would, Jeoffrey. And while you're doing that, may I use your phone?'

'Of course—it's in the hallway.'

Phryne picked up the Bakelite receiver and dialled a certain number she knew only too well.

'City South Police, may I have your name, please?' The voice was gruff, but not inhospitable.

'Hello, this is Phryne Fisher.'

There was an intake of breath.

'I'm a friend of Detective Inspector Robinson,' Phryne added into the silence.

'Yes, Miss Fisher. I know who you are. And what do you have for us this inclement evening?'

'Possibly nothing,' Phryne confessed, 'but I happened to be passing Haggerty's warehouse in Nelson Place, Williamstown, this evening at around quarter past six, and I heard a series of thumps, followed by a most impressive scream. I went straight to Williamstown police station to report this, only to find it closed for the night. I think it might be worth investigating. But of course

I would not wish to pre-empt any operational decisions you might wish to make on this, as you say, inclement evening.'

'Haggerty's you say? Nelson Place? Never heard of it. Look, Miss Fisher, we're short-handed this evening, but I'll be sure to pass the message on. Thank you for your call.'

Phryne replaced the receiver, duty more or less done, and returned to the dining room. On entering, her mouth opened in appreciation. She had not really taken in the contents before, since it had been as dark as the inside of a coal mine. Now it was ablaze with candles in silver candelabra. Tablecloth: white, damask, and spotless. Table: polished mahogany, set for two, with expensive-looking dinnerware and an ice bucket in which perched a bottle of Veuve Clicquot, which awaited its translation into two crystal champagne glasses. Sumptuous scents emanated from under tureens and covers. Her nostrils detected baked salmon with herbs amid the array of dishes. And the dark, brooding, brandy-soaked aroma of what appeared to be Yuletide pudding was definitely among those present. Jeoffrey too was a delicious sight, dressed simply in an open-necked white shirt and plain black trousers, his shoes gleaming with polish.

'So good of you to come, Phryne.'

She approached and extended her pyjama-clad arm.

He kissed the proffered hand gallantly then ushered her to a seat.

'Well, this really is quite something, Jeoffrey,' Phryne said appreciatively. 'It's very good of you to push the boat out like this for me.'

'Being a bachelor gay, I don't entertain all that often, so I thought…why not?'

'Why not indeed?'

As Jeoffrey filled their glasses with champagne, he said, 'There's nothing wrong, I hope, Phryne? That phone call, I mean.'

Phryne sipped from her glass then leaned back in her chair. 'The call I made was to the police. I happened to overhear what sounded awfully like someone being murdered as I was passing a warehouse. I do hope it wasn't that, but you really never know, do you?'

Jeoffrey looked shocked, as well he might. 'Golly, Phryne! Where was this?'

'Just down the road, in Nelson Place. At a warehouse called Haggerty's.'

Jeoffrey made a face. 'That doesn't sound right. Haggerty's closed down a couple of years ago and the building hasn't been used since. It's just waiting for someone to knock it down. Are you sure that was the place?'

'Quite sure. I went to the local police station, but it was shut. If any local criminals want to have their misdeeds attended to, it appears they'll have to wait until office hours resume. So I called City South.' She gave a faint smile. 'They know me there.'

Jeoffrey grinned at her. 'I'm sure they do. Well, Phryne, you've done all you can, under the circumstances. Please, allow me to serve.'

Dinner was prolonged, convivial, and utterly delicious. At one point Phryne mentioned the tale of Bill Crowe, Rosebud, and the opium pipe, and Jeoffrey put down his fork and stared at her.

'I say, Phryne, you really have been seeing life here. I don't like the sound of that broken pipe, though. I hope it isn't the Chinese. We don't want any more scandals about Oriental opium dens, do we?'

'Are there any Chinese in Williamstown? I didn't see any today.'

'Wherever there are ports, you'll find them. And of course there's Hong.'

Phryne lifted a slice of baked salmon to her mouth and swallowed it with infinite delight. Jeoffrey's skill in the kitchen was most impressive. 'Hong? Who's he?'

'He lectures in Chinese. He was born in Brunswick, and his real name is Thomas Browning, but the nameplate on his office door says Thomas Hong. He likes to be known as Hong Huanle T'e Shihch'e.' Jeoffrey reeled this off with admirable facility.

'And what does that mean?' Phryne enquired.

Jeoffrey smiled indulgently. 'Messenger of delight. It tells you a lot about him, wouldn't you say? But his parties are an absolute hoot. I believe he's throwing another one Friday week. Do come. I'll have no trouble getting you an invitation. I'm sure he'd love to meet you.'

'I must admit I'm intrigued myself. How does a Thomas Browning of Brunswick come to adopt the name Hong? It means "red," doesn't it?'

'In certain circumstances, yes. As a surname it means spacious. Or ambitious. His parents took him to China when he was a child, and he grew up there, which is how he came to learn the language. They were caught up in the Boxer Rebellion, and had a rather narrow escape. And, well, I don't really know this for certain, but rumour has it that his parents looted a great many treasures from China and sold them here at an enormous profit.'

Phryne, recalling that she had visited many a stately home crammed with chinoiserie looted without shame from the Middle Kingdom, said, 'Well, thank goodness we don't do that sort of thing anymore.'

'*Tempora mutantur, nos et mutamur in illis?*'

Phryne's Latin was equal to this: *Times change, and we change with them.* A laudable ambition, doubtless; she hoped it was true.

'And now, let us have some of this fashionably late Christmas pudding, shall we?' her host suggested.

It was exemplary, as had been the rest of Jeoffrey's cooking. The pudding was mostly preserved fruit held together with flour and brandy, and the brandied sauce was equally potent. Phryne managed several spoonsful, but at length laid down her cutlery.

'This has been a splendid meal, Jeoffrey, but I couldn't eat another bite. So...what shall we do with the rest of the evening?'

Jeoffrey's eyelashes fluttered. He really did have the most beautiful eyes, she realised. They were blue like sapphires, and glowed with—what, exactly? Not lust as such. More like serious erotic interest.

'I had actually intended to take you for a little walk. Just down to the sea. I never get tired of the sea, you know. That's why I moved here.'

'Well, I'm not exactly dressed for a bracing walk by the sea, but if you'd like to lend me an overcoat, I'm sure we can manage.'

'Not only that, I can lend you some shoes.'

'Surely not—I could put both my feet in one of your shoes.'

'I have a pair which will fit you, you'll see.'

Jeoffrey rose and returned with a large khaki overcoat. Phryne wrapped it around her pyjama-clad frame, and extended her delicate feet into a pair of rubber boots which were a size too big for her—but only one size. Phryne looked at him in the flickering light and raised an eyebrow.

'Jeoffrey? Is there something you're not telling me?'

'Well, if you're asking if I have a secret girlfriend, then no, I don't. My mother has supplied me with a range of her cast-off clothes.' His lips quirked. 'She said a young man never knows when having spare women's clothes might come in handy. She's rather progressive, my mother.'

'And she's a credit to her sex, I must say. Come on, then. Let's have our post-dinner saunter, shall we?'

The rain had stopped, and Phryne saw that Lark Lane by night was a charming scene. Most of the houses were dark, but lights and sounds of general merrymaking emerged from three of the houses there. Phryne craned her ears and heard the thunder of waves breaking on rocks. A single streetlight glowed among the treetops. Shadows lurked beneath dark shrubbery. Phryne took her host's arm and leaned her head against his nicely muscled bicep.

'Lovely, isn't it?' Jeoffrey commented. 'There's a little path along the waterfront. Shall I show it to you?'

'Certainly.'

They reached the path and sauntered along it. Phryne was warm and comfortable for the moment, but this would not last, she knew. She hoped Jeoffrey would be happy with the merest stroll.

'Look, something's washed ashore.' Jeoffrey pointed. 'Perhaps it came off a ship.'

Phryne shivered as they moved nearer. They were far from the streetlight now, and there was neither moon nor stars. But even in the gloom, there could be no doubt that the shape on the shore was that of a man.

'Jeoffrey!'

Alarmed by the figure's stillness, Phryne hastened forward. Dropping to her knees, she put her hand to the side of the neck. There was no pulse, and the skin was as cold as death. And a rent in his jacket showed a stab wound to the heart.

Chapter Ten

'Hello? It's Phryne Fisher. Yes, again.' Phryne was standing in Jeoffrey's hallway once more, speaking into the phone with renewed urgency. 'You must come to Williamstown without delay—I've found a body...No, I didn't imagine it...No, he wasn't sleeping.' The officer on the other end of the line was beginning to irritate her now. 'I have seen a great many corpses in my life, and I assure you, this one's as dead as they come.' Phryne rolled her eyes at Jeoffrey, who was listening to her part of the exchange. 'Look, you'd better come here. Twenty-seven Lark Lane, Williamstown. No, I haven't moved the body, but the tide's coming in. I will go watch over it to make sure it doesn't get washed away by the waves.'

'All right, Miss,' the police officer said reluctantly. 'I'll get someone out of bed. But only because it's you.'

Phryne rang off, and gave Jeoffrey a regretful smile. 'This wasn't how I imagined the remainder of this evening playing out.'

'Nor I. But you really shouldn't be the one to mind the body. I'm happy to do it.'

'That is a most gallant offer, but you are the householder—you should be here to greet the police when they arrive and direct them to the scene. Do you have a torch? I've a small one in my handbag, but I'd like a bigger one if you have it.'

This admirable man reached into a broom cupboard and produced a torch nearly a foot long, and concordantly thick. She tested the switch and a bright beam showed. 'This will do nicely,' she said.

'Are you quite sure you'll be all right on your own?' Jeoffrey asked anxiously.

'Absolutely.' At the front door, she turned and gave him a look. 'Please do by all means wait up for me.'

Phryne retraced her steps to the waterfront. The body was still there, though she could swear it had been moved somewhat by the encroaching tide. She shone the torch onto the man's face and gasped. He was Chinese, beyond question.

An incoming wave splashed over her rubber boots, and she retreated up the shore, keeping the torch beam trained on the unfortunate victim. She had thought to look for clues, but realised there was no point; even if there were any, the waves would have long ago washed them away.

She sat on a rock and stared moodily out to sea. At length, her reverie was disturbed by a voice.

'Evening, Miss Fisher. It's a wet night to be out.'

Phryne turned her torch shoreward to see Jeoffrey standing beside a familiar face. 'Why, hello, Jack. Good of you to drop by.'

In the wavering torchlight, she noted Robinson's twisted smile. 'Well, sleep is overrated, isn't it. Is that our new friend over there?'

'Yes, that's him. He's been dead quite a while, I'd say. Any clues will be long gone. Unless there's something in his pockets, of course.'

Phryne stood up, and her coat fell open. Robinson looked hard at the pyjamas thus revealed, and visibly restrained himself from asking awkward questions. He merely looked from Phryne to Jeoffrey and back again, and gave a brief smile.

'All right, Phryne. I'll need you to make a formal statement at City South, but that can wait till tomorrow. I don't want to interrupt your evening any further.'

'Thank you, Jack. But what are you going to do with this poor fellow?'

Jack Robinson shrugged. 'I've brought an ambulance and some backup. Come see me tomorrow morning. We'll talk then.'

———

Back in Lark Lane, Jeoffrey shut the front door and pulled a deadlock across it. 'I fear your reputation might have suffered, Phryne,' he began. 'I'm sorry.'

Phryne laughed lightly. 'I wouldn't worry about that. Jack Robinson and I have a long history, and he's quite used to me and my idiosyncrasies.' Phryne shook her hair and shivered. 'If there's anything left in that bottle, I think we should drink it.'

Jeoffrey took Phryne's hand and led her back to the dining room. One of the candles had gone out, but the rest still blazed in quiet splendour. 'I can do better than that.'

They resumed their seats at the table, and Jeoffrey poured two glasses of cognac. 'It's probably not what you're used to, Phryne. But it's not bad.'

Phryne took a sip. 'Not bad at all, Jeoffrey. Thank you.'

They sat in silence for some time, savouring the warming liquor. When Phryne had drained the last drops from her glass, she set it on the table and said, 'Towards the end of the war, I was in London. German bombers were becoming a serious nuisance. In fact, I believe that they might have destroyed London. We didn't have enough anti-aircraft defences to keep them off, you know. I think the only reason they didn't bomb us flat was that they knew they were losing the war and they feared our vengeance.'

Jeoffrey nodded. 'That does make sense. After all, the French sabotaged any chance that the Germans might forgive us for beating them. So they didn't want to add our enduring malice to Clemenceau's?'

'Indeed. Anyway, there I was, with a friend, in the middle of London. And we heard a bomber overhead, with its Mercedes engines going *pour-vous, pour-vous* above us. Then we heard that whistling sound that falling bombs make. And my friend looked me in the eye and said, "Phryne? I've been hoarding a bar of chocolate. I think perhaps we should eat it now."'

Jeoffrey's laughter was heartfelt. 'Obviously the bomb missed you, though?'

'It destroyed the building next door. But yes, we were spared.'

Jeoffrey eyed her thoughtfully. 'So we should eat, drink and be merry in the midst of death and destruction?'

Phryne gave him a warm look. 'I believe we should.'

Feeling that more conversation was both desirable and necessary, Phryne sought—after some detailed reminiscences on both sides of London and the Home Counties—to draw him out about himself. On that score he had little enough to say. 'Yes, I really am a bachelor, as I mentioned. It was my mother's idea, and—as you say—I think she was right. As far as I can tell, marriage is no bed of roses. Look at poor old Gerald Street.'

Phryne had met Jeoffrey's colleague while on the trail of the missing *Hours of Juana the Mad*. Viper-tongued with a heart of gold, as she recalled. 'What about Gerald Street?'

Jeoffrey swirled the cognac in his glass and took a sip, then said, 'Gerald really is a splendid chap, you know. Kind, generous, thoughtful—everything you want to see in a colleague. Absolutely first-rate scholar, too. What he doesn't know about ancient manuscripts and Germanic philology you could stick in your eye. His wife, though… Don't get me wrong; she's a decent sort, and a fine scholar in her own way. But her jealousy is terrible to behold. She acts as if she owns Gerald. It's so silly, really.'

Sensing a possible cue, Phryne murmured, 'Well, Jeoffrey, nobody owns me.'

His beautiful eyes opened wider. 'Well, no. I should think not.' He glanced around nervously then, pausing at the clock in the corner and noting, 'My! It's after ten already.'

Phryne rose, and walked around the table. 'So if you're going to make your move, now would be a good time for it.'

She drew him gently to his feet, aware that during the last few hours Jeoffrey's eyes had periodically strayed to her neckline. She had deliberately left the top pyjama button unfastened, so as to give glimpses of creamy delights within, but she had begun to suspect that Jeoffrey Bisset was too well-bred to attempt Phryne's virtue unaided. With the shy and polite, it always paid to be assertive.

He gazed down at her adoringly. 'I say, Phryne, do you mean this?'

'Yes, Jeoffrey, I do. Think of this as akin to the bar of chocolate during the London blitz. Now, please kiss me.'

The kiss was remarkable, and Phryne melted into his strong embrace. His open mouth pressed against hers, waiting for its cue. Phryne's tongue darted between his lips and tangled with his own. His hands deftly unbuttoned her pyjama top and caressed her breasts lovingly. Bachelor you may be, Jeoffrey Bisset, but you are not unpractised in the art of love, she mused, as her senses drowned in ecstasy. Now the difficult bit has been surmounted, the rest will be easy. He kissed her with passionate restraint, then bent over her breasts and sucked them. Phryne closed her eyes in swooning delight.

Then Jeoffrey took her by the hand and led her into his bedroom.

Extracting the long-limbed Jeoffrey from his clothes took some time. When it was done, she gave his body a devouring look, then hastened to shed what remained of her own garments until she stood naked before him.

'Dearest Phryne,' he breathed. With no apparent effort he lifted her, carried her to the bed, and laid her on the quilt. 'Sweet nymph, let me please you.'

Phryne's thighs parted, and felt his skilful hand begin to caress her. She closed her eyes in delight.

———

'That was very well done, Peony. You're truly one of us now.'

'I passed my audition, then?'

'Yes, you did! He's pleased with you.'

Peony reached out to accept the proffered pound note. Then she tilted her chin upwards and gave her lover a passionate kiss.

Chapter Eleven

Phryne awoke the next morning in unfamiliar circumstances. The bed was narrower than her own luxurious brass one, and the mattress rather less yielding to her person. She opened her eyes wide and looked around. The bedroom was painted light green, with a tall bookcase against one wall, filled with Latin texts and other oddments. Detective novels had an entire shelf to themselves, she noted, and there appeared to be the complete works of Arthur Conan Doyle. Next to the closed door stood a small desk and chair. Her previous day's clothes—which appeared to be quite dry, the patent clothes dryer having apparently worked its dark enchantments—were draped over the chair, and her shoes stood on the desk.

She pulled back the sheets and inspected her slender and exceptionally satiated person, smiling to herself as she was flooded with memories of the previous night. She considered dressing, then decided she should wash first. In the meantime, her borrowed pyjamas had been also left for her, so she slipped them on and padded across deep blue carpet to the door. Opening it, she inhaled the scent of frying bacon and eggs. She followed the scent to the kitchen and posed in the doorway.

'Good morning, Jeoffrey. You may colour me impressed.'

He turned his tousled head towards her and smiled. 'Splendid. May I offer you breakfast?'

'I don't usually, but I'll make an exception on this occasion. You don't have coffee, do you?'

The corners of his mouth turned down. 'I'm sorry, but no: I don't drink coffee. Tea?'

'All right. Black, no sugar, please.'

Jeoffrey by morning light was every bit as impressive as he had shown himself the previous evening. He had dressed himself in a plain white shirt and trousers, and exuded a masculine scent of self-assurance and soap.

He waved her to a seat at a scrubbed pine table, which had already been laid with knives, forks, and teaspoons. 'Toast with your eggs and bacon?'

'No, thank you. What time is it?'

'About half past eight. I've been up for an hour or so.' He placed a plate loaded with two fried eggs and three rashers of bacon before her, then slid into the seat opposite and set to work on three eggs and four rashers of bacon, before proceeding to demolish a largeish pile of buttered toast with jam. Phryne had not met such an enthusiastic eater for many a day. It seemed to be contagious, for to her surprise she found herself finishing her serving. She set her cutlery on the plate, and placed her elbows on the table.

'Jeoffrey, you have been an absolute brick.'

Jeoffrey gave her a brief smile, finished off the last piece of toast and jam, and rose to clear away the plates. 'The pleasure was mine.'

Phryne inclined her head, wondering what he would say next. Generally speaking, this was the moment when the eager lover asked when he could see her next. But Jeoffrey did not do so, which was disconcerting. She decided to prompt him. 'Perhaps we should do this again,' she suggested. 'Although without the corpse next time.'

Unexpectedly, Jeoffrey reached out with one long arm, took her hand, and kissed it. 'Phryne, I would love to enjoy more of your wonderful company. But I wasn't going to ask, you know.'

'And why not, if I might enquire?'

'Why, when a goddess deigns to visit, you do not ask for more. You simply accept with gratitude whatever she offers.'

Phryne smiled. 'Very prettily expressed, Jeoffrey. I am astonished that no woman has managed to ensnare you in matrimony, but your explanation last night was cogent. You have certainly delighted me. But now, alas, City South police station calls. Jack will want my statement, I expect.'

'Do you want me to come with you?'

'No, it's all right. I'm sure Jack will be happy to accept my account alone. I'll just borrow your bathroom once more, then I'll be on my way.'

Phryne washed and dressed, and when she was done Jeoffrey offered to call a cab for her.

'No, thank you. I'll take the train.'

—

Phryne caught the Flinders Street train with a minute to spare, and made her way through bustling crowds of commuters to City South police station. As she walked up the front steps, the first person she encountered was none other than Lin Chung. He was dressed in a plain black Western business suit, and his lack of surprise at her arrival suggested he had, in fact, been anticipating it.

'Lin! Are you here about the body I found on the shoreline last night?'

Lin's eyebrows lifted, and he regarded her solemnly. 'I had a phone call from Detective Inspector Robinson this morning asking me to come and identify a corpse.'

'Ah. And did he tell you I'd found the body?'

'He did. I shall repair to the morgue to see if we can discover anything about the poor fellow.' He gave the merest hint of a smile. 'You're here to give your statement, I take it?'

'I'm afraid so. I'm sorry, Lin. And doubly so that you've been dragged into it.'

Lin sighed. 'It had to be someone from our community. Please don't be concerned. We will settle this without incommoding you any further. How did you find him, if I may ask?'

'I was walking along the seashore in Williamstown and there he was. So I called the police and then returned to stay with the body to make sure it didn't get washed away; the tide was coming in, you see.'

As she was recounting this, Lin had taken her arm to escort her up the steps. Having reached the station's front desk, he said, 'And now I must leave. Take care, Silver Lady.'

And with that, Lin was no longer among those present. Phryne leaned against the counter and pondered. That Jack should call Lin was logical enough; he knew that Lin was a respected figure in the Chinese community, and he had to call someone. But Lin's reserve had set her thinking. He had not said the obvious: We all look alike to you Occidentals. But it sounded as though she were being ever so gently warned off. *We will settle this without incommoding you any further.* Did Lin know what this was about? Whether he did or not, his words could not have been clearer. *We Chinese will manage our own affairs.*

'Miss? Can I help you?'

Phryne started at the query from a young constable. 'Oh, I'm sorry. I'm here to see Jack Robinson. He's expecting me.'

The youthful constable went to fetch his superior, and presently Jack appeared. He ushered her into a small room replete with writing implements and closed the door on her. Phryne picked up the fountain pen supplied and began to write. A bald narrative would be sufficient, without corroborative detail. No mention of why she happened to be on the beach at Williamstown in her pyjamas, for example. As she wrote, she wondered why Jack had mentioned to Lin that she had been the one to find the body. Did this mean Jack wanted Phryne to investigate by herself? Jack might have suspected that Lin would not welcome Phryne's investigations. The Chinese were notoriously clannish. Even if Lin wanted Phryne's help, the other families would not. Or would they? It really depended on who had done the killing. If it were an Occidental, then the Chinese would want all the help they could get in bringing the killer to justice. But the fact that Lin had warned her off the investigation did suggest that he at least suspected that the killer was Chinese. In which case they would probably want to fix it up themselves. She could only assume that Robinson was just as eager as Lin to keep Phryne out of the investigation. Well, she would make no promises on that account.

Jack returned and led her to his office. He gestured to a plain wooden chair opposite, and seated himself behind the desk, which had a goodly pile of papers on it, neatly filed inside manila folders. Seen by daylight, he seemed quite unaffected by his night-time excursion to Williamstown. He looked, if anything, quite content with the world. His grey business suit was neatly pressed; his brown hat was, if not jaunty, at least self-confident; and his face had lost its look of haunted persecution. He read through Phryne's statement, witnessed it with a flourish, and stowed it in one of his multitudinous manila folders.

'Thank you for attending the station so promptly,' he said.

Then he fixed her with a shrewd look, 'Now, I have the feeling there's something else you want to share with me.'

'Jack, you do know me well. There was one thing... I found a broken opium pipe in the Williamstown botanical gardens yesterday afternoon. It had been used. And I was wondering if you had heard any whispers about opium in Melbourne. Because this could spell big trouble, you know.'

Ignoring her question, Robinson asked, 'And what did you do with this pipe?'

'I handed it in locally, to a sergeant whose probity was vouched for by a certain local luminary. But you didn't answer my question.'

Robinson smiled wryly. 'Well, as you know, if there did happen to be a police investigation into opium, I couldn't tell you about it.'

'Indeed. But of course if there was not even a sniff of such an inquiry, you would be able to reassure me that this was nothing more than a stray piece of jetsam.'

The corners of the inspector's mouth twitched. 'Then please be reassured. Look, these opium laws are—well, ill-advised is the best word I can think of. It's only encouraging criminals. But I have heard absolutely nothing to suggest cause for concern. And I can tell you with confidence that our city's crime gangs won't touch it. Opium's nothing but trouble, and the profits aren't significant enough to justify it. Nor is there much of a market for the stuff.'

'So despite the fact that I have found evidence to the contrary, you're assuring me that there's no opium afield to speak of.'

Jack Robinson allowed himself a modest peal of laughter. 'That is correct. And if there were any about that I knew of, I'd have to tell you apologetically that I could not possibly comment on a police investigation. Look, Miss Fisher, thank you for the tip-off. I expect the sergeant to whom you gave this artefact has duly filed a report about it, and I expect it will disappear into that great maw of silence which is the police archives.'

He rose. 'Thank you again for the statement. I'll be in touch if you can further aid our investigation.' He sighed. 'And doubtless if that should happen, I will find myself tripping over you constantly in the course of my duties. As usual.'

Phryne took his outstretched hand and shook it cordially. 'I do try my best to make your life interesting, Jack. See you soon, I hope.'

———

Phryne left the building and returned by tram to the beachfront. Walking along The Esplanade from the tram stop, she paused in front of 221B, as her eye had been caught by something sticking from the letterbox. She removed the piece of card and stared at it for a long moment. As before, the message was composed of letters cut from newspapers. *THE WAGES OF SIN IS DEATH!*

Chapter Twelve

'What've you gone and done now, Brown?'

Hammond was furious, and it showed. He paced the room and kicked at a pile of papers on the floor. Rain beat against the windows, and outside waves with grey and white plumes whipped against the rocks.

Brown appeared unmoved by this display. 'I had nothing to do with it.'

Hammond glared at him. 'You expect me to believe that?'

Brown waved a dismissive hand. 'I don't care if you believe me or not, but I'm telling the truth. Look on the bright side; we had no further need of him anyway. His job was to recruit the necessary staff, and he's already done that. Now that he's gone'— Brown shrugged—'there's one less mouth to blab.'

'Well, all right. But if you didn't do it, who did?'

'I don't know, and I don't care. Like I said, it's one problem less to worry about.'

Hammond resumed his seat and folded his hands. 'You reckon you can handle the staff yourself, do you?'

A ghostly smile briefly illumined Brown's impassive features. 'Yes. I've told you this before. I can handle it.'

'All right. Just make yourself scarce till the ship comes in; I don't want to see you back here before then.'

'Why, do you think you're being watched?'

Hammond shook his head. 'Dunno. Just a feeling.'

Chapter Thirteen

While Phryne was wending her way from Williamstown to the city, Ruth and Jane had taken the tram to the Blind Institute, where they found Miss Thomas and reported for duty.

With no suitable classes found for Ruth to assist, she was dispatched once more to Hester in the kitchen, while Jane, as agreed, would be offering her services in the administrative office.

Mr. Blake turned out to be a somewhat ineffectual gentleman of middle age. He smoked a pipe, which necessitated frequent excavations within its dark interior with a small screwdriver kept for the purpose in his wooden desk drawer. Jane's nose wrinkled at the smell. Miss Phryne had once described to her a form of maritime tobacco which was redolent of sailors' pigtails dipped in tar. Jane could well believe that the substance which emerged from the bookkeeper's greasy black leather pouch was of the same genus.

The man was dressed in grey and brown. His face was round, his spectacles likewise, and attached to his nose by a black cord in his coat buttonhole. His eyes were pale blue; he blinked a lot; and more than anything he resembled an affectionate, though not terribly intelligent, black-and-tan terrier. All in all, he seemed the last person in the world to be suspected of embezzlement.

He was delighted to have an assistant, and spent much of the morning fussing over Jane and bringing her tea and biscuits, the former made with the aid of a small electric kettle. And since the kettle had no capacity for turning itself off, Mr. Blake was obliged, as he said, 'to watch it like a hawk, m'dear.'

'If you could add up all the figures in those ledgers while I do it,' he added, 'I'd be greatly obliged to you.'

Adding up shilling and pence in dusty ledgers was well within the grasp of Jane's arithmetic. But there was a great deal to do, and she finished up spending most of the day on it. It was after two when she announced her conclusions.

'Mr. Blake, you've made a few mistakes, but nothing of any consequence. You were only out by a few shillings in most cases.'

Mr. Blake mopped his brow with an enormous white handkerchief and beamed at her. 'I'm delighted to hear it, m'dear. You are a dab hand with the figures, aren't you? It makes me wonder… I don't suppose you could come back again, could you?'

'I will have to ask Miss Thomas's permission, but I can't see why not. Was there something in particular you wanted me to do?'

'Well, m'dear, I don't have your head for numbers, but I have an idea that something is wrong with these accounts, you know.' He shook his head. 'The expenditure seems to have increased since last year, but I can't work out where it's going. I know I should tell Mr. Hedger, but I'm reluctant to do it until I've found out the truth of the matter. But what that is and how to find it'—he shrugged helplessly—'I just don't have a clue.'

'I see.' Jane thought for a moment. 'I suppose one way would be to check all the invoices against the amounts entered in the ledger. Perhaps we could do that when I return next Tuesday?'

'Oh, that does sound like a good plan,' said the bookkeeper gratefully, as the bell announcing the commencement of the day's final class resounded.

'Just out of interest,' Jane continued, 'does this office have a lock and key, Mr. Blake?'

He gave her a startled look. 'It did once, but I'm sorry to say that I've lost the key.'

'Well, never mind—I'm going to sit in on a music theory class now. I'll see you next Tuesday.'

Jane waved the briefest of farewells and exited into the corridor. Having made some progress with one mystery, she was keen to look into the other: the mystery of the ghost in the storeroom, as she thought of it. Students were making their way along the corridor arm in arm, and Jane tagged along behind a group of boys heading for Mr. Findlay's music room.

It took some time for the boys to file in one at a time, and Jane inhaled the scent of them. The boys, she noticed, smelled very different from the girls, who affected the cheaper forms of scent. In both sexes the aroma of soap was pronounced; but the boys mostly had their hair slicked down against the head in the fashionable style. The differing scents of pomade assailed her nostrils, in many cases to an overwhelming degree. Beyond the smell of wax and vegetable oils she noted several varieties of perfumes, including clove, cinnamon, lemon, and orange. Well, she decided, they were welcome.

When the students were all seated at their desks, she inched her way along the wall towards the storeroom. The door was wide open. Mr. Findlay being as blind as his students, she trusted that there was very little risk of discovery, but if she were noticed by anyone, she would brazen it out with the excuse that she had left something of hers there the previous Tuesday.

Under cover of the piano, and Mr. Findlay's strictures to the hapless youth at the keyboard—'No, no, Mr. Roberts! E flat minor, if you please!'—she made her way into the storeroom and quietly eased the door behind her until it was almost, but not quite, closed. By contriving to move only when the piano was playing, Jane managed to explore all the cupboards and boxes of music. There was nothing of interest there. But in one corner she found something which excited her attention. A broken wooden desk had been stored there, and an equally damaged wooden chair—missing some structural support on its left side—rested before it. And a large stack of blotting papers rested on the desktop. There was the usual inkwell in the top right-hand corner. She lifted out the blue-stained china receptacle and sniffed it. There was fresh ink therein, which suggested that somebody had been using the desk recently—which was odd in an institution whose inmates relied on braille.

She examined the top blotter and tried to make out what had been written on it. The script was for the most part too faint and blurred to be legible, but one fragment could be deciphered. *Hawksb 9/7* was written in passable copperplate.

As the piano played on outside, Jane sat cross-legged on the floor to think. The fragment on the blotting paper could mean almost anything. But what it meant wasn't as important as the fact of its very existence. Someone had been using the abandoned desk in the storeroom to copy out—what exactly? Obviously whatever it was required secrecy; the closing of the door on Tuesday seemed to confirm as much. And there was a distinctive scent in the room: something like cinnamon? Was it pomade, or a stray aroma from the kitchen?

Jane was still pondering this when the final bell of the day rang out. She heard the students closing their books and making their way into the corridor. She decided to stay hidden until Mr. Findlay had also left, since she had been lurking in his classroom uninvited. She waited until she'd heard the classroom door close, then she rose to her feet, stiff and sore from prolonged sitting, and returned to the door of the storeroom. But while she had left it an inch or so ajar, it was now shut and—Jane noted with alarm when she tried the knob—locked.

Breathe, Jane instructed herself in the face of rising panic. There was no need to call for help. Not yet, anyway. She turned her attention to the windows, of which there were three. The first she tried would not open at all. The wooden window had expanded in the sash, and it was not going to move however hard she pulled at it. The other two windows were of a type that opened only a little way outwards—not anything like far enough to allow egress.

She sat down on a box of music books and considered her next move. She could break a window. Would this be more compromising than calling for help? Regretfully, she decided that it would. Jane did not suffer from embarrassment, but before she resorted to an action that would draw unnecessary attention to herself, she would attempt to persevere with the windows. Realising that the stuck window might be amenable to Archimedes' Law of the Lever, she found a metal ruler in one of the cupboards and inserted it under the wooden base of the window. But try as she might, she could not move it so much as a fraction of an inch. She only desisted when the ruler began to crush the ageing wood. If she persisted, the window base would crumble away, and probably cause the window to break, which she had already decided would be a bridge too far. She put the ruler away with a sigh. What else could she try?

She turned her attention to the next window along and examined it carefully. There was a small handle which wound what seemed to be a piece of bicycle chain. In this way the window could be cranked open on its vertical axis. Inspecting the chain, she found it was attached to its socket via a small brass pin. She tugged at the pin and found it could move. Carefully, she eased the pin out of its socket, thus releasing the chain. The window, when pushed, now opened wide. She threw her satchel through the opening and clambered after it. With difficulty, and with considerable laddering of her stockings, she shimmied through, and landed on the soft grass with barely a sound. She scooped up her satchel and ran.

Ruth was waiting for her at the front gate, anxious and fretting. 'Janey? Are you all right? I haven't seen you all day. You didn't come in for lunch or anything!'

Jane looked at her sister blankly. 'Oh. Lunch. Do you know, I forgot all about it? I was busy adding up the accounts, and Mr. Blake fed me so many biscuits I was never hungry.'

The pair set off towards the tram stop.

'Did you find out anything?' Ruth asked.

'Not yet. But Mr. Blake himself suspects there's something amiss. And if anyone is stealing money from the Institute, I really don't think it's him. He's quite a dear, really. But Ruth, you'll never guess what happened: I went back to the music room in the fourth period—you know, to see about the ghost—and someone locked me in!'

Ruth gasped. 'Jane, no! How did you escape?'

'I managed to climb through the window.'

'But who could have done it?' her sister asked. 'And why?'

Jane shook her head. 'I don't know. But there's something going on at the Institute, and I'm going to find out what.'

———

Dinner was a relatively quiet affair. Jane and Ruth described the day's events at the Institute to Phryne, who listened with interest, and Dot reported that her mother was feeling somewhat better. Tinker was, as usual, reticent in speech and enthusiastic in appetite, and departed from the table as soon as was polite. Phryne, somewhat fatigued by the exertions of the previous evening, followed suit. She took to her bed at an earlier hour than was customary, and delighted in recollections of Jeoffrey's delectable body. He had smelled of soap, lemon, and urgent maleness, and his ravishing of her had been skilled, solicitous, and indefatigable. It had been a long time since she had been so pleasured. She closed her eyes and drifted off to sleep.

———

She awoke with a start into darkness, her senses suddenly alert. Her eye was drawn to the window, which she had left open for the fresh air. There, silhouetted in the moonlight, was a figure gazing in at her.

'Who's there?' she demanded. Her fingers reached for the bedside lamp, and she switched it on.

There was indeed someone—standing on heaven only knew what, to reach her room on the first floor—staring in at her. The face was wrapped in a long woollen scarf, rendering it invisible save for the eyes. Furious, Phryne seized a book from the side table and threw it. There was an agonised groan, and the intruder disappeared.

Phryne ran to the window and leaned out of it. Below her, the intruder scrabbled for a foothold on the high fence separating the yard from the street.

'If you dare to come back here, I shall shoot you!' she shouted.

The intruder, exhibiting some serious athletic abilities, surmounted the fence, jumped down onto the further side and was off like a rabbit down The Esplanade.

As Phryne subsided onto the bed there was a respectful knock at the door.

'Is that you, Dot? Come in.'

Her companion entered the room, clad in a plain white and exceptionally modest nightgown. 'Miss! What's happened? I heard you threaten to shoot someone!'

'I've just had a nocturnal visitor at my window, Dot.'

Dot sat on the edge of the bed and listened, aghast, while Phryne recounted her misadventure.

'But who could have done it, Miss?' she wanted to know.

'I have a strong suspicion that it's the same person who put another offensive message in the letterbox. He's gone too far now; it's time I reported him to the police.'

'Oh, Miss! Please don't let Hugh find out. It will give him one more reason for insisting that I give up working for you after we're married. He thinks my life's dangerous enough already without this.'

Phryne sighed. She was proud of Dot's determination to keep working, and she certainly didn't want to lend weight to her intended's arguments against it. She came to a decision. 'All right, Dot, leave it with me. I'll see if we can't solve this problem ourselves.'

'Thank you, Miss,' said Dot gratefully. 'I promise I'll help you in any way I can.' And she departed for her own room.

Taking the two previous messages from the drawer where she had secreted them, Phryne added them to that day's offering and contemplated the unpleasant collection.

The problem presented by the warnings she now held in her hand was that the author had taken considerable pains to remain anonymous. She needed someone with a forensic cast of mind to unearth this wretched Pharisee—and fortunately she had one such on the premises. Tinker had managed the affair of the girls' friend Claire's paramour with singular tact and precision, she recalled. She would hand the cards to him and see what he could make of them.

From her wristwatch she found that despite her interrupted slumbers it was not yet ten o'clock. Perchance her budding Sexton Blake might still be up. Donning a dressing-gown, Phryne headed downstairs and out the back door to Tinker's shed. The light was on, and music of some kind was emanating from the open window. It sounded like a string orchestra playing at the bottom of a spiral staircase.

She knocked lightly.

'Who is it?' The voice was a little gruff, as was to be expected. Tinker guarded his privacy with a fanaticism worthy of a Dark Age monk.

'It's me, Tinker. May I have a word?'

There was a short silence. Presently the door opened. ''Course, Miss. Come in.'

Ushered inside, Phryne seated herself on the single wooden chair, and Tinker turned off the crystal set and parked himself on the edge of his bed. He leaned forward, and Phryne surveyed the latest of her adoptions with admiration. Tinker had grown a couple of inches in height and several cartloads worth in self-confidence since taking up residence in her household—or in the shed of such, at least.

'Can I do somethin' for you, Miss?' he asked, giving her a quizzical look.

Phryne handed over the three pieces of card. 'What do you make of these, Tink? They have all been planted in the letterbox in the last week. Ordinarily I would dismiss it as the work of a neighbourhood busybody, but their tone is rather more threatening than that—and after this evening I'm inclined to think the correspondent is a serious menace. Someone climbed up to my bedroom window just now and looked in at me, and I rather think it might have been him.' She nodded at the cards Tinker was holding.

'So that's what it was. I heard ya threatenin' ter shoot someone, but I figured you could handle it seeing as you have your pistol. I don't reckon 'e'll come back in a hurry.'

'Perhaps not, but I don't feel confident predicting what he might be capable of, so I think it's time to put a stop to the business. But to do that, I'll need to know who it is. Is that something you could help me with, do you think?'

Tinker studied each card in turn and then compared them. 'He's usin' at least two diff'rent newspapers, Miss.'

'My guess is that he's local, Tink, as the glue wasn't quite dry on the one he delivered on Monday.'

'That's interestin'. Round here people read *The Sun*, *The Age*, *The Argus*, or *The Hawklet*—or in this bloke's case, two of 'em. Yair, I reckon I could give it a go.'

'Do you have a plan, Tinker?'

'Yair, Miss. I do. 'Cos I knows a bloke.'

'I'm sure you know many blokes, Tink,' Phryne said.

Tinker half smiled. 'That's true, Miss, but *this* bloke's got a paper round. An' if I go see this bloke now and tell 'im 'e can sleep in tomorrow, I reckon he'll jump at it. I'll take over 'is round and find out who gets both the papers what your letter writer has used.'

Phryne found little fault in his logic. 'That's a very good plan, Tink. All right, I'll leave it with you. And if any other cards arrive, I'll give them to you.'

As she closed the shed door behind her, Phryne reflected that Tinker was well on his way to becoming the Sexton Blake character he aspired to emulate. She smiled to herself. She seemed to be raising quite the family of detectives.

———

'*My bounty is as boundless as the sea / My love as deep; the more I give to thee / The more I have, for both are infinite.*'

'That's lovely! Is it a poem?'
'It's from *Romeo and Juliet*. Shakespeare.'
'Oh. Their love didn't end well, did it?'
'No, but Romeo was an idiot, and you aren't.'
'I'm very glad to hear it!'
Laughing, they collapsed into each other's arms again.

Chapter Fourteen

Tinker rose early, when the sky outside his window was still pitch black. He dressed quickly in his work clothes (a buttoned blue shirt, short trousers, and heavy boots with thick woollen socks) and opened the back gate. He heard the milk cart rumbling along the laneway and waited until the Clydesdale horse clopped up to his back gate. The driver looked up with surprise. He was an old man with a cloth cap and a dark woollen muffler around his unshaven neck. His gnarled features twisted into what might have been a smile.

'Morning, Tinker. Jeez, mate, you're up early.'

'Mornin', Sid.' Tinker held aloft the wire milk crate with one hand, and caressed the gently steaming nose of the horse with the other. The horse snuffled, and swished his tail.

The milkman laughed softly. 'Jeez, Tinker, you're game. Hercules gen'rally bites people. 'E seems ter like you, but.'

Tinker refrained from mentioning that three days previously he had given Hercules an apple when his master had been fast asleep on his homeward journey. Horses remember this sort of thing. In the light of the milk cart's lantern, the deep brown eyes gleamed, and the nose lifted in enquiry. 'Not t'day, mate, sorry,' Tinker whispered in the horse's ear, which twitched philosophically.

'Save me the trip, will ya? It's four pints, ain't it?'

Tinker nodded, and strode along the wagon to the rear. Most of the crates were empty now—the milk run must be nearing its close—but there were still several filled cans. He selected a gallon steel can which appeared half-full, carried it inside the yard and returned with the empty, which he loaded into the back of the dray. He stood by the back gate holding his left hand aloft in salute. Hercules clopped along the cobbled lane, and the cart rumbled off into the distance. Tinker tiptoed into the kitchen and stowed the milk in the refrigerator, then helped himself to an apple and an orange from the fruit bowl, stowing them in his leather satchel. Opening the back gate again, he stepped into the now-empty laneway.

St Kilda was utterly silent. Above the Dandenong Ranges he saw the blazing stars of Scorpio rampaging across the eastern sky. Antares gleamed in the scorpion's heart like a fierce ruby. It was quite a sight at the best of times. Tinker had not really noticed the stars during his childhood. Life had been too busy; and besides, the sea mists of Queenscliff interfered constantly with attempts at amateur astronomy. In Melbourne there were more streetlights, but occasionally he would wake early and walk on the beach, and admire the clear western skies above the bay.

Tinker slung his satchel over his shoulder and wheeled out the bicycle he had borrowed from the bloke he'd told Miss Phryne about. It was an old, rusty bike, and he experienced some difficulty getting his right leg over the wooden frame which straddled the horizontal bar. Fred had been emphatic on the subject. 'The papers come in two big canvas bags, and they get put over the frame. If ya don't have the frame, the bags'll fall off and the papers'll get dirty. And then old man Fawkner'll have a fit. 'E's not a bad old codger, but 'e likes to complain and it's best not to give 'im reason.'

In Tinker's limited experience of newsagents they all liked to grumble. It doubtless went with the job. Along with ink-smudged hands—which Tinker now had himself, he noticed, wiping them fruitlessly on his trousers. As well as his bike, Fred had given Tinker some old copies of the various papers he delivered, and Tinker had devoted himself to studying their typefaces closely. The attention to detail had paid off, in that he was fairly certain that Phryne's intruder was a reader of both *The Argus*, which skewed conservative, and *The Hawklet*, a sensationalist gossip rag.

Speaking of which, what else had Fred said about the papers? '*The Sun* goes in one bag, and the rest in the other. And whatever ya do, don't give 'em the wrong paper, or they'll ring up and complain and we all get grief.'

Tinker applied his feet to the pedals and wobbled along the alley, feeling that his kidneys were being battered into submission. At the end of the lane he turned left and headed along the footpath on smooth macadam. He breathed easier. He had ridden bikes occasionally in Queenscliff, and he'd heard that once you'd mastered it you never forgot how. It seemed to be a fact.

Tinker glanced at his watch, which had been a present from Miss Phryne. Quarter past five. Returning his eyes to the footpath, he braked sharply. A dog had erupted out of nowhere, parked itself right in his way, and was barking furiously at him. It was a small, yappy, black creature, and it was very unhappy about something. Tinker rested his hands on the handlebars and gave the dog a severe look.

'Look, sport, ya don't 'ave ter do this. I ain't comin' into your house, all right?'

The dog gave him a puzzled look, then resumed its tirade, though with an undercurrent of uncertainty. Tinker sighed and, skirting the animal (restraining the urge to give it a good kick as he passed), continued along his path.

He arrived at the St Kilda newsagency five minutes early, to be greeted by a fortyish man in spectacles, a grey dustcoat, and a general air of being somewhat fed up with the world. Both hands were on his hips in the time-honoured sugar-bowl pose. 'All right, sonny, what's your story? That's Fred's bike you're riding, I see.'

Tinker dismounted, and leaned the bike against a lamppost. 'Fred came down crook late last night. He didn't want to let ya down, so I said I'd do 'is round for 'im.' This was the best approach, he had decided. Don't ask; just tell Mr. Fawkner what was going to happen. He had learned this from Miss Phryne.

The newsagent took off his spectacles and gave them a rub with a handkerchief whose cleanliness was dubious. 'What's yer name, son?'

'Tinker.'

'Ever done a paper round before?'

'Yair, 'course. In Queenscliff, but.' Another trick Tinker had picked up: if you were going to tell a whopper, make it clear, convincing, and largely unverifiable.

Fawkner looked him up and down impassively. 'Well, you can ride a bike, and you've got the frame on. And you're four minutes early, which counts in your favour.' He paused as a lad erupted out of the shop garage wheeling a bike laden with papers. 'George, make sure number forty-two gets *The Argus* this time! Yesterday you gave her *The Sun* and she gave me grief about it.'

'Yair, I will, Mr. Fawkner.' The boy George gave Tinker a con-spiratorial grin and sped off down the road.

'All right, Tinker. You'll do. Did Fred explain the job?'

'Yair. I reckon I can handle it.'

'Come get your load then.'

Fawkner led the way into the garage, which was lit by a single dim bulb hanging from a cord. Dust and the smell of damp news-print made the place barely tolerable. Cardboard boxes were piled up to the ceiling around the edges. Fawkner bent over and picked up a canvas double pannier. Tinker received it without effort and loaded it onto the wooden frame. Then the newsagent handed him a grubby clipboard with a few pages attached. The street names were underlined in indelible pen, and there were four columns, headed *Sun, Age, Argus,* and *Other.* The last column was for miscellaneous publications, like *The Hawklet,* which were written in by name. For the rest, there were merely crosses marked. Tinker scanned the first page, labelled Hotham Street, and set off. The sky was brightening by now, but as he pedalled through the streets towards his destination, there were still no signs of life.

He discovered that Hotham Street had quite a number of flats, and he quickly grew weary of climbing steps to leave papers outside each door. But as he moved on to Mitford Street and then Dickens, he found the going quicker. He turned over the first page on the clipboard, having delivered all the papers, and eagerly scanned the next page. When he did not see what he was looking for, he sighed.

It wasn't till the last page that he found it: a house which accepted both *The Argus* and *The Hawklet.* He reached into his satchel for the exercise book he had brought and made a note of the address, then ate the apple quickly before continuing on with his route.

It was nearly seven o'clock by the time he returned to the newsagency in Acland Street. Mr. Fawkner was standing outside with folded arms. Two other boys who'd clearly just finished their own rounds were riding off as Tinker approached.

'Well, Tinker?' said the newsagent. 'How did it go?'

'No trouble.' Tinker dismounted and handed the empty

panniers and the clipboard to their owner. 'Pretty sure I made no mistakes.'

'If you had, you'd have run out of something or had spares left over. Since you don't, I'm guessing you did all right.'

'One thing made me laugh, but,' Tinker commented.

The newsagent frowned, clearly unaccustomed to his paper-boys seeing a humorous aspect to their work. 'What was that?'

'One house takes both *The Argus* and *The Hawklet*. Knowin' what those papers are, it struck me as a bit odd. Can't be any others like that.'

'I'm sure there are,' said the newsagent. 'It takes all types, you know.'

'Nah, I don't reckon there could be,' said Tink.

His show of disbelief had the desired effect. Fawkner leafed through his collection of clipboards and quickly identified three other addresses with the same order. 'See?'

Tinker scanned them quickly and tried to commit them to memory. 'Whaddya know?' he said. 'I wouldn't have thought it.'

He took his bike by the handlebars. 'Thanks, Mr. Fawkner. I'd better be off—I've got school today. You can give what you owe me to Fred, and we'll sort somethin' out between us. See ya.'

He pedalled away quickly, reciting the three addresses to himself.

As soon as he'd rounded the corner, he rummaged in his satchel, extracted his exercise book, and wrote the addresses down. Then he rode home along The Esplanade, returned to his shed, and changed hurriedly into his school clothes. Mrs. Butler, who was cooking eggs, bacon, and toast in the kitchen, looked up when he entered.

'Was that you who brought the milk in, Tink?' she asked. 'You've been up and about early.'

Feeling a certain quiet pride swelling within his breast, Tinker nodded. 'Job for Miss Fisher.'

'Ah. Well, would you like a proper cooked breakfast?'

Tinker inhaled the enticing aromas and nodded. 'Yair, that'd be great, Mrs. B. Thanks.'

He sat down and, a little worn out by the morning's endeavours, allowed himself to be made a fuss of.

It was still too early in the morning to be reporting his finds to Miss Phryne, he knew; he trusted the malicious correspondent would refrain from making a repeat visit till Tink had had a chance to enlighten her.

———

That afternoon found Phryne sitting in the parlour, finishing the novel she had flung so precipitously at her night-time intruder. She had found it lying in the front garden and had smiled grimly on seeing the bloodstain on the spine. Her assailant would have a head wound, she judged; while the scarf had been wrapped around his face as far as the eyes, his head had been bare. When she had a firm suspect, she would inspect his head for signs of recent injury. She reached the book's end and laid it down on the sofa next to her. It had concerned the courtship of Edward, a rather gormless youth to whom Phryne had taken an instant dislike, and Amelia, a sweet, trusting girl also rather lacking in gorm. The fly in the ointment was an older man called James who plainly adored Amelia and was always getting her out of trouble. Phryne had hoped that Amelia would eventually have the sense to pick James rather than Edward as her husband, and the girl eventually did so. Phryne herself was partial to comely young men, but someone as naive as the book's heroine really needed a firm hand on the tiller of her life. Generally she preferred women to be self-reliant, in life as in fiction, but the portrayal of Amelia was of a young woman with all the survival instincts of an orchid in a snowstorm.

Dot looked up from her knitting. 'A good book, Miss?'

'Not too bad,' Phryne told her. 'Although I felt like giving the heroine a serious slap around the head. Don't worry about the blood on the spine.'

Dot raised her eyebrows. 'Not your blood, I hope, Miss?'

'Not mine, no. I threw it at our visitor last night.'

Dot nodded her approval. 'I hope it hurt him. Do you have a plan for finding him yet?'

'I've put Tinker on the case,' Phryne assured her. 'And he has come up with quite a clever scheme.'

But before Phryne could expand on said scheme, she was interrupted by the doorbell.

Firm, magisterial footsteps sounded in the passage, and presently Mr. Butler appeared in their midst, ushering in two young women. 'Miss Thomas and Miss Barnes from the Blind Institute,' he pronounced.

Phryne looked the two women over. Both were modestly dressed in long grey skirts and cream-coloured blouses, with flat-heeled, sensible shoes for both. The elder was decidedly plain, with her hair pulled back in a tight bun. The younger was clutching her arm as if it were a lifebelt.

'Thank you for requesting our services, Miss Fisher,' the elder said in a brisk, businesslike tone.

'Yes,' said the younger, in a high, decidedly musical voice. 'I told Ruth and Jane I would love to tune your piano, so I was excited when Miss Thomas told me you'd called.' Her eyes were a striking blue-grey, but entirely expressionless. She was, despite her demure dress, strikingly beautiful. Phryne put her age at about sixteen.

'Please,' said Miss Phryne, gesturing towards the offending instrument. 'Have at it.'

Miss Thomas led her charge towards the piano. Miss Barnes patted the top, felt around it for its general dimensions, and smiled. She then lifted the lid of the keyboard and played an extended arpeggio in F major with one graceful hand.

'I see. Yes, it really does need work, but what a beautiful Bechstein, Miss Fisher.'

'How long will you need?' asked Phryne.

'I think an hour. Perhaps a little less. I cannot be sure as yet.'

Miss Barnes's cheeks coloured slightly. A certain tension in her manner suggested to Phryne that she would prefer to be left alone with her work. Phryne turned to Dot. 'Let us leave Miss Barnes to her work.' She turned to Miss Thomas. 'Mr. Butler will be glad to oblige if you should need anything.'

As they left the room, Phryne turned and noticed that Miss Barnes's tense shoulders had eased somewhat. Miss Thomas had propped open the top of the piano, and the girl was already wielding her brass tuning hammer, reaching around to press a key, which went *plung*.

'That was a kind thought, Miss,' Dot offered when they had closed the door behind them. 'I know she can't see us, but I'll bet she can sense when people stare at her.'

Dot went upstairs to her room, clutching her knitting and the bloodstained hardback, and Phryne was on the verge of following when the parlour door opened. 'Might I have a word with you, Miss Fisher?' It was Miss Thomas.

'Of course,' said Phryne courteously. She waved her visitor into the study, and they each took a chair. 'How may I help you, Miss Thomas?'

Miss Thomas looked at Phryne hesitantly. 'Miss Fisher, as you are no doubt aware, your daughters have been volunteering at the Institute two days this week.'

'Indeed,' said Phryne. 'And I hope they are proving to be of use.'

'They are—they're lovely girls, both of them. But the thing is… Well, I asked Jane for some particular help, and I worry that I might have overstepped. I really should have spoken to you about it before involving her. But I saw an opportunity, and…' Phryne was growing impatient with the woman's elliptical pauses. She decided to help her visitor to move beyond them. 'Are you speaking of the possible irregularities in the Institute's accounts?' she asked.

Miss Thomas's face relaxed into an expression of relief. 'Then Jane has told you of my suspicions already. I'm glad to hear it. I'm sure Mr. Blake, the bookkeeper, is blameless, but I'm afraid he's not really up to investigating the matter himself, and I couldn't do it myself; Mr. Hedger is very fond of Mr. Blake, you see, and doesn't want to give him the impression that there is any question over his work. But the Institute is so desperately short of funds, we really can't afford to be throwing them away needlessly…' The poor woman looked wretched.

'And so you've asked Jane to help,' Phryne finished for her.

Miss Thomas ducked her head. 'When I heard she was a maths whiz it seemed like an answer to my prayers. But I really should have spoken to you about it first. I do hope you don't object.'

'Not at all. But I appreciate your speaking to me about it. And I have perfect confidence in Jane. With any luck, her investigation will soon produce results.'

Miss Thomas nodded. 'Thank you—and I'm sorry for disturbing you.' She rose to her feet. 'I'll go and see how Jennifer—Miss Barnes, I should say—is getting on. She's so clever. She has perfect pitch, you know. And she plays beautifully. Perhaps she could play for you before we leave? The pianos at the Institute are donated, of course, and I fear they aren't of any particular quality. It would be such a treat for her to play on a fine instrument like your Bechstein.'

'Of course she may play it; I'd be delighted to hear her. But if you don't mind my asking, how does she play when she can't see the keyboard? I suppose she knows where all the notes are by touch, of course, but I wonder how she is able to read music. Did she lose her sight only recently?'

Miss Thomas shook her head. 'Oh no. She's been blind since birth. All our students learn to play by touch. Louis Braille was a musician, you know. And he invented braille music notation as well as his letters, because he wanted the best for everyone who'd been robbed of their sight.'

Miss Thomas returned to the parlour, and Phryne headed upstairs to her bedroom; while she was sure Jennifer Barnes was a fine musician, the tuning of the piano in the next room was not making for a pleasant afternoon soundtrack.

She wondered how Tinker had managed his morning's investigation; he would be home from school shortly and she could ask him. His calm and resourceful manner boded well for a future career in detection. He had confided in her his desire to be a policeman. Hugh Collins was something of a role model for him. Her thoughts turned to the detective sergeant, whose absence had grown increasingly noticeable with each passing day. What was behind it? Phryne wondered. If Hugh really had gone off the idea of marrying Dot, it would be a dreadful blow.

Presently there was a soft knock at her bedroom door, and on Phryne's command her companion entered the room.

'Miss Barnes has finished with the piano, Miss, and Miss Thomas said that the fee was ten shillings.'

Phryne reached into her purse for a ten-shilling note and followed Dot downstairs.

In the sitting-room, she found Miss Barnes tearing through the *Moonlight Sonata* in C sharp minor as if running to meet a train at platform four. Her face was fixed in an expression of studied rapture: an attitude very reminiscent of My First Communion. Phryne sat on the sofa and watched the girl.

Miss Barnes played the final chord and bowed her head. Miss Thomas, who was standing nearby, nodded briefly. 'Very fine, Jennifer. But a touch too quick, do you not think?'

'Sorry, Miss Thomas.'

The girl then began on a slow, simple piece. Her sightless eyes closed, and this time, Phryne realised, she was playing a piece of her own choosing rather than one selected by her teacher. Phryne was enchanted, and at the piece's tranquil conclusion she applauded loudly.

'Oh, that was wonderful! What was it? After the Beethoven, I mean.'

'Erik Satie's *Gymnopédie* Number One,' the girl responded.

Phryne noted that Miss Thomas's lips were pursed in disapproval. Good for Jennifer! she thought. Phryne had little time for excessively dutiful students. She had never been one herself, and liked to see a little rebellion in the young. She turned to Miss Thomas. 'Miss Barnes really is a credit to you. She plays superbly.'

Miss Thomas conceded the point. 'She plays well, certainly. But I have no idea where she acquired that piece of...music.'

'I learned it by ear, Miss Thomas,' Jennifer piped up.

'I see. Well, mind that you play the Beethoven piece *adagio sostenuto* next time. We must leave now, Jennifer. We have a tram to catch.' Miss Thomas strode forward and took Jennifer Barnes by the arm.

'Thank you both. And the next time my piano needs a tune, I will ask for Miss Barnes again.'

Phryne noted that a swift, mischievous smile flickered across the girl's features.

Mr. Butler appeared as if by magic, and conducted their guests to the front door.

———

'Alas that love whose view is muffled still / Should without eyes see pathways to his will.'

'Is that *Romeo and Juliet* again?'
'Yes, it is. But we must not be blind.'
'We won't be. And tonight will be splendid. You're doing well.'
'Thank you. Is there to be anyone special in the audience?'
'One of his business partners, I gather. We are expected to be decorative.'
'Then decorative we shall be.'

Chapter Fifteen

Mme Partlett's boutique was everything a French costumier's salon ought to be. Refinement, taste, and discernment radiated quietly from every corner of the store, from the spotless dark blue carpet and comfortable sculpted chairs to the green velvet curtains and elongated windows giving a discreet view of Collins Street without. Elegant women bustled to and fro, wielding scissors, tape measures, and racks of gowns. Madame herself was indubitably French, being slender, clad entirely in black, with prominent black eyebrows, midnight blue eyes, and a sharp nose that looked as though you could carve buttonholes with it.

As Phryne entered and uttered the obligatory '*Bonjour!*' Madame rose from her chair and waved her manicured fingers at one of her assistants. 'Phryne!' she said in a husky contralto. 'How wonderful to see you. And'—Madame's eyelids flickered for a moment, as she waited for memory to place a filing card before her eyes—'the *demoiselles* Ruth and Jane. Am I to take it that new gowns are required?'

Phryne agreed this was the case. Ruth and Jane still loved their original evening dresses in heliotrope (Jane) and cyclamen

(Ruth), which had been discreetly let out here and there by Dot, but both girls had grown such that their hemlines were now insufficiently decorous for formal wear. What they wanted now, Phryne judged, was something similar, with overtones of fashionable grown-up dresses. On the question of colour, Jane still favoured heliotrope, but Ruth had decided her new dress should be amber.

While Madame's assistant—a silent, severe young woman called Simone—was measuring the girls in the sanctity of the back room, Madame and Phryne conducted a lengthy conversation in Parisian French, and between them they decided on a compromise between *à la mode* and *à la jeune fille*. Arms would be bare, but the skirt lengths an inch below the knee. An artificial flower in a complementary colour was to be sewn onto each left shoulder.

Presently, Ruth and Jane returned and approved these arrangements. Ruth's eyes were alive with excitement, while Jane's were abstracted and inward-looking. No doubt she was solving complex equations in her head.

An early lunch at the Windsor followed, with roast chicken and steamed vegetables for the girls, and filet mignon and a glass of champagne for Phryne, followed by crème brûlée. Then, feeling that her adoptive daughters had experienced enough excitement for one day, Phryne ferried them home—sedately enough—in the Hispano-Suiza and turned her mind to the report Tinker had given her that morning, along with four addresses inscribed on a sheet of paper torn from an exercise book.

'Well, Miss?' Dot said as she followed Phryne upstairs. 'Do we have any plans for the rest of the day?'

'Indeed we do, Dot. You might recall that I told you yesterday I had put Tinker to work identifying the writer of those nasty cards? He has performed his part admirably, but the next step is up to us.'

When Phryne explained her intention, Dot was appalled. 'Miss, you can't do that!'

'I can and I will, Dot.' As she was speaking, Phryne had arrayed herself in a respectable grey skirt, a plain white blouse, and an unfashionable black hat which Mrs. Butler had decreed unworthy of her. She wore sensible flat black shoes and stockings and looked as dowdy as was possible for her to look. 'Now listen, Dot—it is bad enough that I should be subjected to the neurotic vapourings of some mountebank who thinks it his place to censure me. But I can certainly not abide incursions upon my property. Heaven knows what he will stoop to next in order to get his point across. We need to find the culprit, and quickly, and my plan is the best means of doing that. And you did say you would help me if I refrained from involving the police, remember.'

Dot had to admit that, in the heat of the moment, she'd made this rash promise.

'All you have to do is look supportive, Dot,' Phryne assured her. 'I'll do the talking.'

And with that, Dot was obliged to be content.

———

At the first address in Dickens Street they drew a blank. It was a shabby weatherboard house with an unkempt garden, in which a few rank geraniums were engaged in a struggle with thistles and weeds. Thus far, they were winning on points.

Dot looked at Phryne dubiously. 'What do we do now, Miss? No one's answering the door.'

Phryne considered the property. 'This house looks to me like the abode of a single man who spends his days either at work or at the pub. See the washing line?'

Phryne drew Dot's attention to a dilapidated side gate leaning drunkenly on its rusty hinges. Beyond it, a four-strand wire clothes line was strung across the yard. It looked depressed, as well it might. 'There's nothing on it, despite the fact that there's a decent breeze which makes it a good drying day. I doubt this is the type of man who sits at home cutting letters from newspapers. Let's go to the next on the list.'

———

The next address—5 Lytton Street—turned out to be a snug bungalow in faced stone, with carnivorous-looking blossoms in riotous bloom. They were being watered, from a shiny new watering can, by a woman with her hair done up in rollers, over which she wore a rose-patterned scarf. She eyed her approaching visitors warily. 'Did you want something?' she asked.

'Hello,' said Phryne brightly. 'My companion and I were wondering if you have considered letting Jesus into your life?' She flourished a bundle of pamphlets which Mr. Butler had given her some months ago. ('Some amusing light reading matter was left here by an enterprising female visitor, Miss,' he had informed her with aldermanic gravity. 'I undertook to pass it on to you.') Instead of throwing the pamphlets away, Phryne had kept them. They were very much standard tracts, urging the wicked to repent. You never knew when such things might come in handy, she had thought at the time, and her foresight had been rewarded.

'Well, where is he, then?' The woman put down her watering can and placed both hands on her hips in a belligerent attitude.

'He is all around us,' Phryne opined, making Promethean gestures with both hands. 'And if you let Him into your heart, then your salvation will be assured.'

The woman made a show of scanning the far horizons. 'I can't see him. Did he catch the wrong tram?'

'Our Lord and Saviour does not trouble with trams,' Phryne persisted. 'He is omnipresent.'

'Omni-what? Listen, are you tryin' to sell something?' She indicated Phryne's pamphlets.

'No,' said Phryne earnestly. 'They're free to all folk of goodwill. My name is—'

Before Phryne could proceed, the woman harrumphed.

'There's not much bloody goodwill around here! Push off!' At which the woman turned her back on her visitors and seized a metal garden rake. She began to rake up fallen leaves with unnecessary severity, grumbling. 'Bloody interfering God-botherers.'

Phryne took Dot's arm and led her back to the Hispano-Suiza. 'Well, Dot. That was certainly illuminating.'

Dot found she was trembling. 'I don't think it's her, Miss.'

'Neither do I, Dot.' Phryne cranked the engine, which roared into life. 'Two more to go.'

———

House number three proved to be a small brick house next to a bluestone church. A young man in shirtsleeves, short trousers, and a towelling hat was bent over a small rosebush, wielding a pair of secateurs with surgical precision. He eyed his visitors briefly, then returned to his labours. Phryne pushed open the low gate, with Dot close behind her, and looked him over. 'Hello,' she said. 'I wonder if you have considered letting Jesus into your life?'

With exaggerated slowness the youth straightened his back and gave her a steady smile. 'I believe others have been before you, Miss.'

Phryne took in the black shirt, with clerical dog collar. 'Oh,

I see, Reverend. Well, there it is. Perhaps a couple of these pamphlets might be of some assistance to your flock?'

He held out his toil-stained hand as Phryne handed one of them over. He peered at it, turned a couple of pages, then returned it. 'No, I think not, Miss. This seems to arise from Mrs. Semple McPherson's evangelical tumults across the Pacific. The lady's oratory is certainly impressive, but her theology is quite unsound.'

'Well, if you should change your mind and would like to know more about Sister Aimee's work, I'd be happy to answer any questions you might have. My name is Phryne Fisher.' She watched him intently as she spoke, but he returned her frank glance with one even more direct. 'Well, thank you anyway, Reverend.' Feeling more was required, she went on. 'Your roses are beautiful. I can see you love them.'

His face was transfigured. 'I love the crimsons best, but I try to tend as many varieties as I can. The lilies of the field are all very well, but roses have the aroma of heaven.'

He inclined his head in polite dismissal, and Phryne led Dot away.

'I think we'll walk to the last one, Dot. It's not far.'

———

The last house was a gloomy, forbidding affair with slate roofing. The windows were shuttered from the outside. The front garden, such as it was, had been paved over save for a narrow strip at the front, which housed a regimented line of miserable-looking flowers. Phryne pushed open the gate, marched to the front porch, and lifted the heavy brass knocker. It fell with a thud like a judge's gavel. The sound made Dot jump, and Phryne patted her hand.

After a moment, they could hear footsteps approaching the

door from the other side. It creaked open, and they were confronted by a bespectacled man in middle age dressed all in black. His clothes looked as though they were begging to be excused.

'Yes? What can I do for you?'

Phryne introduced herself and her companion, and launched into her somewhat breathless routine.

At the end of it, the man laughed scornfully. 'Really? Well, I'm an elder of the kirk, and one of the things you should know, young woman, is that St Paul told women to keep their mouths shut. Speaking on matters of religion is forbidden to the likes of you. I'm sorry, but no. I've nothing to say to you. Good morning.'

And with that he shut the door on them.

Phryne and Dot returned to the car in thoughtful silence. They climbed into the front seat, and Phryne released the handbrake. The Hispano-Suiza rolled forward slowly. When Phryne engaged second gear the motor roared into life.

It was not until they had reached home and were installed in the parlour with cups of tea that Phryne spoke her conclusion aloud. 'Well, Dot, I think we have our man.'

'As you say, Miss. What will you do next?'

'I am going to ask Tinker to tail him. Either we'll catch him in the act of posting inflammatory postcards into our letterbox or leering through windows, or else...I fancy our religious gentleman might have the odd secret of his own, and I trust Tinker to unearth it if there is one.'

'Miss, do you mean to blackmail him?' Dot looked shocked. 'Isn't that illegal?'

Phryne grinned. 'If I have the opportunity, Dot. But I think it's the best option under the circumstances. Unless you would prefer that I seek the assistance of the police?'

Dot shook her head. 'I'm sure your way is best, Miss.'

The sound of the telephone bell prevented further discourse on the matter, and moments later Mr. Butler appeared in the doorway. 'Mr. Bisset on the line for you, Miss,' he said.

'I'll take it in the study, thanks, Mr. B.'

Phryne went next door and picked up the receiver.

'Hello, Jeoffrey. To what do I owe the pleasure?'

'I just wanted to thank you again for your charming company,' Jeoffrey said, 'and express my hope that I might be graced with it again before too long. I wonder if you recall me mentioning a party in the offing?'

'Held by the mysterious Mr. Hong? Yes, I do recall. You have further developments?'

'It's as I thought—he'd be delighted to meet you and will be sending a formal invitation through the mail. It's to be on Friday, the week after next.'

'I shall look out for it,' Phryne promised. 'I do hope there will be a distinct lack of corpses next time we meet.'

An amused chuckle echoed in her ear. 'Speaking of our poor departed friend,' Jeoffrey said, 'did you read *The Argus* yesterday?'

'I'm afraid I didn't.'

'Well, there was a little piece about our man there. It seems his name was Wing Loong, but other than that the article was short on information.'

'Perhaps Mr. Hong knows more,' Phryne suggested. 'It sounds as if he has ties in the Chinese community.'

'So I'll see you at his party?'

'Absolutely.'

Phryne replaced the receiver and went in search of the previous day's *Argus*. Mr. Butler was able to produce it—he had yet to complete the crossword—and his employer took it into the parlour to examine it.

CHINESE FOUND ON WILLIAMSTOWN BEACH

On Wednesday night the body of a young Chinese man was found on the waterfront in Williamstown. He has been iden-tified as Wing Loong, coolie. The man had been deceased for some hours, and it is not known how he met his sad end. Any members of the public in possession of relevant information are urged to contact City South police station.

And that was all. Nothing whatever about the knife wound to the heart. Presumably Jack Robinson was withholding that piece of information.

'All very discreet,' Phryne mused aloud. There was nothing about how she had discovered the body, for which she was pro-foundly thankful.

Hearing male voices conversing in the kitchen—Mr. Butler was, it appeared, thanking Tinker for the gift of some fish he had just caught—she was reminded that she wished to speak with the latter.

She made her way out to Tinker's shed and was duly admitted. She sat on Tinker's chair while he made do with the edge of the bed. As she explained what she wanted, he caressed Molly's head. The dog's tail maintained a steady *ostinato* thump on the wooden floor. When she had finished, Tinker nodded.

'Yair, I can do that, Miss. No worries.'

'You don't mind missing a few days of school?' She felt certain of the answer to this but thought it only polite to ask.

'No, Miss. I don't mind at all.'

'It's your last year of school, isn't it?'

'Yair. Police academy next year, I hope.'

'Well, you may look on this as part of your apprenticeship. Just follow our man for the next few days. Between, say, ten in the morning and ten at night. Assuming it was him, he came to my window at around nine thirty, so it looks as though he keeps regular hours. You can start tomorrow night after dark. I imagine he'll be busy during the day, it being the Sabbath and all. But after he's done praying...'

Tinker nodded. 'You can count on me, Miss.'

Phryne gave Tinker an appraising look. He wasn't greatly interested in Ruth and Jane, she knew well. He accepted them as part of the household, and was always civil to them. This sounded like the fragile growth of the lily of chivalry, however. It made sense to Phryne. Tinker had been the eldest of far too many children. Doubtless it had been drummed into him that girls are to be protected. And with that Phryne returned to her bedroom, well content.

———

'I really didn't like that man.'

'Neither did I. I hated the way he looked at you.'

'Not jealous, are you?'

'No, I'm not. But his eyes are like windows into nothingness. I'm scared for you.'

'Don't be, Peony.'

'Then hold me.'

Chapter Sixteen

On Sunday evening, Jane and Ruth ate dinner in the kitchen (meat loaf with steamed vegetables and rice pudding to follow) with Tinker, who, Ruth noticed, kept stealing glances at the clock.

'Do you have somewhere to be, Tinker?' Ruth enquired with her mouth full of rice pudding.

Jane gave him a steady look. 'I believe he's on a job of some kind,' she said, putting down her spoon.

Tinker returned her look, impassive as a bronze statue. 'Maybe. Gotta go out tonight.'

'Tinker's visiting his girlfriend!' Ruth teased.

Tinker harrumphed, and returned to his bowl.

Later, in the seclusion of their bedroom, the girls discussed the matter. 'Do you know what Tinker's up to, Janey?'

Jane gave the matter earnest thought. 'Last night I woke up because I heard Miss Phryne shouting at someone. Did you hear?'

Ruth shook her head. 'No. I must have slept through it.'

Jane gave her an affectionate smile. 'You're a sound sleeper, of course. Well, afterwards I heard Miss Phryne going out—and I bet she went to talk to Tinker, and now Tinker's going to find whomever it was she was shouting at.'

Ruth nodded. 'He's a good boy, Tinker.'

'A good man, really,' Jane corrected her. 'He's sixteen, you know.'

'We'll be sixteen next year. And of course we've got Frances's sixteenth birthday party next Saturday. I wonder what it will be like? I hope the other guests won't be snobby.'

'I don't think they will be,' Jane said. 'Frances wouldn't have asked us if she was going to be like that.'

'And you really think she's reformed?'

Jane hugged her sister briefly. 'I really do, Ruthie. Come on. Let's play cards.'

'What shall we play? I'm bored with Snap.'

'Let's play poker. With two cards each and five on the table.'

'As long as we're playing for matchsticks, Janey. I can't afford to lose my pocket money to you tonight.'

Jane grinned, and brought out her favourite, unmarked, deck.

———

Tinker, meanwhile, had returned to his shed, where he dressed himself in a dark green shirt and grey trousers. Miss Phryne had taught him about the camouflage tricks she had learned while on a case in Daylesford. Green, grey, and brown were better than black, apparently. He put on black socks and a pair of old brown shoes. Molly looked up expectantly. Are we going out now? she wanted to know.

'Yep. C'mon, Molly. We've got work to do.' He clipped Molly's lead to her collar and looped the other end around his right hand. They padded quietly through the deserted streets to the house in question. The lights were on within, and they settled down to wait.

After half an hour, the front door opened. The man who emerged looked around nervously, and Tinker shrank back into the bushes and kept his hand on Molly's flank.

When he had passed them by—no more than ten feet away from their hiding place—Tinker stood up, holding Molly firmly in check. 'Wait there, Molly,' he whispered. 'We need to keep some distance between us.'

Molly's tail brushed against his leg twice in acquiescence.

They followed their quarry all the way to The Esplanade. He stopped outside 221B and stared up at it. Tinker hid behind a tree belonging to next door, and considered. If the bloke tried to break in again, what should he do? Let Molly off the leash? He decided against it. If Molly tackled the villain she might get hurt, and he couldn't risk that. But he would certainly intervene, and armed with a potentially savage dog he anticipated a swift citizen's arrest without awkward consequences.

They waited, but to Tinker's relief the man appeared to decide against attempting further unauthorised incursions. Instead, he pulled his collar up over his neck, shook his head, muttered to himself and set off towards St Kilda proper. Tinker and Molly followed him from a safe distance.

The object of their pursuit paused at an unpretentious terrace house on a steep hill. The house was a narrow brick affair with two storeys and a tiny park opposite. He loitered outside the house while Tinker, affecting the unconcerned air of Boy Innocently Walking Dog, took up position in the park. The man looked around nervously, then finally made up his mind. Pushing open the wooden front gate, he climbed the steps and knocked at the door of the terrace. Tinker saw the door open and a glow of light stream outwards. A young woman in a red silk dressing-gown surveyed the man from hat to boot, gave him a quick kiss, and drew him inside. Tinker grinned, and settled down to wait.

The moon had come out, and the clouds had parted to make the evening air considerably colder. Molly put her front paws on his lap, and he caressed her head and flanks. He guessed it was around forty minutes later that the door opened. Still in her dressing-gown, the woman waved farewell to her visitor. He wrapped his coat tight around him and scurried on up the hill. The woman stayed where she was, hands on hips, until he was out of sight. Then she called, 'Oi! You with the dog! Come here, I want a word.' The voice was surprisingly rich and fruity.

Tinker grinned sheepishly and crossed the road. As he and Molly climbed the steps, the woman folded her arms and said, 'All right, sonny. What's your game?'

Tinker, aware that Miss Phryne would want to know all the particulars, studied her carefully. About five feet one inches, he estimated, slender build, regular features, dyed blonde hair, dark brown eyes, plenty of what he would describe as sauce, and probably from the posh side of town.

'Just walkin' me dog,' he offered.

She gave him a scornful look.

'I wasn't born yesterday, young man. Come on, out with it. Why're you following that poor bloke? What's 'e done to you?'

Tinker tried to explain it without giving too much away. 'I'm keepin' an eye on him cos 'e's bin doin' somethin' a bit silly. We don't wanna hurt 'im or nuthin. We just wants ter ask 'im ter stop doin' it.'

The woman laughed. 'As explanations go I'm afraid that's rather thin. You'd better come in and try again.'

Tinker fastened Molly's lead around the fence post. 'Stay there, Molly. I won't be long.'

And he followed the woman into her house.

The parlour was unimaginably opulent. A well-stocked wood fire. Silk hangings on all the walls. A silk-covered couch with matching ottoman. Gold ornaments lining the mantelpiece above the fireplace. And an armchair that appeared to have been stuffed by an overenthusiastic taxidermist.

'Take a seat,' the woman said, pointing to the armchair.

Tinker looked at it and shook his head. 'I'd rather not, Miss.'

The woman shrugged. 'Suit yourself.'

He sat on the ottoman, and she parked herself on the couch.

'If you're wondering,' she began, 'I very much doubt he saw you. You're pretty good at remaining inconspicuous. But I have exceptional eyesight, especially in the dark, and I notice things most people don't. So, let's start with names. Yours is?'

Tinker couldn't see any point in hiding it. 'Tinker,' he said.

'Good. I'm Rose. Now, tell me again why you were following my, er, friend.'

Deciding that this straightforward woman might be disposed to be helpful, Tinker decided on a fullish confession, omitting only the identity of his principal.

'Miss, this bloke's bin puttin' threatenin' letters in people's letterboxes. That's bad enough, but one night 'e climbed up to a window at night and stared at a lady in 'er nightdress. That's not on, Miss. Blokes can't be allowed to go round doin' that.'

'I see.' Rose crossed her slender lower limbs. 'Are you sure you have the right man?'

'Yair, Miss, I am. I bin watchin' 'im. And before comin' 'ere tonight, 'e went round to the house of the lady I was talkin' about and stared up at it for a few minutes. I reckon 'e was thinkin' about doin' it again. But 'e came 'ere instead.'

She nodded thoughtfully. 'I'm glad he did.' She gave him a long, assessing look.

'I was going to say that you're terribly young to be a private detective, but you're a very cool customer, aren't you? All right. Now tell me what your employer has in store for him. Does she intend to go to the police? I wish she wouldn't. Despite what it looks like, he's a good man, I think. And believe me, Tinker—I know men down to their foundation garments.' She paused, and lit a cigarette. 'Well?'

Tinker remained silent. It wasn't his place to say what Miss Phryne would or wouldn't do.

Rose leaned over and patted his hand with what might have been affection. 'All right. Allow me to expedite your thought processes, Tinker. Your employer is the Honourable Miss Fisher, private detective. I know all about her, because he calls me Phryne when he's with me. Well, that's no skin off my nose; I've been called worse. Some of my clients are bad men, Tinker. They tell me things which worry me a great deal. On occasion, I even drop the odd anonymous letter in at the police station. But the gentleman in question isn't like that. I'm quite sure he isn't violent. But if he climbed up to Miss Fisher's window, then, as you say, he's going too far. He mustn't do that.'

'His threatening letters weren't too flash either, Miss.'

Rose gave this imperturbable youth a considering look. 'All right, Tinker. Miss Fisher must do what she thinks best. But I hope you'll tell her what I said.'

'I'll do that, Miss.'

She stood up and conducted him to the door, where she gave him a light kiss on the cheek. 'If you ever want to see me on your own account, Tinker, I'll let you have a turn on the house.'

'Thanks, Miss,' said Tinker, trying not to blush. 'That's very kind of you. Molly? We're goin' home.'

———

Phryne put down her book. 'Yes? Who is it?'

'I am sorry to disturb you, Miss.' The voice was that of her imperturbable Mr. Butler. 'But the young gentleman would like a word with you. I informed him of the lateness of the hour, but he suggested that it couldn't wait.'

'Thanks, Mr. B.' Not for the first time, Phryne wondered about

Tinker's reluctance to enter the house proper. It was rare for him to stray beyond the kitchen. She concluded that it was the formation femaleness of the household that put him off. Well, it sounded as though Tinker had News. She wrapped her silk dressing-gown around her person and descended the stairs.

In the shed, Phryne listened to Tinker's account in silence. When he was done, she smiled warmly.

'Tinker, you have done excellently, and I'm very pleased with you. It's very helpful to have a window into this man's character. I expect he's more than usually troubled in his mind.'

'Whaddya gonna do, Miss?' Tinker asked.

Phryne raised her eyebrows. 'Tomorrow I will be paying our chap a visit. And with any sort of luck, that will be the end of this episode. Thank you for doing your part so quickly and well.'

'That's orright, Miss. Er, Miss... It's quite late, isn't it?'

'I suppose it is, Tink,' she agreed. 'I'd best let you get some sleep.'

'It's not that, Miss,' Tinker said hastily. 'It's just... Do I have to go to school tomorrer?'

Phryne smiled. 'Ah, I see. Well, in light of your recent efforts, you do deserve a lie-in. I'll call the school in the morning and tell them you're under the weather.'

Tinker grinned widely. 'I don't 'ave ter stay in, but, do I?'

'No, Tinker, you don't. You can go fishing if you want. And here.' She handed him a ten-bob note.

'Thanks, Miss.' Tinker accepted the folded note and stuffed it into his desk drawer.

Phryne departed the shed, musing over the hypocrisy of a clergyman who frequented working girls and then denounced the sins of the flesh afterwards in order to make himself feel better.

Tomorrow, my fine holy-roller, she said to herself, you are getting the dressing-down of a lifetime.

———

'Peony, I'm scared now.'

'Why? What's happened, Carnation?'

'It's that awful man Liu. He wants me as his concubine.'

'Well, he can't have you. You're mine now.'

'Peony, you don't understand! I told him I didn't want anything to do with him, but do you know what the boss said?'

'What did he say?'

'He said I had to go with him! I think he's afraid of Liu.'

'You don't have to do what he says!'

'I'm afraid he might make me. I don't know what he might do!'

'Just tell him no.'

'It's more complicated than that, Peony.'

Chapter Seventeen

'Dot? I'm going to wrap up the case of the threatening letters. Are you coming?'

Phryne had dressed modestly for her visit. Black trousers, black silk jacket, dark blue hat, and her favourite flat boots. Dot, in shades of beige, stood before her with her hands folded. 'Yes, Miss.'

'It's just as I suspected, Dot: our fellow was indeed incubating a disreputable secret. So now we have him where we want him, I'm going to administer the *coup de grâce.*'

'Very good, Miss.'

———

Dot's mouth opened in surprise as the Hispano-Suiza began to climb the hill towards the bluestone church. Phryne parked on the roadside, switched off the motor, and gestured to her companion, who alighted and followed Phryne to the wooden gate. Phryne knocked on the front door with her gloved hand. It was the same small brick house she remembered. A wooden signboard announced that the Reverend TJ Winsome presided over Matins, Evensong and Holy Communion, and the householder answered the door himself. Now that he was no longer in his gardening garb, she could see that the young, athletic-looking man with straight, black, closely cropped hair had a reddened scab on his forehead. He blinked brown, expressionless eyes at Phryne as she stood in his doorway.

Phryne gave him a winning smile. 'I'm Phryne Fisher—you might recall that we met the other day. May I come in, Reverend Winsome? We have matters to discuss.'

The man nodded, then turned and led Phryne and Dot into a shabby living room. 'May I offer you tea?' It was a beautiful voice, too: soft, yet carrying. He indicated the least threadbare armchair. Phryne sat in it and waved for him to take the chair opposite. Dot remained standing, since there seemed to be no other furniture available. He did as instructed and brought both hands together in prayerful supplication. And stared, as Phryne reached into her gold mesh handbag and produced a trio of cards.

'No tea, thank you, Reverend. But you can perhaps explain why you placed these cards in my letterbox, prior to visiting one of the working girls of St Kilda.' She frowned at him, her brow furrowing with displeasure, and fanned the three cards outwards. 'Pick a card, Mr. Winsome. Any card! *Repent? Whore of Babylon? The Wages Of Sin Is Death?* And please, save yourself the bother of prevarication. The wound on your head is where I beaned you with a hardback novel when you so far forgot yourself as to spy on me through my bedroom window!'

Too surprised to protest, the Reverend Winsome sat in meek submission. Phryne clasped her gloved hands together. 'Now explain yourself, sir. You have seriously inconvenienced me, and I do not like to be a means of therapy for confused young clergymen. Whatever penitential complex you are currently working through, please leave me out of it in future. So far as I am concerned, you may cavort with as many working girls as you think you can afford—although your flock would be amused to hear of your adventures.' She smiled, but the menace in her voice was unmistakable.

Winsome sat transfixed, like Saint Sebastian awaiting the final arrow of martyrdom. Finally he appeared to recover himself and leaned forward, hands turned outwards in mute supplication.

'H-how did you know it was me?' he managed.

'The letters were cut out of *The Argus* and *The Hawklet*,' Phryne explained. She saw no reason not to let the man into her confidence. The higher opinion he had of her investigative abilities, she reasoned, the less likely he would be to wish to re-enter the lists against her. 'Uncommon bedfellows, I would say. I don't know why you take that grubby rag, Reverend. I suspect it has given you improper ideas. I have visited everyone in this neighbourhood who takes both of those organs, and you were the only credible suspect. It needed a youthful, light-boned figure to balance on my narrow wall like a trapeze artist.'

The Reverend Winsome put his head in his hands and let out a sob. Just one. It was more like a hiccup. Then he lifted his gaze to hers and gave her a steady, frank look. 'Miss Fisher, I do most humbly apologise, and abase myself. I have done you great wrong, and I regret it exceedingly. I have no defence whatever. I will not beg. I leave it entirely to your discretion whether or not you acquaint the police with my misdeeds. But I—that is, I regret to have to inform you that my flock is small, and apathetic. St Kilda is fallow ground for the Word of the Lord, and on my small stipend, I cannot afford a wife. And so...'

Phryne grasped what he was trying to convey. 'And so you cavort with ladies of the street when the temptations of the flesh become too much for you to bear. Believe it or not, Reverend Winsome, I do understand, but you must see that you can't expi-ate your own sins by castigating me for mine—not that I accept such a characterisation of my private concerns, which are none of your business. The Gospel of John, you know.'

'*He that is without sin among you…*' the man murmured wretchedly. 'I'm sorry, Miss Fisher. One of my parishioners is a neighbour of yours who declared herself scandalised by your lifestyle. But, as you say, I should have paid more heed to the Gospel of John and less to scurrilous gossip. Can you forgive me?'

Watching him, it seemed to Phryne that this was a young man to be pitied. 'At this moment, I am not inclined to report you to the police…'

The fellow's eyes widened hopefully.

'But I will be dropping a word in the ear of my friend the bishop.'

The wide eyes of hope became the wide eyes of surprise and dismay.

Phryne smiled. 'That's right. I am not without influence.' She was momentarily distracted by a memory of Lionel's golden body, before returning abruptly to the present scene.

Winsome was blinking rapidly. 'Oh, Miss Fisher! Well, you must do as you think best. And I apologise once more for my aspersions upon your character. I don't know what I was thinking. I'm a despicable person. Deplorable. I—'

Phryne rose, cutting short his self-abasement. 'Well, Mr. Winsome, I'm sure you know best in that regard. And please, don't trouble to stand. We shall see ourselves out.' She fixed him with a gimlet eye. 'Oh, and Reverend? Do remember what I said the other night. If you come back, I will shoot you. Please do not imagine for an instant that I was joking. I keep a pistol under my pillow, and I will not hesitate to use it.'

The Reverend Winsome put his head in his hands once more and groaned.

———

Dot was silent all the way home. Phryne sat on the sofa in her parlour, and accepted a cup of Greek coffee from Mr. Butler. 'Well, Dot. That went well, didn't it?'

'But, Miss, how did you know it was the clergyman? I thought you meant the Presbyterian.' Dot was agog to hear, and Phryne was only too glad to explain.

'As I indicated to the Reverend, the housewife and the kirk elder didn't seem capable of scaling the garden wall so nimbly. And they were both bare-headed, with no visible wound. The Reverend Winsome, on the other hand, wore a towelling hat.'

Phryne paused, sipping at her thick, reviving coffee. She wondered how much more to tell Dot, but decided to omit only the young woman's offer to Tinker. As she related Tinker's adventures, Phryne watched as Dot's eyes grew round with astonishment.

'Oh, Miss Phryne! Tinker is becoming quite the detective, isn't he!' Dot considered the young clergyman's confession, and shook her head. 'But are you really sure the reverend is a good man, given those awful cards and that he's been, well, consorting with fallen women?'

'Yes, Dot, I am. People do have their virtues and vices all mixed up together. I was worried, though. Anyone who can work themselves up into such a ferment might not be safe to have around. But I don't think he's capable of personal violence, though given all the trouble he went to, projecting all his own internal torments onto me, we might certainly have been due a painful scene or two.' Phryne put down her cup. 'I'm going to leave our clergyman friend where he is for the present. If he really does repent, and stay repentant, then when I have words with his superiors—which I shall, Dot—then I will also report his demonstrated penitence. And just as I promised, Dot, we managed to fix our little problem without police help.'

'Yes, Miss. I'm glad. Hugh wouldn't have liked it.'

'Have you heard anything from him lately?'

'He did send a note to say he's sorry he hasn't been around, but he's been working nights...'

Dot allowed the sentence to hang in the air, almost as if she suspected Hugh of serving up the standard excuse for extracurricular romances. Phryne decided to squash that idea; if Dot hadn't been so upset by his absence, she would realise herself just how out of character that would be for her intended.

'Dot, he's a sergeant now,' Phryne said briskly, 'and that comes with extra responsibilities. And don't worry: he won't always be working nights.' This seemed to meet the bill for the present, so Phryne changed the subject. 'Now Jane and Ruth have two more visits to the Blind Institute this week, so I'm hoping Jane will discover what's what with their accounts. And on Saturday I'll take the girls into town to pick up their new dresses. I intend to drive them to their party that night. Turning up in the Hispano-Suiza should impress the upper crust no end.'

'Indeed, Miss.'

Phryne heard the postman's whistle outside, and a few minutes later Mr. Butler appeared in the parlour with the mail.

'Anything special, Mr. B?'

'Aside from communications from tradesmen, Miss, just the one.' Phryne accepted a purple envelope with considerable interest.

Dot craned her neck to see. 'What is it, Miss?'

Phryne scanned its contents and handed it over. Dot stared at it. 'Miss? It looks foreign.'

It was certainly that. There were expertly calligraphed Chinese characters in gold ink across the top and bottom, and what looked like archaic pictographs. In the centre was the following:

HONG requests the pleasure of the Honourable Miss Phryne Fisher's company to help celebrate his birthday. Dress: semiformal. Dinner and refreshments will be served. No presents by request. 78 The Strand, Williamstown. Tel AW 872

The date named was Friday week, at seven p.m.

'Who is Hong, Miss?' Dot asked.

'He's a lecturer at the university, Dot. I had been expecting this.' She smiled to herself at the thought that she would meet Jeoffrey again at the party. She was looking forward to seeing that admirable man.

Dot handed the invitation back. 'Miss, it looks overdone. It looks to me like someone pretending to be Chinese, only he isn't, really.'

Phryne nodded. 'That's what I think too, Dot. I mean, purple and gold? I thought that was only for Assyrian cohorts. Overdone is exactly what it is. So while I intend to go to this party, I am going to talk to Lin first to see if he knows anything about this Hong.'

———

Phryne waited until the early evening before she dialled Lin's number.

'Hello?' Pure Oxford in both syllables. You could almost hear the dreaming spires in the distance.

'Lin, it's Phryne.'

'Silver Lady! How splendid to hear from you. How are you?'

'Just about as well as any woman could ever be, Lin. And you? And how is Camellia?'

There was a brief silence in which Phryne examined the telephone cord, wondering if mice had nibbled through it. 'We are both well, Phryne. Have you called to ask after our, er, unfortunate labourer?'

Phryne noted that Lin did not use the word 'coolie.' Interesting. While she hadn't called on that matter, curiosity led her to say, 'Well, yes, Lin. Have you found out anything?'

'He certainly met with misadventure, but I'm afraid we're no closer to knowing why, or who the perpetrator might have been.'

'I think misadventure is putting it mildly,' Phryne remarked, recalling the stab wound to the heart. 'You know I would be happy to investigate, Lin. I could—'

But Lin interrupted. 'Phryne, please—leave it to the police. I fear there might be…awkwardness if you should become involved in this distressing matter.'

Phryne frowned. It was clear that Lin considered this to be an internecine Chinese feud. If that were the case, she would be well advised to take Lin's advice. She spoke a smattering of Chinese, thanks to her association with him, but she was nowhere near fluent. In any case, it was one thing to speak the language, and quite another to appreciate the cultural nuances of a tight-knit community that would not exactly welcome a stranger poking her nose into their affairs.

'All right, I'll leave the sad case of poor Wing Loong. But, Lin, is there something else on your mind?'

'Why do you say that, Phryne?'

'Well, you're tense and not like your usual urbane self. Something else, perhaps?'

Lin sighed. 'Phryne, I probably shouldn't be telling you this, because you'll probably want to investigate this too, and again I would ask you to refrain.' Another silence.

'What is it?' Phryne prompted. It wasn't usually this hard to get information out of her beloved.

'It's Camellia's sister. She's gone missing.'

'I'm sorry to hear it. But I would've thought her family would welcome my assistance, Lin.'

'These are inauspicious times, Silver Lady. Please, I want you to leave this be for now.'

'All right, Lin. I'll respect your wishes. For now. Oh, one more thing—do you know of an Occidental gentleman who calls himself Hong?'

There ensued another prolonged silence; Phryne had never known a conversation so full of them. Finally Lin made a sound redolent of acute indigestion. 'Why do you ask?'

'I've received a party invitation from him.'

'Are you going to accept?'

'I certainly am. You make him sound very mysterious—and you know how I love mysteries.'

'Well, I will not attempt to dissuade you,' said Lin. 'I think that would only be counterproductive. But may I please implore you to be careful?'

'I'm always careful!' Phryne protested.

'Be more so,' her paramour urged. 'I do not know the gentleman in question to speak to, but he is regarded as untrustworthy.'

Lin thereupon rang off, sounding more out of sorts than Phryne could ever remember him. She replaced the receiver and pondered the lexicographic significance of the word 'untrustworthy.' Phryne knew enough about the Chinese to know that studied understatement was the hallmark of their public utterances. So 'untrustworthy' would fall somewhere between receiving stolen goods and axe murder by night. Phryne shook her head and climbed the stairs to her room. It was sensible of Lin not to labour the point, which would only have put her back up. How much trouble could a party invitation from a university academic entail, anyway? It distressed her that Lin was being so distant and uncommunicative. He had always been frank with her and shared his troubles unreservedly. Now he was warning her off. Warning her against trying to investigate Wing Loong's murder; warning her not to attempt to find Camellia's sister; warning her against the mysterious Hong.

What could have happened to Camellia's sister, anyway? Chinese girls were generally kept under close supervision. Could she have run away? Well, even if she didn't search for the girl herself, one thing she might do was drop a quiet word in Hugh Collins's ear, asking him to keep an eye open for a stray Chinese girl. It would also give her an opportunity to see if she could discern the reason why he was also proving so elusive of late.

She lay on her bed and stared at the spotless cream-coloured ceiling, considering the male species. She had on occasion heard them bemoaning the complexity of the female mind, but it seemed to her that they were infinitely more complicated. She indulged for a while in thoughts of Lin's beautiful person, then lingered unexpectedly over Jeoffrey Bisset. Following which, she mused once more on the hapless Reverend Winsome. Under other circumstances, Phryne might have found him attractive. But he really was an awful mess. The Reverend Winsome clearly lusted after Phryne's body. (She allowed herself a brief smile. He wasn't alone there, she was delighted to say.) But anyone who externalised their guilt to the extent this man had done was not safe to approach. Anyone capable of inserting threatening letters into their adored one's letterbox was a disaster waiting to happen. Would he have attacked her that night had she not thrown the book at him?

There was a question. You'd think not, but you never really knew. She had downplayed the danger when speaking to Dot, but under the influence of guilt, shame, and lust, men were capable of truly desperate deeds. Letters cut from newspapers were clear evidence of premeditation. Which meant that she could not trust him. She had the impression he had taken her threats seriously, but who knew? If he showed his face in her vicinity again, then Dot or no Dot, she would report him to the police.

———

After dinner, Phryne knocked on the girls' bedroom door. 'Jane? May I have a word?'

'Of course, Miss Phryne.'

Phryne entered the bedroom and sat herself on one of the two chairs. The girls were sprawled on their beds, wrapped in their flannel nightgowns and woollen dressing-gowns. Ruth was brushing her hair with a pearl-handled hairbrush. Jane did not need to, as she had kept her hair short ever since an impudent boy had tied her plaits around a lamppost. She was reading a textbook on pathology, but laid it aside and sat up.

'Is this about tomorrow, Miss Phryne?'

'Yes, Jane. Let us review our case, shall we? We think there's something wrong with the accounts. If anyone is stealing from the Institute, it's probably not Mr. Blake. He sounds pleasant but incompetent. But he thinks something's wrong, too, and he doesn't want to tell Mr. Hedger until he knows what's been happening. He probably fears he will be fired.'

Jane considered Mr. Hedger's likely reaction to the news that his beloved institution was being defrauded while his book-keeper was apparently asleep at the wheel, and nodded. 'I think he's right to be worried. So what do I look for in the accounts, Miss Phryne?'

'Check the accounts against the two years previous. What we should look for is whether the amounts are being falsified—you'll notice if the amounts paid to certain suppliers have increased dramatically, for example—and also if there are invoices coming in from suppliers who didn't appear in past ledgers. These are the main methods used to defraud a business. Perhaps someone is sneaking into the office late at night, or early in the morning, and fiddling the books—perhaps while hiding in the storeroom you were locked in last Thursday.'

Jane thought about this. 'I was able to read the words on the blotting paper,' she remembered. 'They weren't in braille. So they must have been written by someone who isn't blind. And there aren't that many sighted people at the Institute. We can probably rule out Miss Thomas and Mr. Blake; they both seem determined to discover the truth about the accounts. It wouldn't be Mr. Hedger himself, surely?'

'It's possible,' Ruth mused. 'But it doesn't make sense. He's quite forceful, isn't he? And he's got such a—well, a presence. If he wanted to get rich, he'd be in business, wouldn't he?'

'I should think he'd be very successful if he was,' Phryne agreed.

'No, it can't be him,' Jane concluded. 'So we have to find out how many sighted employees there are, and who among them would have access to the office.' She looked up at Phryne. 'Oh, I don't believe I told you this, Miss Phryne: Mr. Blake said the office used to have a key, but it's gone missing. I wonder if our culprit stole it so that Mr. Blake couldn't lock the office?'

Phryne thought it over. 'Possibly, Jane. But I can't see how we'd find out who had the key. I think our answer will be found in the accounts. You mentioned there were some missing invoices? Try matching up those you do have against the ledger and work out which are missing and to whom the payments went.'

'And then?'

'If you can give me their names, I'll have a go at tracking them down. All right, girls. Sleep well, and good luck tomorrow.'

———

'No, I am not in love with him! Absolutely not, in no way whatsoever!'

'He thinks you are. Everyone's talking about it.'

'He's an arrogant, conceited man with delusions of grandeur!'

'Have you told him you don't love him?'

'Yes, but he didn't believe me!'

'Well, in that case he won't be able to make you do anything you don't want to do.'

'Maybe. I hope not.'

Chapter Eighteen

Tuesday saw Phryne spending a lazy day in bed, dozing and reading. In due course, she heard Ruth and Jane arrive home and waited for them to come make their report, which they promptly did. They stood before her, bashful but quietly triumphant.

'You look as though you have news,' Phryne observed.

Jane handed over a fresh exercise book. 'Here's a summary I made of all the invoices for the last three years, Miss Phryne. The ones with asterisks are new payments for this year and last year which don't appear in the 1927 accounts. Some of the invoices are missing, but not all of them. I think there really has been an attempt to cover up fraudulent payments, Miss Phryne. Miss Thomas was right.'

'Good girl, Jane! Now, obviously you couldn't take the invoices away with you. Did they look phony?'

Jane thought this over. 'Not really, Miss. If they're fakes, they're pretty good ones. But I found four business names for which Mr. Blake has paid invoices that look suspicious. I've written the names and the amounts over the page.'

Phryne turned the page and stared at the list. None of the

amounts were substantial, but there seemed to be a great many payments made to Windsor Smallgoods, Prahran Packing, Hawksburn Greengrocers, and Armadale Butchers. 'Are you sure these aren't legitimate bills, Jane?'

Jane gave a quiet smile. 'I'm sure they're fraudulent, Miss Phryne, because the amounts are identical to those invoiced by other businesses in the same line of work.'

'So Mr. Blake suspected nothing, paid them, and when the real bills came in he forgot that he'd paid them already. Does he sign the cheques himself?'

Jane nodded. 'Yes, he does. He carries the chequebook in his inside coat pocket.'

'Oh, dear. This doesn't look good for Mr. Blake, does it?'

The two girls shook their heads sombrely.

Phryne tapped the exercise book. 'Jane, this is an excellent piece of detection. Tomorrow I'm going to investigate these businesses, and with any luck we shall find out where the money went. Then I am going to see Mr. Blake. I'd like to spare him from the consequences of his negligence, if possible. Oh, I asked you to find out about the sighted employees. How did you go with that?'

This was where Ruth came in. 'I asked Hester,' she said. 'There aren't any obvious suspects, though. There's Mr. Hedger, Miss Thomas, and Mr. Blake, of course, and some of the teachers too, apparently. And all the gardeners are sighted too.' She frowned. 'But I don't think it's likely any of the gardeners did it.'

'And there's Hester herself, don't forget,' Phryne added.

Ruth opened her mouth to protest but before she could Phryne continued, 'A cook is well placed to skim off excess cash just by saying, "Oh, we need this and we need that." Then she could pretend that all the duplicate goods and services had duly arrived.'

Jane took Ruth's hand. 'It's true, Ruthie. All the same, I don't think she's our suspect. Just keep it in the back of your mind.'

'All right,' said Phryne. 'Well done, girls. Now go and have some lemonade and cakes. You deserve it.'

As the girls departed, Phryne lay back on her bed and stared at the ceiling. Hester really might be the culprit. Not having met the cook, Phryne was entirely dependent on the girls' second-hand accounts. But if both of them thought Hester was honest, well, she trusted their judgement. They were level-headed and sensible, Jane especially. Tomorrow she would see what she could discover. When in doubt, she reminded herself, follow the money.

———

The next morning found Phryne at the Companies Office. An hour or so later saw her pushing open the heavy door of the Blind Institute, having left the Hispano-Suiza parked in a nearby side street. She had dressed with some care in black trousers, flat shoes, a grey blouse, her brightest floral jacket in pure silk, and a fashionable purple cloche hat, and wore a tasteful but expensive string of pearls around her neck. Nothing like pearls to convey wealth and respectability, and those she intended to visit would be suitably respectful in the presence of serious money.

The first person she encountered was none other than Miss Thomas. 'Oh, Miss Fisher! I wasn't expecting you. Have you any news?'

'I believe so. Would you be so good as to summon Mr. Blake for me? I need him to accompany me on a small excursion. I expect him to be absent for an hour or so.'

Miss Thomas's eyes widened. 'Of course, Miss Fisher. Please wait here.'

Presently Mr. Blake joined Phryne by the door. 'Miss Fisher, isn't it?' he asked breathlessly, blinking at her. Jane was almost certainly right, Phryne decided at once: whoever was stealing from the Blind Institute, it was exceedingly unlikely to be this brown-coated picture of abject ineptitude.

'Indeed it is, Mr. Blake.' Phryne gave his hand a perfunctory shake. 'Before we head off, I think I should mention that four of the business names you've been feeding with your company chequebook are almost certainly bogus.' She watched his face intently as she delivered this news.

He blinked, swallowed, and wiped his forehead with a hand-kerchief pulled from his pocket. 'Oh dear,' he managed. 'I'm in a lot of trouble, aren't I?'

'I cannot promise you anything at this point. Fortunately for you, neither I nor my daughters believe that you are involved in this fraud. For fraud it is, Mr. Blake—in excess of two hundred pounds thus far, over the last two years.'

'Oh dear. As much as that?' The man drooped. He looked so wretched that Phryne took pity on him.

'Well, we will do what we can. Which branch, and which bank, if you please?'

'The Bank of New South Wales, Prahran. It's in Chapel Street.'

———

Chapel Street was a hive of activity. Cars motored, boys on bicycles delivered things, women hurried past with brown-paper parcels, and the buzz of commerce was almost deaf-ening. Phryne swung the Hispano-Suiza into a parking spot outside the bank, then, with Mr. Blake scurrying behind, swept through the hallowed portals and marched straight up to a self-important-looking young man who was hover-ing in the foyer. She reached into her purse and took out a business card.

'Hello,' she said brightly. 'Please give this card to the manager immediately. I wish to see him, without delay, on a most delicate matter.'

The youth was shocked. He was dressed in his best grey suit, with polished black shoes. His hair was slicked back with expensive unguents, and it was his job to overawe customers. The fashionably dressed woman in black trousers and a bright, floral jacket seemed not to have received the memorandum, however. He gaped at her as she tapped her foot on the polished stone floor.

'Well, hurry up, young man. Don't stand there looking like a statue. Get cracking!'

To his own amazement, he found himself hurrying to the manager's office. Taking his courage in both hands, he knocked twice.

'Yes, who is it?' came a querulous voice from behind the oak door.

'It's Hopkins, sir. A lady has demanded to see you without delay, sir. She's asked me to give you her card.'

'Really? Well, come in, Hopkins.'

Hopkins opened the door and approached Mr. Rogers's desk tentatively. It was a desk designed to intimidate, with a vast expanse of polished mahogany, a bound pad of blotting paper, and a fountain pen and ink set mounted in what might have been gold. Mr. Rogers was a round-faced gentleman in a grey suit, with blue cravat, wavy grey hair, and a bristling grey moustache. He glared at his subordinate, and reached out his chubby hand for Phryne's business card. Hopkins watched Rogers's face change colour. It began white, shaded with crimson, but within moments all the blood had drained out of his features, leaving a grey look of naked terror. 'Better show her in, Hopkins,' he said hoarsely. 'And we are not to be disturbed for any reason.'

The brilliantined youth re-emerged into the foyer, and ushered Phryne and Mr. Blake behind the counter, to the considerable interest of the common customers obliged to stand in line like everybody else. Hopkins gave Phryne an obsequious smile, pushed the bank manager's door open, and evaporated.

Phryne entered first, to see a nervy bank manager raise himself to his feet behind his desk. 'Miss Fisher? I am Archibald Rogers. To what do I owe the pleasure?' His voice had a rift in it.

Phryne waved a gloved hand. 'Mr. Rogers, this is Mr. Blake, who represents the Blind Institute, and we are here to seek your help in unravelling a complex web of deceit and fraudulent transactions. I am hoping, at this stage, that we will be able to solve this without calling in the police just yet. But,' she added winningly, 'I cannot make any promises.'

Mr. Rogers resumed his seat, and waved at the two chairs in front of his mighty desk. 'Please, do sit down. Anything I can do to help, I will, naturally. But I do hope this turns out to be an innocent mistake.' He gave her a direct look of honest helpfulness, seemingly much calmer now.

Seating herself next to Mr. Blake, Phryne realised in a flash of inspiration that Mr. Rogers was expecting a private detective on some other business. Adultery, possibly? Now it was merely a case of possible fraud, he seemed to be breathing easier. Phryne smiled to herself.

'Thank you, Mr. Rogers. Now it seems clear enough that the fraud does not originate here. The fact that bogus invoices have been paid by your branch is not in itself evidence of criminality on the part of this splendid institution.'

Rogers nodded mechanically.

'It is the recipient of these stolen funds who interests us. You will be able to find out where the money went, will you not?' Phryne drew out a sheet of paper and placed it on the bank manager's desk. 'These are the amounts, dates, and alleged recipients we would like to examine.'

Rogers plainly did not like it. He adjusted his cravat twice, and ran his hands over the grey corrugations of his hair.

'That's all very well, Miss Fisher, but we don't—that is to say, I can't go fossicking around in some other bank's records to find out where the money went.'

Phryne leaned forward with her elbows resting on the mahogany desk and her chin resting on her hands. She gave him a penetrating look.

'Well, ordinarily, no. Of course you wouldn't. But just because you *wouldn't* doesn't mean you *can't*. I'm sure you are able to find out where the money went, aren't you? And when you do, you're going to tell me, or else I will be back to talk to you about the other matter...' She left a significant pause in which she had the satisfaction of seeing the bank manager blanch. Whatever it was she was pretending to know certainly had him running scared. 'Now, I've already done half the job for you. I have checked the registry of companies and business names, and these quaintly named and railway-inspired companies have but a spectral existence. Hawksburn? Windsor? And other stations on the Frankston line? I hope to find out who is behind this scheme to defraud a very worthy charitable institution—and I am offering you the chance to mount your white charger and ride to the rescue, Mr. Rogers. Don your white armour, girt yourself with shield and lance, and get on that gallant steed.' She rose, waving Mr. Blake to his feet. 'I will give you until Friday at noon to tell me where the money went.'

Mr. Rogers rose too. 'I will do my best, Miss Fisher,' he stammered. 'I shall telephone by Friday, without fail.'

As they walked back along the corridor towards the main atrium, Mr. Blake mopped his brow. 'Miss Fisher,' he said in an awed whisper, 'you were magnificent! Thank you! I don't know what I would have done without you.'

Phryne patted his arm kindly. She knew only too well what he would have done: the same as a rabbit on the highway faced with the unexpected apparition of an approaching vehicle by night with blazing headlights. He would have stared at the oncoming danger, dazed, until it squashed him flat.

———

Mr. Rogers was better than his word. At five past three on Thursday afternoon, she was sitting in her parlour reading when Mr. Butler opened the door and bowed with becoming gravity. 'A Mr. Rogers on the telephone, Miss. He said it was urgent.'

Phryne took the call in her study, and listened to the bank manager's report with avid interest, making extensive notes with one hand while the other held the receiver. 'Thank you very much indeed, Mr. Rogers. You have been most helpful.'

Glancing at her watch, Phryne noted there was just time to sally forth to the address Mr. Rogers had supplied.

———

Not long after her return, Ruth and Jane arrived home, weary and a little downhearted. Their time at the Blind Institute had come to an end, with no apparent resolution of the mystery. Fortunately, Phryne was able to report that she had made significant progress at her end.

'It turns out that the proceeds of the false invoices have been siphoned off into a special account called Mont Albert Forty-ninth, Proprietary Limited, which is a standard shelf company with two statutory officers. One of these appears to be in a nursing home, clutching his seventy-nine years to himself like a gold watch. I found that out by visiting Mont Albert's official address, which is attached to a quite different company—which is against the law, you know. When a company—even a shelf company—changes its official address, the Companies Office must be informed. Clearly the Mont Albert director, a Mr. Tobias Shenton, did not do so. He did, however, leave a forwarding address with the new proprietors of the premises.'

'So this Mr. Shenton could be the mastermind behind the fraud?' Ruth asked. 'Be careful, Miss Phryne.'

'You might better warn Mr. Shenton to be careful of me, Ruth,' said Phryne, with a smile which had just a hint of bared teeth.

———

In the event, Phryne was baulked of her prey.

Tobias Shenton lived in Mont Albert, perhaps not all that surprisingly. His was a modest-looking house which had once had pretensions to grandeur, but had fallen from its formerly exalted state. The aged stone of its construction had cracked from the encroachment of ivy, there were slates missing from the roof, and two of the front windows were boarded up. Only the garden looked well tended. When Phryne rang the doorbell, she was greeted by a smartly dressed young house-keeper who informed her that Mr. Shenton was out of town until Monday.

'Shall I give him a message, Miss?' the housekeeper enquired, looking at the obviously wealthy visitor with open curiosity.

Phryne decided against giving Mr. Shenton advance warning of her return.

'It's all right,' she announced. 'Nothing important.'

She returned to St Kilda in a tolerably vexed condition.

———

'There, that wasn't so bad, was it? And you danced beautifully.'

'So did you.'

'And Liu wasn't there after all.'

'No. Perhaps he's forgotten all about you.'

'I really hope so.'

'Hold me in your arms again.'

Chapter Nineteen

On Saturday morning Mme Partlett was busy with another customer, but Simone—still in her severe black—ushered the girls
into a dressing-room. Phryne sat at her ease and considered
the party she herself would be attending in the not-too-distant
future. She found herself looking forward to it very much. This
Hong was probably just a raffish academic of a type familiar
to her, but she had, thanks to her long acquaintance with Lin
Chung, acquired a taste for chinoiserie, and she was curious to
know how an Australian would manage it. And there was the
prospect of Jeoffrey Bisset to contemplate, of course. She enter-
tained further designs upon him, and Hong's party would offer
her the chance to advance them. Should she order a new dress
herself? she wondered, casting an eye around the boutique.
But she quickly dismissed the idea; she already had a galaxy of
costumes with which to dazzle the eyes of potential admirers.
There was a time in every woman's life, she reflected, when she
finally had enough clothes.

But that couldn't yet be said of her adoptive daughters, who
had exited the dressing-room to stand before her in their gowns
of heliotrope (Jane) and amber (Ruth). As she and Madame had

discussed, artificial flowers (purple for Jane and apricot for Ruth) adorned each left shoulder. The hems, perfectly straight, hung precisely one inch below the knee. The effect was magnificent. The two girls posed balletically, bare arms uplifted, and grinned at Phryne.

'Wonderful!' Phryne clapped her hands. 'Are you happy with them?'

Ruth's face was glowing with delight. 'Thank you so much, Miss Phryne.'

Even Jane looked pleased as she too murmured her thanks. She had changed her stockings, and consigned the laddered ones to a wastepaper basket. By common consent, Ruth and Jane carried a spare pair with them at all times.

Madame Partlett extricated herself from her insistent customer—a loudish, tiresome woman with evident social pretensions—and pronounced herself satisfied. '*Magnifique*,' she said. 'You agree, Miss Fisher?'

'*Je suis d'accord, madame.*' Phryne paid the bill in cash (five pounds ten shillings) to audible sniffs from Madame's other customer, who muttered something about modern girls and their lack of shame.

Phryne turned on her. She was a woman of around forty, whose pearl necklace had probably cost if not a king's ransom, at least that of a marquis. Her hair she wore long and plaited in cornrows, which might have been attractive on her a number of years ago. Her face was square and appeared to have been designed for digging trenches. She wore plain black—presumably in mourning for something or someone; possibly her sense of humour—and she was holding up an elegant evening gown in the style of Erté by one hand as if it were a dubious fillet of fish.

'*Pardon?*' Phryne said, looking the woman full in the face. '*Avez-vous dit quelque chose?*'

'I'm sorry,' the woman sniffed, surveying Phryne's elegantly shocking clothes. She saw a youngish woman in blue trousers, flat patent leather shoes, an apricot silk blouse, an emerald-green silk scarf, and a smart black beret. She exuded wealth and power from every pore of her slender figure, and the woman pursed her thick lips. 'But I don't speak French.'

'*Dommage*,' Phryne consoled her. 'That gown will suit you. *Très mouton habillé en agneau*.' She turned to the girls. 'Come, you must get changed again, and allow Simone to box up the dresses for you.' Phryne cast a quick glance at Madame, whose eyes had widened by a millimetre or so at Phryne's remark. Phryne winked at her.

On the way home, Jane, in the back seat clutching her cardboard box with its precious cargo, asked, 'Miss Phryne, did you tell that woman that she would be mutton dressed as lamb?'

Phryne laughed, and spun the steering wheel, narrowly avoiding a youth on a bicycle. 'Indeed I did. Now don't try that on your teachers, girls. It's not very good French, anyway. But I wanted to say something she might be able to work out for herself later. She was quite rude to you girls, though you may have missed it.'

'Why, what did she say, Miss Phryne?' Ruth asked. Her own box was resting on her knees, and she was holding it tight with both hands.

'Nothing of consequence, Ruth. But I felt it meet and right to put her in her place.'

Ruth coloured. Of course Miss Phryne would never allow anyone to be rude to them in public. She had still not got used to having such a tigress of a protector. Jane merely smiled to herself. She was largely indifferent to other people and their absurd opinions, but it was amusing to watch their adoptive parent squashing rude remarks from others.

On their return home, Phryne and the girls rested until a light meal around four o'clock. 'We may assume this party includes dinner,' Phryne told them, as they tucked into fresh omelettes, 'but it might not be served till late, so it never hurts to have a little something before you go.'

After the girls had risen from the table, Phryne shared her intentions for the evening with Dot. 'I'm driving the girls to their party, and I'll pick them up at midnight.'

'That's very late, Miss,' her companion observed.

'It is, but these are fashionable people from the top end of town. Keeping late hours is part of their conspicuous consumption. The girls will love it—and acceptance by the upper crust will secure their futures. I will be fascinated to hear how they go tonight.' She paused, reflecting on her own transformation from Richmond guttersnipe to English boarding school and debutante balls. She had little use for fashionable society, but she wanted Ruth and Jane to have the same opportunities she had been afforded.

'Miss, what about the birthday present? I hope the girls bought her one.'

'Yes, they did. Ruth asked Frances what she wanted, and apparently it was an expensive picture book with coloured plates—which the girls bought with their own money. Now I'm going to have a nap.'

———

At five forty-five the girls came downstairs in their new dresses, where they were admired by the rest of the household.

'Well, you do look a treat,' said Mrs. Butler warmly.

Even Tinker came in from the shed to see and offered his gruff approval.

As Mr. Butler cranked the Hispano-Suiza into life, Phryne

arranged the girls and their dresses in the back seat before slipping behind the wheel. Having consulted her map, she'd decided that avoiding the city and the more noisome inner suburbs would be a wise precaution. She would travel along Balaclava Road as far as Hawthorn Road, then turn north and so come to Glenferrie Road, which would take them eventually to the vertiginous heights of Kew. The party was to be held At Home, in Banool Avenue, which Phryne recalled hearing was the highest point in Melbourne. Top of the town, verily.

The journey was uneventful in the early evening. The sun was setting in cloud ahead of them as Phryne turned into Cotham Road and began the ascent to the giddy heights of Kew. She turned right into Banool Street. The engine was protesting so much she found she had to engage second gear. Even that needed a severe pumping of the throttle to climb the vertiginous hill.

Number forty-seven turned out to be a considerable mansion just below the summit. It faced the street, and was so lofty that on the upper side it was a single storey, while on the lower side there were two spacious storeys, with an open garage below housing two brand-new motor cars. It appeared that the Reynolds family were very wealthy indeed, and not afraid to show it. Phryne drove to the very summit, which appeared to be a public park, and turned around so she would be able to bump-start the engine again. As she switched off the engine, sounds of ragtime piano wafted through the open windows. Within all was light and splendour, with coloured lanterns hung from the balconies. Elegant boys in evening dress and girls dressed in the height of contemporary fashion lined the balcony and waved.

Ruth waved back, her eyes shining. 'I'll return for you at midnight, girls,' Phryne reminded them. 'Have fun!'

As they stepped out of the back seat, three youths strode across the manicured lawn to gawp at the Hispano-Suiza. One of them lifted his hand to the flying stork hood ornament. He caught Phryne's eye, grinned sheepishly, and removed his hand hurriedly. 'Ruth, isn't it?' said another, an impossibly tall lad of around sixteen. 'May I have your arm?'

Ruth bowed her head. 'So long as you give it back, then by all means.'

Another youth offered his arm to Jane, who glanced at him sharply, shrugged, and extended hers.

Phryne engaged the clutch, and let it out. As the motor roared, a ragged cheer broke out from the balcony. Phryne waved her hand gaily and proceeded down the hill in second gear. Only time would tell, but it certainly looked as if the girls' society debut had begun propitiously.

———

As Ruth and Jane entered the house, they found Frances standing by the door. She looked at Jane, who was holding the wrapped gift in her left hand, and gave her a seraphic smile. 'Presents on the sideboard,' she said. 'We open them after dinner.'

Frances Reynolds was transformed in her party dress. Jane had always assumed that the purpose of school uniforms was to level the competition in conventional good looks. Frances was slender, long-legged, black-haired, and regular-featured. In her school uniform she did not exactly stand out. In her fashionable party dress, complete with feathered fascinator on her headband, she might have stepped straight out of a fashionable party in New York or London. Her face shone with health, and undeniable make-up. Her eyes—deep brown—sparkled with a determination to enjoy herself. She was utterly beautiful, and she gave Jane a look of penetrating intelligence. She inclined her chin somewhat. 'I'm so glad you both could come,' she said. 'You look wonderful.'

Her tone was sincere, unquestionably, and Jane was convinced immediately that Frances was indeed extending an olive branch. 'And so do you, Frances. Your dress is quite stunning.'

Not just stunning but surprising, Jane thought. After the care Phryne and Madame Partlett had taken not to transgress the bounds of modesty with Ruth and Jane's dresses, Frances had come to her own party clad in a glittering silver dress whose hem ended at mid-thigh, and below that there was nothing but slender tassels extending to three inches below the knee. Well, Jane decided, if you couldn't wear a racy dress at your own party, then when could you? Frances was a sporty girl, and her taut, muscular thighs were arguably worth showing off. Correctly interpreting the direction of Jane's thoughts, Frances met her gaze with an amused smirk, and took her arm.

'I want you to meet my parents. Do come.'

Jane deposited her parcel on the side table among a goodly pile of colourfully wrapped boxes, then she and Ruth followed Frances towards the elder Reynoldses.

Mr. Reynolds proved to be a tall, slim man in a blue three-piece suit. His handshake was firm, polite, and perfunctory. His mind, Jane decided, was somewhere far away; possibly on a yacht in the bay. He had that windswept look one associates with amateur sailors. Mrs. Reynolds wore a dark blue dress cut to the same length as Ruth and Jane's. Her eyes were a startling blue, and she gave both girls a firm handshake and a swift examination that missed nothing. A decisive nod of her pointed chin pronounced herself satisfied with the girls' presentation, as if she had concluded: expensive, fashionable yet decorous, with no attempt to outshine my beloved daughter on her birthday.

'I've heard so much about you both,' Mrs. Reynolds told them. 'It's a delight to meet you. Was that you in the Hispano-Suiza? It did seem to attract a great deal of admiration.'

'Miss Phryne loves her car,' Ruth conceded.

'Of course, the famous detective. Charles did tell me about her today.'

She nudged her husband, who, summoned back unexpectedly from the mysteries of sailing, snapped into life.

'Oh, yes. The Honourable Miss Fisher is a famous detective. And you're her daughters, I take it? Well done.'

Having wandered into the thickets of social complexity, Ruth looked at the man gratefully. While this had been a slightly awkward interpolation, Frances's father had managed to glide over the irregularities of adoption as though sailing a dinghy around a breakwater in a light zephyr. His wife cooed and placed her ring-encrusted hands together. 'Well, yes. Blood will out, you know. Anyway, dinner is at eight, then dancing. The pianist is from the Blind Institute—Frances mentioned you've been volunteering there. And we have another of their charges here tonight.' She gestured vaguely to a far corner of the room. 'Donald's over there, with the white stick. He's someone's brother, you know, and Frances said we must invite him.' Mrs. Reynolds paused to draw breath, then beamed on them anew. 'We had the Blind Institute's jazz quintet for Robert's eighteenth last month,' she explained, 'and Frances was so impressed with the pianist she asked for her specifically. Perhaps you recognise her?'

Amid a cascade of jazz harmonies, Ruth and Jane looked over at the smart young woman seated at the grand piano. It was Jennifer Barnes. Her hair was plaited in two cornrows and she wore a light grey dress. She seemed to be enjoying herself, as she was smiling broadly.

'We do know her!' Ruth exclaimed. 'We met her at the Institute, and she tuned our piano last week.'

'How splendid!' said Mrs. Reynolds. 'Now you must excuse me—I really should go and greet the new arrivals. Have fun, ladies.' Ruth and Jane found themselves backing towards the nearest available wall. Beside a magnificent dark wood dresser piled high with silverware, they spied a couple of chairs. While Ruth went to claim them, Jane made a short detour to a sideboard where a magnificent punchbowl in chased silver was filled to the brim with fruit cup, in which floated strawberries and other dainties. She brought back two glasses and they sat and sipped contentedly, looking around them at the vast living room. There were around forty guests all told, and nearly all of them fitted comfortably into this cavernous space. From the polished wood floor to its high, chandelier-crowned ceiling, everything spoke of aristocratic luxury. There were sculptured carpets at intervals. There were round tables, currently pushed against the walls and laden with silver services, napkins, and crockery. The room was, Jane estimated, about forty feet by twenty-five. A harmonious proportion approximating the Golden Mean so beloved of the Greeks. It must take up most of the lower floor. Presumably all the bedrooms were upstairs, and the kitchen and other facilities behind the three white doors which opened off the living room.

As Jane was assessing their surrounds, Ruth's attention was on the punch. She detected not only ginger, but cinnamon, allspice, and possibly clove. Bursting with flavour, certainly, but not too sweet. She speculated that mineral water had been used instead of lemonade. She took another sip to be sure—yes, definitely mineral water—then turned to Jane. 'Well, what did you make of all that, Janey?' she whispered. 'Our hosts, I mean.'

Jane put her head to one side consideringly. 'I believe Frances's regard for us is genuine. She truly wants to be friends. As for her parents…' She shrugged. 'Mrs. R is a well-meaning hostess doing hostess things. It's probably not easy making conversation with people you've never met before.' Jane was not in the habit of attempting such herself, but she could imagine that it might prove troublesome. Her private view—that Mrs. Reynolds was probably not very bright—she kept to herself for fear of being overheard. 'Now that Mr. Reynolds is a clever man. They didn't want to bring up the matter of our adoption, but Mrs. R was finding it hard to avoid, so she called upon her husband to help out. He doesn't particularly want to be here, but he knows the right sorts of things to say even when his mind's elsewhere. My guess is he'd rather be sailing.'

'What makes you say that?' Ruth asked.

'He's wearing yacht club cufflinks. But I say, fancy Miss Barnes being here! And isn't she doing well?'

At that moment, Jennifer Barnes launched into a jazz version of 'Rule Britannia,' which evoked a good deal of laughter. She followed this with 'Old Hundredth' in ragtime, 'Waltzing Matilda' and, finally, 'Let's Misbehave.'

Jane and Ruth leaned forward in their chairs to listen. By this time, Jennifer had a crowd gathered around her, boys and girls alike urging her on. Frances moved through the throng and clapped her hands after the final chord.

'Jennifer, that was wonderful! Now, we're going to have dinner quite soon, but I wonder if you'd care to try one of your improvised duets with me?'

'Of course,' Jennifer said agreeably. 'What would you like to play?'

'How about the *Moonlight Sonata*? Can you work around that?'

Jennifer grinned. 'I can try.' She stood up, steadied herself on the piano, and Jane saw Miss Thomas breaking through the scrum to assist. She was wielding another piano stool and parked it next to the other, before retreating to the ring of spectators.

'Left or right?' Frances enquired.

'I'll start on your right,' Jennifer proposed. 'Then we should swap.'

Frances played the piano moderately well, having recently passed her fifth grade exam, and the Beethoven sonata offered few difficulties. After all, most of it was played on the black notes. Jennifer paused for a moment, then began to improvise some jazz melodies beyond the treble clef. At one point she burst into a brief, tinny rendition of 'God Save the King,' which caused a general intake of breath and sidelong looks among the spectators. Her eyes were firmly closed, and she was plainly thinking ahead to whatever lay on the next page. A broad grin crossed her face, and she launched into a reprise of 'Rule Britannia,' which somehow fitted Beethoven's melody perfectly, if you overlooked the fact that it was now in a minor key. The end of the sonata was reached, to general applause, while Jennifer concluded with a flourish from 'The Star-Spangled Banner.'

Frances rose, taking Jennifer's left hand in hers, and with difficulty they swapped places, whispering to each other. Frances began again from the top, while Jennifer hovered over the deep bass notes, interpolating sinister arpeggios at intervals, which slowly became Parry's 'Jerusalem.' As she segued into 'Pop Goes the Weasel,' Frances burst into delighted laughter, but without missing a beat. The applause when they had finished their second run-through was loud, prolonged, and well-deserved.

As the recital concluded, some of the young men were pressed into service shifting the tables into the centre of the room for dinner. Within sixty seconds seven tables had been assembled around the room. There were name cards at every setting, and Jane and Ruth found themselves on table three. They were pleased to find they had been placed next to Jennifer Barnes and Miss Thomas.

Dinner was superb: small pastries with chicken and vegetables; soups (mushroom or French onion); roast beef with steamed vegetables; and ice cream or sorbets to follow.

'What a coincidence that you should be here!' Ruth said to

Jennifer, who was managing her knife and fork with considerable dexterity.

Jennifer smiled. 'The Reynolds family have given generously to the Blind Institute.'

Miss Thomas, to Jennifer's right, nodded. 'Indeed. But oh, Jennifer, I had no idea you were so clever! That duet you did with Frances was wonderful! But please—don't do that sort of thing when Mr. Findlay's around. He would disapprove.'

'I'm not so sure,' Jennifer countered. 'I think Mr. Findlay has hidden depths. He might act very prim and proper in class, but I suspect he has a sense of humour.'

'If you say so.' Miss Thomas didn't seem quite convinced. 'But how did you combine all those tunes with the Beethoven? That's so creative of you.'

Jennifer smiled, and her nose crinkled. 'I know the piece very well, as you're aware. But it would be easier with a major key.' She closed her sightless eyes for a moment, listening to the slackening conversation around her. 'Could you assist me back to the piano, please? I will be needed in a moment, I think.'

She had judged the tenor of the conversation accurately. Moments later, Mr. Reynolds made a short, decorous speech, in which he congratulated his daughter on having attained the age of sixteen without undue mishap, and expressed his wish that she continue in this vein. He thanked the guests for coming; he thanked the hired caterers for their excellent service; and he thanked Miss Barnes for her imaginative entertainment, declaring that he looked forward to more of the same after dinner was concluded. Waitstaff passed among the tables with champagne flutes, and a modest amount was poured into each glass from silvered ice buckets laden with bottles of Moët & Chandon.

Mr. Reynolds raised his glass. 'To Frances!'

'To Frances!' the assembly chorused, and sipped at their

champagne; and from the piano, Jennifer struck up the intro-
duction to 'Happy Birthday,' which was sung in a variety of
contiguous keys.

'And now'—Mr. Reynolds returned his empty glass to a passing
waiter—'if you would all rise, we shall clear the floor for dancing.'

As everyone rose, Jane noticed Frances sitting by the blind
boy her mother had pointed out earlier. He was not unhandsome,
with regular features, a wide mouth, and a prominent nose. As
she watched, Frances assisted him to his feet and led him across
to a chair by the wall. Jane approved. Frances Reynolds really was
putting her back into turning over her new leaf.

Jane looked around the party guests, seeking the other members of the coterie of mean girls who had so tormented poor
Claire. Josephine and Charlotte in particular seemed notable
absentees. It was quite likely that Claire's death had shaken up
the furniture in Melbourne's youthful high society.

Ruth nudged Jane. 'This is a lot more grown-up than I thought
it would be,' she confided. 'I was expecting Pass the Parcel and
Musical Chairs.'

Jane nodded. 'So was I,' she admitted. 'But there is a pleasant
undertone to all of this, isn't there? These people really do like
each other. I haven't heard a single catty remark since we arrived.'

'I haven't either.'

The girls watched as Frances led a tall, lissom youth into the
middle of the floor. Jennifer Barnes began to play a sprightly jazz
tune which Jane recognised as the Charleston. With a whirling
of random knees the pair broke into the accompanying dance.
Ruth found herself drawn onto the floor by one of the inter-
changeable young men present, and did her best to emulate the
others around her. Jane saw a slender arm extended towards her
and shook her head.

'I'm sorry. I don't dance.' She gave the boy a quick once-over, noting his hangdog air of disappointment without regret. Instead, on a whim, she made her way to where the blind boy was sitting. His hair was plastered down thickly with pomade, which filled his immediate vicinity with the scent of vegetable and mineral oils and, for some reason, cloves and cinnamon. 'Hello,' she said. 'Donald, isn't it? My name's Jane.'

'Pleased to meet you,' he answered mechanically. 'Are you one of Frances's schoolfriends?'

'Yes, we both go to PLC. And Mrs. Reynolds mentioned you're at the Blind Institute?'

'I would've thought that was pretty obvious,' he responded, raising his white stick by its handle.

'It is a bit of a giveaway,' Jane agreed. 'I've seen a lot of blind people who don't use them, though.'

Donald's lip curled at one corner. 'No, most of us don't like the stick. It's advertising our affliction rather too ostentatiously. Besides which, if a truck wants to run us over, the stick's not going to be much help, is it?'

Jane laughed. 'No, I suppose not.'

'But I find it useful,' he added. 'And I really don't care what others think of me.'

'You must know Jennifer Barnes. Isn't she a brilliant pianist!'

The boy's face seemed to harden. 'Yes. She's very clever.' He rose suddenly. 'Excuse me,' he said. 'I need to go to the bathroom.'

With a flourish of his white stick, Donald made his way across the room. Jane watched him for a moment, then she went back to her seat by the wall.

Ruth was having what appeared to be the time of her life on the dance floor. She grinned at her partner, her eyes sparkling with delight. As the dance ended, she whispered something to him then resumed her seat next to Jane.

'Was that fun?' Jane wanted to know.

'Yes, it really was. And Charles is lovely. I like him.' Ruth looked at her sister. 'I noticed you talking to Donald. Was he nice?'

Jane raised her eyebrows. 'He was…interesting. But I'll tell you about him later.'

They watched the dancing in companionable silence, sipping at their champagne. One glass for a birthday party and no more, it seemed. Very much the attitude of Miss Phryne, Jane noted. On special occasions she and Jane were given champagne, despite their being only fifteen.

After a while the dancing was brought to a close, and the Opening of the Presents was announced. Ruth and Jane paid little attention. Most of the gifts were books, although some were perfume or pottery. Ruth held her sister's hand tightly as their gift was unwrapped. Frances gave them a wide smile. The book had cost two pounds, which seemed a lot of money to Jane, but it was worth it for that wide, heartfelt smile. It was a book of Italian painters from long ago, with forty colour plates. There were no duplicate gifts at all. Jane deduced from this that Frances had asked everybody for different things. Either that, or else a great deal of covert negotiations among her friends had occurred.

Miss Thomas brought Jennifer back to sit next to Ruth, and she herself took a seat on Jane's other side. 'We haven't had a chance to talk since you finished at the Institute,' she said in a low voice. 'Have you anything to report yet?'

'We have made progress,' Jane assured her. 'But we're not quite ready to speak of it yet.'

'Good for you!' Miss Thomas gave an approving nod, possibly for Jane's reticence as much as anything.

Meanwhile, Ruth's curiosity had been aroused by her sister's cryptic comment about Donald.

'Do you know a guest called Donald?' she asked Jennifer. 'Apparently he goes to your school.'

Jennifer shivered imperceptibly. 'I wouldn't say we were friends or anything, but we're acquainted. He's always struck me as very cold. Why?'

'I just wondered.' And then, since the subject seemed to be an awkward one, she added, 'I say, your playing was wonderful tonight.'

Jennifer's lips twitched into a smile.

After the presents, more ice creams and sorbets were served. Frances and Jennifer took turns at the piano, eventually giving way to Frances's dance partner, who flexed his hands ostentatiously and made a reasonable fist of some jazz tunes. Before they knew it, the clock—a huge grandfather clock in the hallway—tolled out midnight. Frances stood at the door to farewell her guests, thanking them all for their presents.

Farewelled and thanked in their turn, Jane and Ruth stepped outside. It was a cool night, and the lights of Melbourne shone like diamonds in the distance. 'Come on,' Jane said, taking her sister's hand. 'There's Miss Phryne.'

And so she was: sitting at the wheel of the Hispano-Suiza, with the acetylene lamps blazing.

The girls walked down the stone steps to join her, well content with their society debut.

———

'So who is coming to this party on Friday night, Carnation?'

'His work colleagues.'

'Are they all Westerners?'

'I believe so, Peony. I shouldn't think there'll be any trouble.'

'Good.'

Chapter Twenty

'Jane, are you sure?'

Even though it was well past their bedtime, Jane and Ruth were still hovering in Phryne's parlour, unwilling as yet to doff their party dresses. And Jane had caused Phryne's eyebrows to shoot upwards.

'Miss Phryne, I can't be absolutely sure. But his hair oil is very distinctive. Lots of the boys wear their hair slicked down like that. But his blend of clove and cinnamon is very unusual. And it's the same smell as I found in the storeroom.'

Phryne sat up in her chair, watching the girls on the sofa opposite her. 'What did you make of him, Jane?'

Jane thought for a moment. 'I had the impression of someone cold and arrogant. I asked him if he knew Jennifer Barnes, but he doesn't seem interested in other people. If anything, he seems to scorn them and think himself superior.'

'What about you, Ruth?' Phryne asked. 'Did you speak to him?'

Ruth shook her head. 'I was too busy dancing.' She blushed. 'But I did ask Jennifer about him. She doesn't like him.'

'Did she say why not?'

'It was like Jane said: she called him cold.'

Phryne thought this over. Cold, indifferent to others. Thought himself superior. She knew Tobias Shenton of Mont Albert Forty-ninth Pty Ltd couldn't be working alone; he would need to have accomplices inside the Institute. This Donald sounded a likely candidate…if only he weren't blind.

'What are you thinking, Miss Phryne?' Jane asked. 'Is it something to do with the mystery at the Institute?'

The clock in the corner chimed once and Phryne stood. 'I am going to visit Mr. Shenton again on Monday. With any luck he will be at home this time. Come on, girls. It's time you were in bed. You've had a big day.'

———

Phryne went for a long walk on the beach on Sunday while Dot did her Sabbath duty at church. She felt frustrated at not being able to pursue the case of the Institute's fraudulent accounts immediately, and was still put out by Lin Chung's reticence on the matters concerning him. She was cheered by dinner, which was a splendid meal. Mrs. Butler had quite surpassed herself. Now that summer was over, roast dinners were back on the menu. In this instance it was roast lamb with a rosemary and cranberry glaze; potatoes both sweet and ordinary; steamed beans and carrots with honey and sesame; and a rice pudding to follow. Ruth and Jane tucked in with a will, and even Phryne ate more than usual. This sheep had certainly given its life in a good cause, she decided.

The only missing element was Tinker, who occasionally arrived fashionably late. But never this late, and Phryne was on the point of sending out a search party when he arrived, tired, dusty, and apologetic. Mrs. Butler scolded him gently and disappeared into the kitchen in order to retrieve the plate she had been keeping warm for him. He sat down, accepted a glass of lemonade, and gave Phryne a significant nod. When Mrs. B placed his plate before him, he set to as though coming off a Lenten fast.

Phryne slept heavily that night, but awoke refreshed. She peeled back the covers, surveyed herself in her Chinese silk nightgown, and smiled complacently. She turned her gaze towards the window, which she had left open. A modest sea breeze wafted in, scented with salt, seaweed, and the undertones of early autumn. Australian summers still took some getting used to, but today it was mild, cool, and pleasant. Phryne lay back on her emerald green silk sheets and sighed with contentment. In due course Dot would arrive, with coffee and perhaps a croissant, and thereafter she would have a pleasant day's detecting.

Dot's arrival was heralded with a tentative knock on the door, and Phryne smiled to herself. Dot's morning knock was always somewhat hesitant, doubtless a result of having more than once discovered a beautiful naked man in her employer's bed. 'Come in, Dot,' she called.

Dot entered, wearing her customary shades of brown, and looked at Phryne with an affection laced with relief at finding Phryne alone.

As predicted, the silver tray she set on Phryne's bedside table was laden with both coffee and a croissant.

When Dot had left the room, Phryne sipped at the coffee, feeling more alert with each injection of caffeine, brewed to perfection in the Greek style by Mr. B. The croissant was likewise excellent, and would have passed the approval of the most exacting pâtissier in Paris. Croissants should be crisp and flaky on the outside and meltingly light within, and this achieved its aim on both counts.

It was ten to ten by the time Phryne pushed the tray away. An idea had begun to germinate, and she nodded in satisfaction as she rose, shed her nightgown, and headed for her bath.

When she had completed her ablution and donned clothes appropriate for the business ahead, she sought out her companion. 'Dot, I'm going to see the director of Mont Albert Forty-Ninth. Do you want to come?'

Dot, who rather enjoyed seeing her employer dishing out justice in her own inimitable style, did.

———

As Phryne made her way across the suburbs—sedately, in deference to Dot's apprehension for their safety when her employer was behind the wheel of the Hispano-Suiza—she glanced over at her companion. Noting that, though the hands clenched in her lap were white around the knuckle, Dot's brow was remarkably unfurrowed, she asked in a flash of insight: 'Have you heard anything from Hugh?'

Dot relaxed in her seat and smiled. 'He came to mass yesterday, Miss.'

'I'm pleased to hear it, Dot. How was he?'

'He looked really tired, Miss, but he said he came because he wanted to see me. He didn't take Communion, of course, but he sat with me through the service and gave me some flowers to take home.'

Phryne hadn't noticed any additional floristry about the house, but presumed that the flowers now adorned her companion's bedside table. 'That was very sweet of him, Dot.' Phryne reached over to pat her hand.

'Thank you, Miss—Miss, the truck!'

Phryne returned her left hand to the wheel and steered adroitly around the vehicle that pulled out from the kerb suddenly. She heard Dot whisper fervently under her breath; no doubt a prayer that she would live to see her wedding day.

—

'Miss Fisher? Private investigator? Well, really, I don't see how I can help you.'

Tobias Shenton was not at all what Phryne had expected. For a start, he was seventy if he was a day. He was dressed in aged tweeds, and sported a snowy beard and thinning white hair. His mild blue eyes had an expression of honest puzzlement that had to be genuine. Far from resembling a criminal mastermind, Phryne would have taken him for a retired theatre critic.

They were sitting in the man's study. It was small, containing a fireplace innocent of either wood or coal, and tall bookcases reaching almost to the ceiling, filled with what appeared to be adventure novels and books on gardening. The windows— also tall and narrow—had not been cleaned for some time. An inoffensive-looking spider had taken up residence in one corner of the ceiling, and had spun itself a respectable little web. He had offered tea, which Phryne and Dot had refused.

Phryne leaned forward and cut to the chase. 'Mr. Shenton, you are listed in the Companies Office as one of the two statutory officers of Mont Albert Forty-Ninth.'

'Ah...' The man's face cleared and he tapped his walking stick against his trouser leg. 'I think you have confused me with my nephew George, Miss Fisher. He's the one who does all the business stuff in the family. I hold a few directorships for him and attend the odd board meeting, but'—he gave a self-deprecatory laugh—'I have to say I never really understood what those other fellows were talking about. My main interest is roses.'

'So you would be surprised to learn that you are listed as the company secretary of this enterprise?' Phryne persisted.

He shook his snowy head. 'I think you must be mistaken, Miss Fisher. I have a small annuity, and that suffices for my modest needs. I have no business interests worth the name. I'm sorry. Would you like to see my roses?'

Phryne stood up. 'Some other time perhaps, Mr. Shenton. I'm sorry to have troubled you.'

He showed them out, and Phryne and Dot made their way back to the Hispano-Suiza.

'Well, that was odd, Miss,' Dot observed as Phryne cranked the starter. 'He seemed to have no idea what you were talking about.'

Phryne gave a taut smile. 'Mr. Tobias Shenton, as you must have gathered, Dot, is being used.'

'But wouldn't he have had to sign something, Miss, when the company was set up?'

Phryne grimaced. 'I expect his signature was forged. Either that, or he's forgotten all about it. I don't really know, and I doubt it matters much.'

'So where are we going now, Miss?'

They were currently roaring down the hill through Deepdene.

'To the Blind Institute, Dot—after I make a certain telephone call... Ah, there's a phone box.'

Phryne parked on the roadside verge and Dot watched her as she conversed. Her employer was doing most of the talking. She was animated, her eyes sparkling, and Dot knew what this meant: Miss Fisher was about to happen to somebody.

———

Later that afternoon, Phryne and Dot sat in the office of Stanus Hedger, director of the Victorian Institute for the Blind. The students had been dismissed for the day—all bar one. George Shenton, summoned from his city office unexpectedly, sat next to his son, his face a study in grey-faced terror. Phryne and Dot sat nearby, but a little apart. All of them were looking at Mr.

Hedger. He was livid. Normally, brown eyes do not blaze like comets, but his did so now. He glared at the Shentons *père et fils*. 'I've been hearing things about your son, Mr. Shenton,' he began, quietly enough.

There was a terrible, dread-inspiring pause. Nobody breathed.

Mr. Hedger gestured towards Phryne and Dot. 'Allow me to perform the introductions. This is the Honourable Phryne Fisher, and her assistant Miss Williams. Miss Fisher, as you may be aware, is a private detective of some note in this city. She has been investigating some financial irregularities in the Institute's accounts, and those investigations are now complete.' He thumped his fist on the desktop. 'So, Mr. Shenton: tell me all about Mont Albert Forty-Ninth.'

Mr. Shenton was doing his best to present a facade of Pillar of the Community, in his black business suit with slender black tie, though his jug-eared look marred the effect somewhat.

'Mont Albert is a vehicle I set up for my son, Donald,' he explained, resting both hands on his knees. 'I am a stockbroker, sir, and I wish my son to follow in my footsteps. I believe his disability should not disqualify him. So eighteen months ago, I set up a company for him, with silent partners as directors, and staked him fifty pounds. I believe he has doubled his money since then. I am very pleased with his progress. Clearly he has shown considerable financial acumen.'

When *père* had wound down, Phryne turned her attention to *fils*, who was sitting calmly, clutching his white stick. 'Fortunately I was able to track down one of these silent partners,' she said. 'Your great-uncle Tobias. If not for that, you might perhaps have got away with it—since as well as financial acumen, it appears you show considerable aptitude for crime. According to your father, there is currently a hundred-odd pounds in Mont Albert Forty-Ninth, but you've embezzled a lot more than that, haven't you? Where is the rest of the money, Donald? Mr. Hedger would rather like it back.'

'Too bloody right I would!' roared Mr. Hedger, and slammed both hands on the desk now.

Mr. Shenton quailed, but his son, Phryne noted, did not. It was barely noticeable, but the corners of his mouth were curled in a supercilious smirk.

'Tell me what you've done with it, you miserable blackguard!' the director demanded.

'I don't know what you're talking about.' He directed his sightless gaze towards Hedger. 'Embezzlement is a serious accusation. What evidence do you have connecting me with this?'

The director looked at Phryne, who regarded both Shentons with a look of disdain. 'Mr. Shenton, your son concocted a remarkable scheme involving four bogus business names.'

The man blinked at her, then bowed his head in naked horror and shame.

Phryne nodded silently. It appeared that Daddy had no prior knowledge of his son's crimes.

She looked hard at Donald. 'Windsor Smallgoods, Prahran Packing, Hawksburn Greengrocers, and Armadale Butchers.' As she pronounced each name, the boy recoiled slightly. It was enough to confirm her suspicions. 'He gained access to the Institute's accounts and issued duplicate invoices for goods which had been supplied by other businesses. He used the music storeroom as his office, and when one of my assistants was on his trail he decided to give her a scare by locking her in, in true bully fashion.'

Donald laughed. 'Come off it, Miss Fisher! You seem to have forgotten something: I'm blind, remember? Were these invoices you speak of written in braille?'

Phryne silently stood up and advanced on the youth. She raised her right hand and made as if to give him a ringing slap.

Donald flinched.

Phryne resumed her seat. 'Ah, but you aren't completely blind, are you, Donald? I think you can see rather better than you've been letting on.' She paused to give this time to sink in.

Mr. Shenton stared at his son, aghast. Mr. Hedger's look was one of utter loathing.

'You've been having us on, you little swine!' he bellowed.

'Please!' Mr. Shenton stood and extended both arms in supplication. 'Mr. Hedger, I hardly know what to say. It is clear enough that my son has committed great wrongs.' As his son made to interrupt, he held up a hand. 'Silence, Donald! If the money went into your account, then you are guilty as charged; I neither know nor care how you managed it. And may I remind you that you are seventeen years old: you could be sent to prison for this. Everything you stole must be restored at once, along with an additional contribution, which I personally will supply.' He turned back to the director. 'Please think of it in the nature of punitive damages, Mr. Hedger. I do hope that this, along with a full confession, might persuade you to let the matter rest here.'

There was a long and painful silence. Finally Donald threw his white stick onto the floor. 'I made a mistake on the bond market,' he announced in a voice as flat as the Nullarbor. 'I lost twenty quid in the first week. I was wondering how to get it back. At first I thought maybe there was a safe in the office I could break into, so I dropped in to talk to Blake and have a surreptitious look. I noticed how he was struggling with the accounts and realised the answer was right in front of me. He never even noticed!' The youth had the impudence to laugh.

'Neither did I,' said Mr. Hedger in a low, quiet voice. 'We were all at fault. Go on, son.'

Donald shrugged. 'There's nothing else to tell. Once I'd set the scheme up, it ran itself.' The boy really did seem pleased with himself.

'Really?' Now Hedger's voice was almost a purr. 'Well, Mr. Shenton, I haven't made up my mind what to do about this. It's clear enough to me that you're remorseful, but it's equally clear that your son isn't. I'm more than half inclined to send the little swine to prison.' He nodded to the door. 'That'll be all for now. I'll be in touch.'

The distraught father bent to pick up his son's white stick from the floor and restored it to him, then, taking Donald by the arm, he escorted him from the room. The door closed behind them, and Phryne gave Mr. Hedger a sharp, inquisitive look.

'Well, that was interesting. It's not really my business, of course, but I'd be interested to know how you intend to play this.'

The director gazed back at her. 'I'm most obliged to you and your daughters for your assistance.' He gave a short laugh. 'What I don't understand is how you came to notice something amiss in the first place. Did Miss Thomas put you up to it, by any chance?'

Phryne leaned forward, feeling that she should put in a good word for the woman; without her, after all, Donald would have continued to bleed the Institute dry. 'She did mention that she suspected something wrong with the accounts, but apparently she couldn't persuade you to listen to her. Why was that, I wonder? Because you didn't believe a woman could understand finances?'

Hedger continued to stare steadily at Phryne for several seconds, then he leaned back in his chair, put both hands behind his head and nodded. 'As you say. But it turns out she was right.' His forehead corrugated. 'I'm thinking our friend Mr. Blake needs a change.'

'You're not going to sack him, are you? He was very cooperative.'

'No, Miss Fisher, I won't. I look after my people. But I can't keep him on in the office.' He tapped the desktop, thinking. 'Blake's an amateur gardener, did you know?'

Phryne didn't. 'Do go on.'

'I feel Charlie could use some help with the grounds. I'll put Blake out to pasture there.'

'And the office?' Phryne persisted. 'Do you have any plans for that?'

The director gave a reluctant smile. 'I think I'll ask Miss Thomas to give it a go.'

'That sounds like an excellent idea, Mr. Hedger. But what are you going to do about Donald?' On receiving a forty-watt None Of Your Damn Business glare, she added: 'I merely need to know if the girls or I will be required to give evidence. We were thinking of taking a holiday.'

Mr. Hedger offered a conciliatory nod. 'All right, that's fair enough. Look, I don't want a scandal any more than Shenton does, but I'm hoping he won't realise that, because I want him to feel inclined to make a very generous donation.'

'And Donald? You won't keep him here, surely?'

The light of battle flashed momentarily across the director's features. 'Oh, I will. I know he's able to see better than he's been letting on, but I reckon his eyesight's still bad enough for him to be considered legally blind. That means he comes under my jurisdiction.' He showed his teeth for a moment. They were porcelain-white, and reminded Phryne of a shark she had once met in Port Phillip Bay. 'I've got plans for Donald. He needs to learn a trade, and he's not too young to start in my brush factory.'

Phryne burst out laughing. 'Far better than prison! Good for you, Mr. Hedger. Well,' she said, rising to her feet, 'I think my work here is done.'

Hedger rose also, and they shook hands. 'You'll send me a bill for your investigation, I trust—it's only fair.'

'By no means,' said Phryne crisply. 'And I shall continue to employ your piano tuners, and your musicians, too.'

'That's very kind of you.' He touched his heart briefly. 'Thank you.'

As Phryne led Dot from the great man's office, she felt the exhilaration she invariably experienced at the successful conclusion of a case.

As she cranked the engine of the Hispano-Suiza to life, Dot, who had been mulling things over in silence, spoke up. 'It doesn't seem right, Miss,' she said. 'Shouldn't Donald be put on trial?'

Phryne accelerated away from the kerb. 'No, Dot. It's like Mr. Hedger said: a trial would mean a scandal, and the Institute can't afford that. If everyone knew that donors' money had been embezzled, they'd stop giving. Now, my next stop is the police station; there's something going on in the Chinese community—first the murder of that poor labourer and now a missing girl. I want to ensure something is done about it and it's not just swept under the rug. Do you want to come with me? I'm hoping to speak to Hugh.'

'Better I don't, Miss. I don't think he's comfortable mixing his work and his private life.'

'As you wish, Dot. I'll drop you home first.'

———

Phryne had a wait of forty minutes before Hugh Collins finally appeared in the foyer at City South police station. It was clear that he and his razor had not been on speaking terms that morning. He appeared to have slept in his clothes, and his dark-ringed eyes suggested he had spent the night staring into the abyss. 'Miss Fisher,' he greeted her, in a tone that was markedly chilly and formal. 'What can I do for you?'

'Detective Sergeant Collins.' Phryne decided to see his

formality and raise it. 'I was wondering if there was any news regarding the corpse I found on Williamstown Beach.'

Collins gave her a long, considering look. 'I'm afraid not. Enquiries are continuing.' If his manner had been any more wooden you could have made a chest of drawers out of him.

Phryne gave him a bright smile. 'I could help with this, you know, what with one thing and another.'

She paused for a response. Hugh's silence was deafening.

'And I wondered if you had come across any stray Chinese girls in your travels,' she continued. 'If you should, I'd be obliged if you would let me know at once.'

'Have you filed a missing persons report?'

'No, I haven't, because I'm not the one who lost her. But she belongs to one of the more important families in Chinatown, and they are no more anxious than you are to share information around. Nevertheless, Sergeant, it would be a better world if we were all prepared to help each other out on occasion.'

This was met with another stony silence.

Finally Collins said, 'May I help you with anything else, Miss Fisher?'

'It really doesn't sound like it.' And Phryne swept out, in no good temper.

———

'Well, Liu, do you still want the girl?'

'Carnation? Why, certainly I do. But will she agree to it?'

'I can be very persuasive.'

'I'm glad to hear it. All right. After your little celebration, then?'

'Agreed.'

Chapter Twenty-One

Dusk was falling as Phryne climbed out of Bert's taxi on the Friday of Hong's party. She handed him a ten-shilling note. 'Bert, are you sure you don't mind collecting me later?' She had decided against driving herself; if Hong's hospitality proved as lavish as promised, she might not be in a suitable state to do so.

Bert rolled his cigarette to the left corner of his mouth. 'She'll be sweet, Miss Phryne. We bin workin' nights lately, but we'll be home by midnight. Just call any time after that if you want a lift. We'll be up.'

She looked around her. Like much of Williamstown, The Strand seemed to contain a strange assortment of bedfellows. 'What is that place over there?' she asked Bert, pointing to a weather-beaten shack that showed signs of life.

Bert's eyes flickered towards it. 'That's the Anchor. Some of the Comrades drink there. If you're thinkin' of payin' a visit, be a bit careful.'

'The natives aren't friendly?'

'I wouldn't say that. Just...be discreet.'

'You know me, Bert.'

As the cab sped away, Phryne ran her hands down her

glimmering evening dress by Patou, smoothing invisible creases. It was tunic-cut, loose yet clinging in all the right places, and daringly beautiful with silk the colour of grapevines gloriously ablaze in their autumn reds. A cunningly wrought headdress encircled her gleaming hair, ending with a cluster of amethyst grapes that highlighted the elegant arc of her neck. Phryne smoothed her long satin gloves, admiring the glow of her golden slippers in the light of a lantern above. She had momentarily considered dressing in Chinese costume, but decided against it. There would be others similarly attired, and Phryne preferred to stand out from the crowd.

In the early evening light, Hong's house looked agreeably festive. Coloured lanterns hung from the trees, and all along the upper-storey balcony. The front door opened, and jazz-flavoured music wafted out to meet her. Before she could open the gate, another taxi pulled up outside, and the tall, elegant figure of Jeoffrey Bisset emerged. 'You come most carefully upon your hour!' Phryne declared, and offered him her arm.

Jeoffrey's handsome features lit up, as he entwined his arm with hers. Jeoffrey wore standard evening dress—white tie—and looked the picture of excitable elegance. 'I say, Phryne, you do look smashing. Come and meet the birthday boy.'

Silhouetted in the open doorway was a man rather under middle height, dressed in pale blue silk brocade robe that might have befitted a Chinese magistrate. Exotic creatures—dragons, Phryne thought—adorned its sleeves and hems. On his head was a black skullcap of some sort.

As Phryne and Jeoffrey climbed the four stone steps leading up to the porch, Hong raised his arms in welcome. He looked… smooth was the *mot juste*, Phryne decided. He was quite young, in his early thirties or thereabouts, and his face was unlined. His black hair was cut short. 'Jeoffrey!' he announced in a cultured voice. 'How splendid of you to come! And your lovely companion must be the famous Miss Fisher.'

He bowed from the waist (no more than fifteen degrees), and Phryne offered her hand. His lips brushed her knuckles, and he clicked his heels together. Western shoes under the silk robe, Phryne noted.

'Very pleased to meet you, Hong.' Phryne withdrew her hand gracefully. 'Many happy returns.'

'You are too kind.' Hong half turned, and ushered them both over the threshold. 'The party is upstairs. I believe you already know some of the guests, Miss Fisher—from the university's arts faculty.'

The interior was opulent beyond words. As they ascended a dark staircase, Phryne saw the walls were hung with plaster masks of fearsome-looking deities, ranged just above head height. They looked down with what the onlooker hoped was benevolence, although some of the masks' features were quite terrifying. Moustaches made of human hair were very much in evidence. 'The Eight Immortals, Phryne,' Jeoffrey murmured. 'Supposed to bring luck.'

The house itself was modernist to a degree, with a single large room occupying the entire upper storey. It was a ballroom, probably fifty feet by thirty, and the ceilings at least twenty feet high. The walls were hung with artworks in which *arts décoratifs* was the dominant style. Hong had made no attempt at faux Orientalism, Phryne noted approvingly. The furniture was exquisite, and modern. Restrained blackwood vied with chrome, while the wall hangings were crimson, blue, and purple. The tableware was mostly silver, which earned another nod of approval from Phryne. A tasteless parvenu would have gone with gold, which Phryne considered vulgar.

The next thing Phryne took in were the scents. Small porcelain incense burners were arranged around the walls and tables. Phryne's nose detected sandalwood, camphor, and frankincense, and a number of other scents she could not identify. On closer inspection, she realised that what she had taken to be incense burners weren't the usual wooden sticks at all. Small candles burned in the vessels, and a little pool of liquid above the candles provided the aromas. Phryne was impressed, and said so. 'Oh, my. I say, Jeoffrey, this is very special.'

On a low stage, an orchestra was playing—mostly male, although the big bass drum was being beaten into submission by a young woman in a purple silk dress wielding two enormous drumsticks. There were odd-looking stringed instruments, and some utterly outré woodwinds. The male members wore Western evening dress, and they scraped, bowed, blew, and thumped along in an extraordinary mixture of what seemed to be tolerably authentic Chinese music and New Orleans jazz.

From stage right, a bevy of danseuses emerged, dressed in gloriously expensive-looking silk dresses in light blue, light green, red, and yellow which showed a relatively demure amount of thigh. The girls waved their long fingernails in agreeable patterns, and their slender hips swayed appropriately. Their smiles might have been painted on with a trowel. Jeoffrey ogled them good-humouredly, and turned and whispered to Phryne, 'This fusion of Chinese music and dance with jazz is very much the thing in Shanghai, I'm told.'

'I see. It is certainly unusual.'

Phryne gazed around at the other guests, more of whom were arriving every moment. The arts faculty of the University of Melbourne was well represented, she noted. She recognised Gerald Street, accompanied by a woman Phryne presumed was his wife, judging by the way she clung to his arm. They were simply dressed: he in tweed jacket and grey trousers; she in a demure black dress which might have been fashionable in 1918.

At the gentle urging of their host, the company dispersed to small round tables arranged around the edges of the room. There were a dozen of them or so, of polished dark wood, each comfortably seating four. Phryne found she had Jeoffrey to herself for the moment; Gerald Street had made as if to join them, but found himself forcibly detained by his consort, who, it appeared, had not the slightest intention of allowing her husband anywhere near the exotic bloom that was the Honourable Miss Fisher.

Two Chinese waiters in plain black jackets buttoned to the neck moved around the tables with trays of champagne glasses of the Marie Antoinette design and laden ice buckets. Phryne and Jeoffrey both accepted Veuve Clicquot, and clinked their glasses together.

Jeoffrey looked into her eyes. 'A good year, I hope?'

Phryne laughed. 'I don't know, Jeoffrey. I didn't see the bottle. But I would say so.'

Before settling down for what she hoped would be a pleasant evening à deux, she deemed it meet to circulate. 'I can see refreshments being prepared, stage right. During the interim, let's go and say hello to your colleagues, shall we?'

'Oh, rather,' Jeoffrey assented, with rather less enthusiasm. He rose to his feet and followed in Phryne's wake.

A plump man of middle years in ill-fitting evening dress was talking to a bird-like woman in a blue satin sheath dress. Both looked familiar from her visit to the faculty. Memory supplied the name of Mr. Katz, commonly known as Kitty. 'Kitty and Veronica,' Jeoffrey whispered in her ear. Phryne nodded her thanks.

Sensing their approach, Kitty turned to meet them, and his mouth opened wide in delight at the sight of Phryne. 'Why, Miss Fisher! What a splendid surprise! We've met before, remember? I'm Kitty—English literature.' He gestured to his companion. 'And this is Veronica—European history, you know.'

'It's lovely to see you both again,' said Phryne. 'And what a wonderful party.'

'Indeed it is,' Kitty enthused. 'Now, Jeoffrey, I really need to ask you something.' Kitty manhandled Jeoffrey away to the side of the ballroom, talking earnestly all the while. Phryne transferred her attention to Veronica. She had a pleasant and highly intelligent face, Phryne decided. Blue-eyed, with long blonde hair hanging down below her waist.

'I seem to be missing some context here, Veronica. What was that all about?'

Veronica rolled her eyes. 'Kitty is such a duffer. He fears that I have designs on him, and he has annexed your companion in order to escape me.' She laughed softly. 'I don't know what it is about male scholars. They seem to believe the women of the world are lining up to bask in their glory.' Her eyes darted briefly towards Jeoffrey. 'It's funny, really. The only one of them who is genuinely attractive to women has practically none of that absurd vanity. These facts may, of course, be related.'

'Jeoffrey? Yes, he is becomingly modest. I take it you have no interest in Kitty?'

Veronica's golden waterfall of hair swayed from side to side as she shook her head. 'None whatever. I only came to talk to him to ease him into the party. He may be an abysmal idiot where people are concerned, but he's a good scholar. And, more to the point, he is a genuinely pleasant and kind man. In arts faculties, that is quite uncommon.' She looked sidelong towards the Streets. 'Gerald is also a man of quality: brilliant, generous, and kind, if a little sharp. Pity about the wife.'

'I'm seeing invisible handcuffs and leg irons,' Phryne ventured.

Veronica laughed aloud. 'Silly, really. Incidentally, Jeoffrey is looking increasingly besieged. I think it would be an act of kindness to rescue him.'

'I shall do so forthwith. Thanks for the chat.'

Veronica bowed slightly.

Impressed by the young woman's sangfroid, Phryne walked straight up to the learned gentlemen and detached Jeoffrey by the arm. 'Sorry, Kitty, but I saw him first.'

Kitty's mouth opened and closed like a blowfish in shallow water as Phryne swept away with Jeoffrey in tow.

Seated once again at their table, Jeoffrey took her hand and squeezed it fervently. 'Thank you, Phryne. The man was just babbling. I don't know what's got into Kitty tonight.'

Phryne explained. Jeoffrey's eyes widened. 'No! Really?'

'That is Veronica's view. I believe her.'

'Dear me. Silly man! She's a good sort, you know. One of the faculty wives told her to her face that her hair was ridiculously unfashionable. Know what she said?'

'I believe I can guess. Something along the lines of: *Yes, it is, and I really don't care.*'

'Pretty much that. Spiffing champagne this. I wonder if we can get some more.'

Phryne waved at one of the waiters, who hurried to refill their glasses. No sooner had he departed than a remarkably beautiful Chinese girl undulated towards Phryne and Jeoffrey. She bore a large silver plate on which were arrayed dumplings, spring rolls, glazed chicken wings, rice balls flavoured with Phryne knew not what, and other delights. She smiled prettily, and they accepted small porcelain bowls from a miniature pagoda on the left of the tray, and filled them with a modest assortment of dainties.

'Would you like a spoon and fork?' the girl wanted to know. Her accent was pure Oxford, without a trace of singsong.

'No, thank you.' Phryne selected a pair of bamboo chopsticks and glanced enquiringly at Jeoffrey, who shook his head and selected another pair. The girl returned to the rest of the company, swaying on a pair of high heels which looked dangerously unstable to Phryne's disapproving eye, and dispensed further largesse.

The food was utterly superb. 'I say, Jeoffrey, this really is rather good, you know,' Phryne observed, tackling a chicken wing. She contrived to separate meat from bone with her chopsticks and lifted it to her mouth. Garlic, certainly, but a number of other intriguing spices too.

'It is!' Jeoffrey appeared to be attempting to swallow a spring roll whole. 'And this is only the first course. There are several more to come.' He was staring at the dancers now, mouth slightly open, and Phryne followed his gaze.

'Oh dear.' Phryne laid down her chopsticks. 'The girls don't look happy, do they?'

Jeoffrey raised his eyes from their legs to their faces and frowned. 'No, they don't.'

The dancers had paired off and assumed position for what appeared to be a cross between the tango and Irish country dancing. It ought to have been excitingly risqué, but it just wasn't, though the women went through all the rituals of clothed Sapphic passion.

'It almost looks as if they're afraid,' Jeoffrey observed.

'Of whom?' Phryne wondered. 'Our host?'

Looking around, she spied Hong lounging very much at his ease in a capacious armchair. Seated next to him was a young Chinese woman in a red silk dress. He was murmuring to her in an undertone, and she was laughing freely at what were presumably his jokes, but her eyes did not smile. Instead, they flickered to and fro across the room unceasingly. Phryne turned back to Jeoffrey and saw he was looking down at her all but empty bowl, and the chopsticks laid neatly beside it.

'I see you have experience of Chinese food, Phryne?'

Phryne smiled complacently, thinking of Lin Chung and her many banquets in his delectable company. 'Oh, yes. And you?'

Jeoffrey smiled. 'I spent time in Shanghai when I was in the merchant navy,' he confessed.

Phryne's eyebrows rose appreciably. 'Really? But I thought… That is to say…'

Jeoffrey laughed. 'I know. Everyone thinks we scholars hatch out of magic toadstools. But I've had a satisfyingly chequered life. I was in the war, of course. As a sailor. When it was over, I thought I'd better earn some money to finance my studies, so I joined the merchant navy. That took me to many strange and wonderful places.'

Phryne gave him a sidelong look. 'And I am sure you saw many unusual things in Shanghai.'

He eyed her with amusement. 'I saw many all-female dance troupes, mostly wearing a great deal less than these girls are.' He waved a hand at the stage, where the women had by now disengaged and were now presumably evoking the opening of the chrysanthemums in springtime. 'And they all looked a lot happier than this mob. I wonder where Hong found them.'

'Indeed.' Phryne reached for her cigarette case. At once Jeoffrey laid his hand on her arm and shook his head.

'I'm sorry, Phryne, I should have told you. Hong can't stand the smell of tobacco.'

Phryne sighed and looked towards the street-facing balcony. 'What about out there?'

Jeoffrey shook his head. 'Not even there. You'll have to go outside, I'm afraid, if you really must.'

'Oh, but I must. I'll be back soon.'

On her way downstairs she exchanged grimaces with the Eight Immortals. At the foot of the stairs she stopped and turned away from the front door. Her eyes followed a high-ceilinged hallway plastered in pure white. Beneath her feet, she noted, was a deep, multicoloured sculpted carpet in blue, red, gold, and purple. Hong's private means—apparently looted, if rumour was to be believed—must be substantial indeed if he could afford all this. His university salary would barely cover his champagne bill.

Curious, Phryne walked down the passageway, which had rooms leading off; some of the doors were ajar, and she glimpsed a library, bedrooms. At the end was a plain white door, which was shut. On impulse, Phryne tried the handle. It was locked from the inside. Smiling at her own lack of manners, she made her way back down the hall and slipped through the front door, ascertaining that the lock was snibbed before closing it behind her.

Outside, full night had fallen, and stars gleamed intermittently through the clouds. Phryne lit a Sobranie then walked down the steps to the footpath and set off along the road towards the docks. She had always loved harbours. This one appeared unusually quiet. A large vessel lay at its moorings along the pier. She would have expected there would be stevedores about, but there was no activity of any sort.

Strolling back along The Strand, she lit another gasper. She had no desire to re-enter the party as yet. Instead, she walked along the grass verge. A hundred or so yards ahead, a dark, wooden building glowed with yellow light and she walked towards it. But as she drew near, the windows were suddenly blacked out, as if her presence had been noted.

Phryne shivered. The night was coming in cold now, and she was in need of another drink. She made her way back to Hong's residence. In the darkness the coloured lanterns made the house look like a welcome refuge. The front door was still unlocked, so she entered and climbed the stairs towards the party on the first floor. Sounds of music and merriment wafted down towards her. Returning to the party she saw Jeoffrey Bisset at the table where she had left him, accepting more food from a beautiful waitress, his eyes lingering on her with guileless fascination. Well, he was certainly welcome to admire. One of the most agreeable things about Jeoffrey was his enthusiasm.

Catching sight of her, he stood. 'There you are, Phryne! May I fetch you another drink?'

She nodded. 'Thank you, Jeoffrey. Anything with alcohol in it.'

Jeoffrey set off in search of refreshment, and Phryne resumed her seat. She found her gaze drawn to a young Chinese woman. She wore a long silk dress of emerald green, and was sitting alone at a side table in a pool of silence. Phryne thought she might be one of the dancers, though she could not be certain. Her hair was plaited closely against her head. Her eyes were half closed, her legs crossed, and no one made any move to approach her. Just for a moment her eyes opened wide and she met Phryne's stare before closing them again. Thereafter Phryne had the impression that the girl was continuing to watch her covertly. Phryne felt, for a moment, adrift on uncharted seas.

Jeoffrey returned with another glass of champagne, which Phryne half drained in one gulp. 'Thank you, Jeoffrey. Tell me, what have I missed?'

Jeoffrey settled himself in the seat beside hers. 'Well, the dancers and the orchestra are having a bit of a break, but apparently they'll be back later. If you're wondering if we're going to have speeches and the like, then no. That's not Hong's way.'

'I see.' Phryne took another sip of champagne.

A waiter brushed past their table and appeared to drop something. Phryne looked down at the polished surface and discovered a folded note. She looked sharply at the waiter, but he had melted into the crowd. The girl in the emerald dress, too, had vanished. Mystified, Phryne unfolded the note. It was on quality cream notepaper, and contained just three words printed in capital letters: PLEASE LEAVE NOW.

She handed the note to Jeoffrey, who read it then looked up at her. 'Phryne, would you care to hazard a guess as to what is going on?'

Phryne shook her head. 'I have no idea, Jeoffrey—but I sense that something is wrong here, and I intend to find out what it is.'

Jeoffrey raised an eyebrow. 'So we're not taking the hint we've just been dropped?'

'I'm not,' Phryne replied. 'On the contrary. But you may do as you like, of course.' She reached into her handbag beneath the table and her hand closed around her gold-handled pistol.

Seeing the set look on her face, Jeoffrey's own expression grew serious. 'Are you anticipating danger?'

'Does the idea worry you?'

Jeoffrey didn't bother with false bravado. 'I believe it does—but if you're staying, then so am I.'

At that moment the orchestra reappeared and resumed their melange of Oriental jazz fusion. The young woman playing the bass drum began to beat it as though sounding the alarm for a house fire, while a young man, dressed all in black with a black cap covering his head, skipped off the stage to where Hong reclined in his easy chair and stabbed him once in the heart with a long, gleaming knife.

———

Hammond pondered the news he had just been given, then presently he rose and left his office, locking the door behind him. If a man were quick, then a very considerable prize might be there for the taking. The barge, he knew, was ready and waiting. He could take it upriver to another place he knew. Haggerty's warehouse was no longer safe, but there were other options available.

Chapter Twenty-Two

Phryne gazed at the scene in horror. The orchestra continued to play—Phryne would remember that later, how bizarre it seemed. One or two women screamed as dark, arterial blood seeped from Hong's body. He lay sprawled on his sofa, his expression more surprised than alarmed. His mouth was open, and his face blanched white. It was clear that he had perished instantly.

Hearing a gasp beside her, Phryne noted that Jeoffrey was slumped in his seat, apparently rendered unconscious by the sight of so much blood. She turned towards the gathering. Hong's guests were milling around, looking lost and bewildered.

Phryne waved to Gerald Street for assistance. He at once abandoned his wife's hysterics and came to throw a strong arm around Jeoffrey and carry him to a nearby sofa.

Veronica was next to arrive, breathing deeply but seemingly in control of herself. 'I've sent Kitty to call the police,' she reported. 'And we should at least attempt to stop anybody leaving, don't you agree?'

'Good thinking,' said Phryne as she discreetly drew her revolver from her handbag. 'If you and Gerald could take care of that, I'll take care of the other.'

'What oth—'

But Phryne was already racing down the stairs. As she rushed through the front door and down the steps to the street, she could see the killer barely a hundred yards ahead of her. She saw him cast something aside as he ran; the knife, she presumed. Putting on a burst of speed, she managed to close the gap to about forty yards, but was forced to stop abruptly as five black-clad figures appeared from out of nowhere and fanned out in front of her, barring the way. The man in the middle was the only one not holding a weapon.

The quintet were an ill-assorted bunch. Two carried hatchets, which gleamed in the distant streetlight. Two more carried long knives. One of the hatchet-wielders barked a question, and hefted his weapon experimentally. The leader—assuming it was he—shook his head.

'Hello,' said Phryne smoothly. 'Beautiful evening, isn't it?'

The leader glared at her. '*Kung mou!*' he said. It had the ring of a direct order.

'*Kung mou?*' Phryne repeated, to be sure.

This earned an emphatic nod. '*Kung mou!*' the unarmed man repeated. He waved a peremptory hand. The other four surrounded her in complete silence. The leader held Phryne's gaze with his own. In the dim light, his eyes appeared as black as jet.

'*Kung mou!*' the man stated a third time.

Phryne surveyed the assembled knives and hatchets and carefully concealed her pistol in the folds of her tunic. This was no night for shooting.

'Very well.' She motioned with her head back the way she had come. 'I'm going back to my party, which has been broken up with much-admir'd disorder.' She smiled at the men. 'Have a pleasant night.'

Phryne turned on her heel and walked back towards the

residence of the late—whether he would be especially lamented remained to be seen—Mr. Hong. Occasionally, her shoulder blades prickled, as if expecting to take receipt of a thrown battleaxe. She steeled her nerves and walked on without a backward glance.

———

'Ah, Miss Fisher! How did I know you were going to be here?'

Jack Robinson surveyed the ruins of the birthday party with a tired glance. Uniformed constables were interviewing guests and staff alike. This, Robinson considered, was every copper's worst nightmare. The Caucasian guests—well, they would at least be capable of answering questions. So far the Chinese had been less than forthcoming. Who knew if they even spoke English? Robinson was certain that some of them at least must speak English well. Did the police force have a Chinese interpreter? Even if they did, would it help? Jack really hoped this did not signal the start of a triad war in his city.

Phryne nodded at the detective inspector. 'Well, Jack, I'm glad I've made your night, anyway. Are you going to question me yourself, or would you rather leave it to one of your minions? Because I have plenty to tell you.'

Robinson ducked his head in acknowledgement. 'I'll speak to you in a moment or two, Miss Fisher, if you'd care to wait here.'

'Don't leave it too long, Jack. I want to show you something.' Phryne sank into a chair. This blatant murder had shocked her profoundly. She breathed deeply for a few moments and watched the activity around her. It was Gerald Street's turn to be questioned by a uniformed constable in one corner, she noted. The rest of the party guests milled around disconsolately, having been forbidden to leave a party that was now far from festive. Jack

Robinson exchanged a few words with a uniformed constable then strode towards Phryne.

'All right, Miss Fisher. What did you want to show me?'

Phryne picked up her handbag. 'Come with me, Jack—I'll explain on the way.'

As they walked down the stairs and out through the front door, Phryne gave the detective inspector a concise summary of her concerns.

'Jack, do you remember when I called to report the discovery of a deceased Chinese man on the beach?'

The inspector nodded. 'You were in pyjamas, as I recall.'

'Not my own,' Phryne added, recalling the flop-eared bunnies. 'Well, as you'll recall, that wasn't my first communication with City South that evening.'

'I don't know what you're talking about, Miss Fisher. Are you saying you called earlier? What about?'

'I was passing Haggerty's warehouse an hour or two before-hand when I heard a scream come from inside. And then, only a short time later, a dead body turned up on the beach. I think it's reasonable to assume that these two events were connected, don't you? I'm sorry not to have mentioned it in my statement the next day, but I thought my message would have been passed on. I suppose police resources aren't infinite, but I would have thought the homicide on the beach might have jogged someone's memory. So, if you haven't investigated Haggerty's warehouse already, then I'd suggest you do so tonight. That's if you can spare the manpower, of course.'

Jack said nothing, but turned and called up to a uniformed constable on the upstairs balcony. 'Smith? Come down here, will you? And bring Corbett.'

As they waited for the constables to arrive, Jack said, 'So the warehouse is what you wanted to show me?'

'Oh! No, it was something else—just up here.'

As she led him further up The Strand, she described how she had chased the murderer, only to be dissuaded from further pursuit by a gang of what she presumed were his compatriots.

She stopped walking. 'As I was chasing him,' she explained, 'the killer threw aside the weapon. It should be right around here…'

But though she, Jack, and the two uniforms scoured the surrounds, there was no sign of the knife.

'They clearly had the foresight to remove the evidence,' Jack commented with a sigh. 'All right, let's see about this warehouse of yours.'

As they walked across the park towards the warehouse, he asked, 'So this phrase the leader kept repeating—do you know what it means?'

'I am not fluent in the language,' Phryne confessed, 'but I believe I have heard those words uttered before. I believe they might be Cantonese for *Say nothing*—an embargo I have clearly breached.'

Approaching the deserted warehouse, Jack observed, 'No obvious signs of life.'

Phryne followed him to the building's front door. Robinson produced an electric torch from his coat pocket and switched it on. The door was not only locked, but fastened with a heavy chain and an impressive padlock. He frowned, and turned to one of his two minions. 'Do you by any chance have your lock picks with you, Corbett?'

'Yes, sir.' Corbett produced a jangling set of steel lock picks. He began to prod and poke at the lock.

Robinson stood over him, watching impatiently. 'We haven't got all night, Corbett. Do I need to go and get some boltcutters?'

Corbett did not seem to have heard. Muttering under his breath, he jiggled some more, and at last the lock snapped open. 'There you are, sir.'

'Good man, Corbett. Now we shall see what we shall see.'

Robinson pushed open the door and shone his torch into the space to reveal...nothing. The warehouse was empty, and appeared to have been so for some time.

Robinson frowned darkly at Phryne. 'Miss Fisher, if it were anyone but you, I would wonder if you'd had one too many drinks and imagined you'd heard a scream.'

Ignoring him, Phryne kneeled down on the floor, heedless of her costume, sniffed, and wiped her finger across the concrete. 'Jack, someone has washed this floor very recently. Smell this.' She held up her finger for his inspection, and Robinson's nose twitched. 'Dry-cleaning fluid. Nothing like dry-cleaning fluid for getting rid of bloodstains.' She picked up two short, straw-coloured twigs and displayed them. 'And these are from a standard laundry scrubbing-brush. Someone has been cleaning up in here. One has to wonder why. May I?' She took Jack's torch and moved the beam around the warehouse.

It was indeed empty—except for some heavy mats piled up in a corner. Phryne walked across to them, bent down, and sniffed. 'Come and have a whiff of this, Jack.'

Robinson sighed and crossed the floor to join her. He rubbed his finger along the mat obediently and brought it to his nose. 'Miss Fisher, I don't want to pour cold water on your enthusiasms, but that's tea you can smell. Ordinary black Indian tea, I'd say.'

He turned and began to move back towards the door, his heavy footsteps echoing on the bare concrete. Phryne stayed where she was, sniffing hard. There was something else, she was sure of it... After a moment she rose.

'Jack,' she called to the inspector's back, 'there is a faint under-tone of something here that isn't tea. If I were you, I would put my own padlock on this place and interrogate the mats thoroughly. I don't trust them.'

Robinson turned and fixed her with a look. 'Miss Fisher, are you quite well?'

Phryne shrugged. 'Despite having been threatened with knives and hatchets and witnessing a brutal murder, I am well enough, thank you for asking. And I really do recommend that you beat those mats and test what comes out of them. You see, Jack, whoever was here must have left in a considerable hurry—presumably to dispose of the corpse of Wing Loong. Perhaps these mats were too heavy for them to remove in their haste, so they left them behind. But someone sprinkled them with dried tea-leaves first, hoping to disguise the underlying scent of...'

'Of what?' Jack demanded.

'Jack, I suspect this warehouse has been used for storing opium.'

Robinson returned to Phryne's side and bent over the mats once more. He sniffed hard, then shook his head. 'No, I can't smell it. Perhaps the business with the broken pipe has made you suspect opium where none exists?'

'Not at all,' Phryne said firmly. 'I agree that it's a very faint scent, but what have you got to lose? Beat the mats and have the residue tested. And if I'm wrong, well, I'd be glad of it. Because if we do have opium smuggling here in Melbourne, then things are going to get very ugly. I don't like this at all.'

Robinson gave her a long, considering look. 'No. Neither do I. In fact, it might be worth keeping a watch on this place, just in case someone should try to retrieve the evidence.'

He turned to his underlings. 'Smith, I want you to watch over the place from a discreet distance. If anyone attempts to enter it, blow your whistle. I'll be back as soon as we've finished questioning the party guests and seen the body dispatched to the morgue.' He gave a heavy sigh. 'I have a feeling we're going to be here all night.'

Leaving the stolid Smith to watch over the warehouse, Robinson led the way back towards the Hong mansion.

'Jack,' Phryne said, 'While I'm sure you'll want a written statement from me—another one—could we perhaps leave it until tomorrow?' She was feeling rather worn out. Not even the prospect of sharing Jeoffrey's bed held more appeal than the thought of her own.

The inspector gave her a level look. 'I'd be prepared to agree to that if you promise me you won't go investigating any more crime scenes between now and then.'

Phryne inclined her head. 'I promise,' she said solemnly.

Jack and Corbett climbed the stairs to the front door of the Hong residence, and Phryne walked towards the phone box she had spied further down the street. She would call Bert about a lift. Then, remembering that he had said he wouldn't be home before midnight, she glanced at her watch. It was only ten. She hesitated. She could return to Hong's house and wait out the hours there, but she didn't really relish the thought. Glancing around for inspiration, she spied the shack she had asked Bert about when he'd dropped her off. The Anchor, he had called it— and if the comrades drank there, it couldn't be all bad, could it? Perhaps they had the makings of a gin and tonic. Provided she were—as Bert had warned—discreet, surely they wouldn't mind.

She followed a small towpath to the rundown shack. There was a sliver of yellow light visible beneath the rough-hewn door, but no sounds emerged. She knocked.

'Hello?' she called. 'I was wondering if I could get a drink?'

There was a sound of boots clomping on wooden flooring, and the door opened a fraction. A grizzled face stared at her. 'Flamin' hell,' it said, gaping at her.

The ensuing silence was broken by three other voices, which uttered respectively: 'Who is it, Kev?' 'Do we know 'em?' and 'Sorry, luv, we're closed!'

Kev's face turned from the door towards the speakers. The ear facing Phryne had a bright gold earring set in the lobe, indicating a sailor past or present. Or someone who wanted to be thought of as a sailor. Whipcord muscles strained beneath a blue-and-white-checked flannel shirt which gave off an overpowering scent of stale beer and tobacco. 'It's a posh sheila,' he told them in a voice one part wonder and two parts awe.

'Well, open the bloody door and let's have a squiz,' urged one of the voices within.

Kev did as asked.

Framed in the open doorway, Phryne's apparition caused a silent sensation. Finally someone muttered, 'Gawdstrewth!'

The barman put down the length of lead pipe he was brandishing and whistled softly. ''Old on,' he said. 'Don't I know you?'

Phryne drew herself up to her full five feet two inches and gave the barman a regal look. 'I really couldn't say. Listen, are you going to let me in or not? It's bloody freezing out here, and I'd like a drink.'

There was a muttered conversation, then one of the bar's patrons—dressed as were the others in blue trousers, a blue-checked shirt, and massive leather boots with visible steel caps—gave her a gap-toothed smile.

'I reckon yer right, Stevo—we do know 'er. It's that friend of Comrade Bert and Comrade Cec, isn't it? The Honourable Phryne Fisher. Well, m'lady, if ya don't mind the decor and the company, yer as welcome to drink 'ere as anyone.'

Phryne entered. Kev shut the door behind her and turned a key in the lock.

She appeared to have interrupted a poker night, as the company were assembled around two card tables in various stages of play.

'Care fer a 'and?' called a man from one of the tables. 'Twos and threes wild, three card draw.'

'A drink first, I think,' Phryne said. She approached the bar, and a bottle of port was produced by the barman. 'Three and six, luv. Best plonk we've got.'

Phryne smiled her gratitude but said, 'I'd rather a gin and tonic, if you can manage that.'

She noted the presence of a large tray of sandwiches under a colander on the end of the bar. They appeared to date from the Carboniferous Era, but they were, after all, only there for show. Owing to a curious quirk in the licensing laws, it was possible to sell alcoholic beverages after six to bona fide travellers, provided that food was being served as well. Phryne was happy to be classed as a bona fide traveller any day of the week, but those sandwiches would be best approached with flame-proof gauntlets.

The barman put a small glass on a dirty towel and reached under the bar, from whence he produced a bottle of what Phryne sincerely hoped was gin; it was hard to tell, the label having been torn off. He opened a small bottle of Indian tonic water with a screwdriver, and assembled a gin and tonic. He even found a slice of lemon to go with it, which floated uneasily on the gently effervescing surface. 'That'll be tenpence, luv,' he said.

Phryne handed over a shilling, and shook her head when the barman went through the motions of rummaging for change. She tasted her drink warily, and found it surprisingly palatable.

As she sipped, she watched the poker games with idle interest. As one concluded at the nearest table, she called, 'Deal me in?'

Room was duly made for her at the table, and the company was introduced. There was a Bluey (red hair), a Curly (bald), and a Tiny (six feet three). Phryne then spent the next hour happily playing poker with The Men in an atmosphere of beer and roll-your-owns. She ensured that she lost the first few hands, which endeared her to the company, and thereafter played steadily, winning twice and recouping some of her losses. With twos and threes wild it made straights and flushes far more common than they would otherwise have been. Generally, it took a full house, at the very least, to gain victory. This took some getting used to.

She ordered another gin and tonic as play proceeded, and sipped it conservatively. She had almost finished it when she saw one of the men from the other table lay down his cards and leave the pub without comment. He returned a quarter of an hour later with his face set in a frown. He whispered something to the barman, who nodded and raised his right hand to the company.

As if by silent consensus, both tables laid down their cards, and Phryne found herself looking at a room filled with steady, thoughtful faces. The gap-toothed man Bluey appeared to have been appointed spokesman. 'All right, Miss Fisher. Ya can play cards, and comport yerself with decorum appropriate to the occasion, and ya don't ask inconvenient questions. But ya ain't here by accident, are ya?'

Phryne smiled. 'Well, yes and no. I did indeed come here seeking a drink, as stated, but it would be disingenuous to pretend I wouldn't welcome information about certain local incidents if anyone were in a mood to offer it. As you are doubtless aware, I am a private investigator.'

'Yair, we know. So what would you be privately investigating around here, Miss?'

'Oh, this and that,' said Phryne airily, as two recent murders sprang to mind. 'But let's start with the existence—indeed, the disappearance—of certain…Stuff.'

This produced a chorus of comprehending nods.

'Well, the thing about Stuff is that it does move about, Miss,' Tiny volunteered. 'That's what happens at docks.'

'Well, yes,' Phryne conceded. 'And most of the Stuff that moves about is no concern of anyone's outside their lawful owners. But I am speaking particularly about a large consignment of Stuff which until recently might have been held in a warehouse just next to the park down the road.'

The tension in the room increased.

'You'd be talkin' 'bout Bad Stuff, then?' Bluey ventured.

'Definitively Bad Stuff, yes.'

'We don't like Bad Stuff,' Curly interjected.

'I'm not surprised,' Phryne answered. 'Because Bad Stuff attracts unwelcome attention and awkward questions. Anyway, this particular Bad Stuff was in the aforementioned warehouse, and I suspect it was moved in considerable haste. Would anyone care to tell me where it might have been moved to?'

Apropos of nothing in particular, the man who had left the premises then returned said, 'There's a big stakeout goin' on tonight—down the road at Haggerty's.'

Bluey fixed Phryne with a glittering eye. 'Friends of yours, Miss?'

She returned his stare with a broad smile. 'Very possibly.'

'Yeah, well, they're wastin' their time there. It's not likely anyone's gonna return now that the Bad Stuff has been moved on.' He gave her a gold-toothed grin. 'Ever bin to Wallace's boatyard, Miss?'

'I don't think I have, Bluey. Do you think it's worth a visit?'

'Might be. It's not far from here. Just down past the yacht club.'

Phryne nodded thoughtfully. 'Thank you. I'll bear that in mind.' She turned to the company and inclined her head. 'Gentlemen. Thank you for a splendid evening.' Then she rose, approached the bar, and handed the barman a ten-shilling note. 'Next round's on me.'

As Phryne closed the door of the Anchor behind her—hearing from within the turning of key in lock—she noted from her wristwatch that it was just after eleven o'clock. Now she would have to find Jack, who would be watching Haggerty's, without getting herself arrested or shot, and divert him to Wallace's boatyard. She flitted across the park, moving from tree to tree and scanning the shadows for hidden sentinels. There was little street lighting, but her eyes adjusted quickly to the gloom, and lurking beneath a tree ahead she could discern a lean, elegant figure that looked familiar. She stepped soundlessly towards him and paused, holding her breath. When she reached the tree's penumbra she whispered in the silence.

'Jack? Is that you?'

Jack Robinson turned. 'Miss Fisher? I thought you'd gone home!'

'I thought better of it. And just as well—I have news.'

'News that warrants interrupting me at a critical time?'

A possum skittered in the branches above their heads and they both flinched.

'I rather think it does, Jack. Informants have advised me that you're in the wrong place. You need to get some people to Wallace's boatyard immediately.'

In the dim light, she saw his brow furrow. 'What informants would these be?'

Phryne shook her head. 'Sorry, Jack. I will say that they're well placed to advise you.'

'All right, Phryne. We'll play it your way. So where is this boatyard?'

'I'm told it's next to the yacht club.'

'Very well, Wallace's boatyard. I'll give the orders to the men.'

———

'I'm so sorry, Peony, but I had to do it! He'd arranged for me to be kidnapped. He told me Liu's men were waiting for me outside! So…I killed him.'

'Oh, Carnation! But how did you get away? I've been so worried!'

'I think his employees have taken the law into their own hands. They helped me get away.'

'Not your father?'

'Oh no, I don't think that's likely. Father wouldn't break the law, nor allow anyone else to do so. But I recognised the man who was leading them. His name is Ming. I think he's in charge now.'

'You mean he killed Wing Loong?'

'I think so. But the others were in on it, I believe. Some of them are working for...for somebody else. I don't know who. Look, Peony, we can't stay here—or I can't, anyway. The other dancers and the musicians in the orchestra will have to give their names and addresses to the police, and they'll come here looking.'

'Yes, you're right. But I'm coming with you, Carnation. Wherever you go, I go.'

'Don't make promises you can't keep, Peony. Come on, hurry—we must pack our belongings and leave at once.'

'Where will we go?'

'To Little Bourke Street. They won't look for us there. And even if they do, we all look the same to them.'

'But...my father will find us.'

'Don't worry, Peony—we can stay with Aunty Ma. Only the workers go to Aunty Ma's noodle shop, and they won't tell.'

'How will we get there?'

'By train. It's early yet. Now hurry!'

Chapter Twenty-Three

Jack Robinson led the way along the Strand's footpath. A late moon was rising above the bay and shimmered on the water's surface. Phryne noted that Jack had dropped his earlier insistence that she keep her nose out of police matters. She grinned to herself. If nothing else, she would be available as a scapegoat if they drew a blank yet again.

They passed the yacht club, and came up against a wire fence. Robinson took out his torch and flashed it on the sign: WALLACE BOATYARD. There was a heavy chain with a padlock on it, and the fence was at least ten feet high. 'Where the hell is Corbett with the lock picks?' the inspector muttered.

'No need for Mr. Corbett, Jack.' Phryne removed a hairpin from under her headdress and inserted it into the lock. A few twiddles and the lock obligingly sprang open. 'Never say I don't do anything for you.'

Robinson pulled the chain from the gates and pushed them open, and directed his men to spread out and search the premises.

It was soon obvious the boatyard was deserted. Phryne followed Jack as he flung open the door to the office and switched on the light. Then he swore. The floor was covered in dust, but there was a large oblong patch of dark wooden flooring which told of a recent load sitting there.

'It was here all right—but it's bloody well gone!' he fumed. 'Come on, Miss. Let's get out of here.'

Outside in the darkness, the sound of a diesel engine rumbled into life, and they hurried towards it. Standing by the water's edge, they watched a flat barge with a low cabin in its middle recede from the Wallace slipway and head out towards the bay. Phryne cursed volubly. 'Oh, Jack. I'm so sorry. We're too late.'

But to her surprise the detective inspector was sanguine. Putting a hand on her shoulder, he said, 'Not to worry, Miss Fisher.'

From his pocket he produced his policeman's whistle and blew three long blasts on it. Phryne saw a vessel further out in the channel change course to intercept the barge. From near its mast, a searchlight flashed three times. The barge wheeled around and attempted escape, but it was no match for the other. Orders were barked through megaphones, and within minutes dark-uniformed men swarmed aboard the barge. Flashlights were shone. There was even the glint of handcuffs.

Phryne watched it all unfold in stunned silence. When it was done, she turned to her companion. 'All right, Jack. Now I really am impressed. That would be the water police, I suppose?'

Robinson allowed himself a small self-satisfied grin. 'Mostly. But they have a man of mine aboard. Someone you know.'

The impounded barge was apparently fitted with an electric light hung from its stubby funnel. This was suddenly switched on as the barge returned towards the slipway. And beneath its brilliant, actinic glare was a black-coated figure Phryne recognised. He looked towards the shore and held both thumbs upwards. He looked exhausted, grimy, yet triumphant. Phryne's mouth made an *O* of surprise. Of all the people she had expected to encounter tonight, Dot's intended wasn't in the top hundred.

The meeting by the slipway was, in its way, a masterpiece of Antipodean understatement. Detective Inspector Robinson looked upon Detective Sergeant Collins and said, 'All right, Collins. You've made the pinch. You can tidy all this up. You've earned it.'

'Thank you, sir.' Then Hugh noticed Phryne and his eyes widened. 'Miss Fisher, is that you? I didn't expect to see you here!'

'Try to keep me away, Hugh.'

Collins grinned, then turned away and began to issue orders.

Jack led Phryne to the base of an elm tree, where they sat in the dark on the verdant grass.

'I suppose I owe you an explanation, Miss Fisher.'

'You owe me nothing, Jack, but I would certainly appreciate it if you would enlighten me. I have the sense I've been groping in the dark. Clearly you know something I don't.'

Robinson chuckled heartily. 'Well, that makes a pleasant change, doesn't it? The boot's been on the other foot often enough. But we couldn't have pulled this off without you, so— strictly off the record, you understand—I'll put you in the picture.'

So Robinson began his story. 'All right. Now, at first we didn't take much notice of that stray opium pipe you found. It was just one of those things. But it was officially classified as curious.'

'Curious?'

'Yes. Just that. Something which might mean nothing, but which should be filed away in case it became important. Sergeant O'Flaherty from Williamstown police station rang me and reported it straight away, as it happens. I wouldn't go so far as to describe the man as imaginative, but he's a decent sergeant and he knows his job. We've worked together on occasion, and I trust him.'

'I'm glad to hear it, Jack.'

'Meanwhile, we've had clear evidence of opium percolating

through the suburbs and around the city. Not just Chinese, either; a few Occidentals have been found under the influence—a fact we managed to keep out of the papers. Hugh Collins has been on the case for some time, ferreting out opium dens and asking questions, trying to discover the source. Given the discovery of the pipe, I had a quiet word with the deputy harbourmaster here, a man who's been helpful in the past, but he assured me with absolute confidence that there was no opium passing through the docks of Williamstown. Then tonight you come barging into the picture talking about Haggerty's warehouse and insisting I beat those mats. So we do, and we find evidence of opium, despite the confident assurances of the deputy harbourmaster that there is absolutely no opium hereabouts.' Jack nodded towards the activity by the waterfront. 'That's him being taken away in handcuffs now, by the way.'

'Oh, my.' Phryne put her hand to her mouth. 'After what happened to Hong, I presumed he must have had something to do with it. And he clearly had a great deal of money, so I did suspect... How deeply involved was he, Jack?'

'Oh, he was up to his neck in it.' In the darkness, Phryne felt rather than saw him lean a little closer. Jack Robinson smelled primarily of soap and gingernut biscuits. It was not an unpleasant combination. 'By the way, where did you get the idea about beating the mats?'

'I'm not exactly sure, but I think it was one of the stories—' Phryne paused; she had better leave Lin out of it, she decided. 'It was a story one of my Chinese friends told me. Did you know that in Imperial China, the magistrate was also the detective?'

'High, middle, and low justice? Sounds good to me.'

'Well, yes and no. The downside was that he had to get it right. If you tortured a confession out of someone who turned out to be innocent, whatever you'd done to him was done to you. *I acted as I thought best* didn't meet the bill apparently.' She heard Jack stifle a gasp. 'Anyway, my friend told me a detective story from old China in which someone was smuggling salt, and the magistrate had the mats beaten.'

'I see.' Jack leaned back on his elbows. 'Well, like I said, I had put Collins on to this case. Now one thing we found out the hard way is that when the Chinese talk about the police they don't distinguish between branches. So our Oriental friends, who were as keen as we were to rid the city of the scourge of opium, swore blind that they'd reported this man Hong to what they described as The Police. I can tell you, we wasted a lot of time on that. But eventually we found out that the person they'd reported to was none other than our handcuffed friend. The harbourmaster is an amiable drunk who doesn't know what day of the week it is, so his deputy, Hammond, has been running the show. Collins discovered that Hammond was being paid off by a Mr. Brown...' He paused significantly.

'As in Mr. Thomas Browning, born in Brunswick, perchance?' Phryne ventured.

'Quite—who was then able to bring in the stuff unhindered. We knew there was a big shipment on the move, but we hadn't been able to find it. Collins has been patrolling the bay every night for the last fortnight with the water police, but nothing doing. Then, when Hong was assassinated by person or persons unknown earlier this evening, Hammond must have conceived the bright idea of pinching the swag for himself. He no doubt thought that he had better move it tonight, before an investigation into Hong blew their conspiracy wide open.'

'I see. And that's why the water police were conveniently located offshore.'

'Indeed, but unfortunately we had no leads. You were able to introduce me to Haggerty's warehouse, which—trusting your hunches as I do—confirmed that the opium was indeed in the vicinity. And we knew they hadn't shipped it out of Williamstown, since we had the harbour under surveillance, so it was clear that it was here somewhere. But we just couldn't discover where the stuff was. The only thing I could think to do, as I told you, was watch the warehouse in case someone came back for the mats. But, of course, you have unorthodox means of obtaining information which are unavailable to humble policemen, and you brought us here in the nick of time.'

Phryne stretched out her legs, which were becoming cramped. 'Jack, one thing that bothers me is why the Chinese didn't report Hong to head office, as it were. After they went to this Hammond person—who turned out to be as bent as a hairpin, as you say— and saw that no action was taken, why not pay a state visit to police HQ and tell their story there?'

Robinson gave a low chuckle. 'You can blame that on an over-zealous detective sergeant with friends in high places. Someone well known to Sergeant Collins, I might add.'

'Oh no! Not that chinless wonder who gave Hugh such a hard time when you were seconded to that crime task force?'

'The very same. Just between us, Fraser was responsible for the Victoria Police laughing off the idea of opium smuggling in the first instance. While he was still working on the task force in question, he conducted a raid on Little Bourke Street. A number of premises were searched, including that of your friend Mr. Lin, because that half-witted officer was convinced that his silk shop was a front for opium smuggling.'

'Dear me. I take it the raid was a fiasco?'

'Oh, completely. Apparently a number of silk bolts were damaged. So your friend Lin paid a visit to the Commissioner and lodged an official complaint. I believe he will be duly compensated.'

'And Fraser?'

Jack smiled. 'He's off the underworld task force. I believe an up-country transfer is on the cards.'

'Anywhere special?'

'Mildura has been mentioned.'

'Oh, dear. I hope he likes fishing. All right, Jack. Now I understand. Melbourne's Chinese community feel they have been let down by the Victoria Police, so they decide that there's no point reporting anything at all to you. Now it makes sense.'

'It does. Now I have a question for you, Miss Fisher. How on earth did you find out where the opium was tonight? Perhaps it was through your contacts in the maritime industry...'

Phryne grinned to herself. Now there was a sentence with a barbed hook on the end of it. 'Bert and Cec's contribution this time around was restricted to driving me here in their taxi. And dispensing general advice.'

'They might also have given you a passport to a certain hostelry not a million miles from here,' Jack suggested.

'I couldn't possibly comment on that, Detective Inspector.'

'Don't worry. We know about the Anchor, and we leave it alone. There's nothing much happening there that need concern the Victoria Police.'

'I am very glad to hear it, Jack. All right. I'm wet, cold, and uncomfortable, and it's time I went home.' She stood up slowly and stretched her limbs.

Robinson rose too. 'I fear our chances of finding Hong's assassins are small, but it's an imperfect world. Thanks to you I at least have something of significance to show the Commissioner. According to Collins's hand gestures, it sounds like about a hundredweight of opium. So if you'd like a lift home, I expect we can run to that.'

Phryne inclined her head. 'Thank you, Jack. I will accept your kind offer.'

Chapter Twenty-Four

Phryne awoke early next morning, cross and out of sorts with the world. 'Dot? I really hope it's an earthquake that is causing you to rouse me at such an ungodly hour. Anything less and I will not be a happy person.' She glanced at her bedside clock, which announced the hour of nine in the morning. An hour which, in Phryne's estimation, was best devoted to lying abed, thanking her fortunate stars that she didn't have to get up and go to work, and laying her head back on its rightful pillow.

Dot, standing in the doorway in her customary palette of beiges and browns, looked at her employer with an ever so slightly reproachful eye. 'Oh, Miss Phryne! I know it's early, but you really need to get up.'

Phryne gently ushered her sleeping cat to one side, threw off the blankets, and frowned. 'So it is an earthquake? Has an exasperated demigod stricken down this city of iniquity? Has the Temple curtain been rent in twain? What is going on?' Phryne indicated an affronted Ember, now giving himself a thorough wash, pausing occasionally to cast disapproving glares at his mistress.

Refocusing on her companion, she noted one of Mr. Butler's best silver salvers in Dot's left hand. An ornate calling card rested upon it. Phryne wondered if the inscription belonged to one of the Horsemen of the Apocalypse.

Without a word, Dot handed her the card, and Phryne read the legend _Mrs. Camellia Lin_ in a modestly serifed font. Dot's evident discomfiture was now explained. While Dot was aware of the unorthodox relationship existing between Phryne, Lin, and Camellia, her staunch Catholicism found this digestible only when contemplated in the abstract. Confronted by what she could only envisage as a vengeful betrayed wife, Dot's emotional resources had reached their point of overload. 'Miss, she says she'll wait. But you must see her this morning.'

Phryne managed a smile. 'Very well, Dot. Ask her to wait for ten minutes, and see if Mr. Butler can manage some Chinese tea and sliced fresh fruit. I seem to remember that this is the Confucianist prescription for unexpected home visits.'

Dot exited the room, seemingly grateful for any directions in this suddenly over-complex situation. Phryne forwent her toilet, beyond a brief scrub-down with a face washer. She chose a black silk Chinese jacket with embroidered birds, plain black trousers, and unobtrusive flat shoes. (Without stockings, because she could not be bothered.) She looked into the mirror, applied a soupçon of lip salve, gave herself a wink and walked downstairs to face the music.

In her downstairs parlour Phryne discovered that the Butlers had excelled themselves. Phryne's best porcelain tea set was on the table, with slices of fresh melon and yellow peaches. There was even a plate of melon seeds, to which her guest had already helped herself.

Camellia was dressed in purely Western attire: a long black skirt, white silk blouse, a plain black silk jacket, and tiny black leather shoes, with stockings that were undeniably silk. Her pregnancy was visible, but it did not seem to incommode her in any way. On Phryne's entry, she rose at once to her full height of per-haps four feet ten inches, and offered a polite smile and her hand. Phryne took the hand, gave it a slight squeeze, and sat herself in a chair opposite. Camellia at once resumed her seat and began to speak in clear, unaccented Oxford English. She began by asking after the health of Miss Jane and Miss Ruth, then complimented Phryne on the excellence of the tea and refreshments. Phryne made the appropriate rejoinders, and asked after Camellia's health and the progress of her pregnancy. Camellia replied that she was well, then gave a decisive nod, satisfied that the formalities had been safely negotiated.

'Miss Fisher, I know it is most irregular that I should come to you, but that cannot be helped. I am aware that you have an honoured place in my husband's affections, and it is because of this that he finds himself unable to confide too closely in you in this'—there was an awkward pause—'this difficult matter. Also, my husband is watched day and night. His association with you is widely known, and as a result, were he to come here it would be discovered at once. There might even be'—Camellia took another deep breath—'unfortunate repercussions. Whereas I...'

'Being a mere woman, may go where you please, since who would suspect a woman of independent action?' Phryne finished.

Camellia gave a nervous smile. 'Indeed. All our people will assume that I know nothing of importance.'

'I see.' Phryne eyed her guest carefully, utterly unsure of how to proceed. 'Camellia, I will honour your confidence in this difficult matter. May I assume that you have come to see me regarding recent incidents in Williamstown?'

A ghost of a smile passed across Camellia's perfect features. 'You may.'

'And the Lin family is concerned by what happened there?'

Camellia showed a glimpse of gleaming teeth between her

cerise lips. 'Not merely the Lin family, Miss Fisher. My own parents are also greatly troubled, as is everyone else in the Chinese community.'

Phryne nodded, recalling what Jack Robinson had told her about the Chinese distrust of the police. She leaned forward in her chair. 'I gather, then, that you are aware the police are investigating the assassination of Mr. Hong—whom, I gather, is no great loss to any community. But no doubt you would like to see justice done for poor Wing Loong, too?' Phryne put her hands on the table and regarded her visitor earnestly. 'I understand why you've come, Mrs. Lin, and I can assure you that I will investigate both deaths thoroughly.'

Camellia gazed unblinkingly at Phryne for a moment. 'Justice *has* been done in both cases, Miss Fisher.'

'Oh!' said Phryne, as realisation dawned. 'Are you telling me he was part of Hong's smuggling gang?'

Camellia inclined her head. 'He was not merely part of it, Miss Fisher—he was the organiser! He corrupted the workers. He bribed them with cash—and opium—to do his bidding. Hong was the mastermind, certainly. But Hong could not have done all this without a local Chinese to make the arrangements. Despite his avowed love for our culture, no one in our community trusted him.'

'And so Wing was killed by members of local families here, lest he bring disgrace and ruin upon all Chinese in Melbourne?'

Camellia smiled faintly. 'That is certainly a theory, Miss Fisher.'

'Ah.' Phryne reached forward and took a slice of peach from the blue porcelain dish. It tasted like the incarnation of summer. 'And nobody saw anything, and nobody heard anything, and nobody knows anything?'

Camellia's smile broadened for a moment, then vanished. 'That is indeed possible. What do you know of the Opium Wars, Miss Fisher?'

Phryne recalled history lessons from her English boarding school. Miss Plunkett had waxed eloquent about this outrage. 'I seem to recall that the British wanted to allow opium to be imported into China, and enforced it with gunboats?'

Camellia raised a delicate eyebrow. 'That is the official version. The so-called Opium Wars were not about opium at all. In any case, the sale of opium was perfectly legal until the local Commissioner decided to prohibit it. What the British wanted was to have China opened up for trade, and to protect their innocent civilians from harassment by the Chinese. And when the Commissioner did impound the opium, the traders wanted Britain to reimburse them. This was not palatable to the British government, as you can imagine.'

'Paying out of the Treasury to opium dealers? No. I can imagine how the House of Commons would have reacted to that.'

'Young Mr. Gladstone was very eloquent on the subject. He was a romantic. He had no idea what was happening. An agreement between the local merchants and the local Chinese was made, and both governments rejected it. The dispute arose because neither side understood the other.'

Phryne remembered that Miss Plunkett had been an ardent admirer of Mr. Gladstone, though everything Phryne had read about the man suggested he was a pompous fool, greatly inferior to his archrival Disraeli. She gave Camellia a penetrating look. 'Forgive me, Camellia, but I am a little surprised. You seem very well informed about this.'

Camellia laughed, and helped herself to another slice of peach. 'My husband does not believe that his wife should be kept ignorant of men's business, Phryne.'

'Good for him!' Phryne ate some more peach herself. It tasted heavenly: soft, perfectly ripe, and dripping with nectar.

'And besides, Phryne, do you know the name of the man who impounded the opium?'

When Phryne shook her head, Camellia said softly, 'He is remembered as Commissioner Lin.'

Phryne stared at her. 'Oh, my. So, this is family history for the Lin clan?'

Camellia pressed her slender hands together and leaned forward. 'Indeed it is. The Lin family knows the truth, which is not as discreditable to Britain as the Chinese government would have us all believe. But since we are Australians now, we do not have to pretend.' She smiled ruefully. 'However that may be, can you imagine what the popular press will say if these events in Williamstown become common knowledge?'

Phryne pondered for a long moment, during which Camellia helped herself to more melon seeds, which made a faint popping sound as she cracked them with expert fingers. 'Let me see if I have this straight,' Phryne said. 'An Australian purporting to be a great friend of your community wants to smuggle opium into our ports to sell to the Chinese, and he suborns a local Chinese to organize the operation. Both he and his agent are murdered. And the press will have conniptions, and blame everything on the Chinese, even though your people had nothing to do with Hong's plans, and stood to suffer the most from his operation.'

Camellia sat up straight, clasping her hands in front of her. 'Yes. Do you not believe we will be punished terribly? And yet we told the police what Hong was doing! All we wanted was that the law should be enforced!' Her shoulders slumped. 'But they did nothing. The first consignment of opium was distributed, and we have dozens of opium addicts now.' Camellia's expression was distraught now, and she gave Phryne a beseeching look. 'I swear to you that the Lin family had no part in the killings. But'—she hesitated—'others decided to take the law into their own hands.'

Phryne gave her a shrewd look. 'I have the impression this is personal for you, Mrs. Lin, over and above your concern for your people.'

Camellia nodded. 'My sister Peony ran away from home recently, and I heard that she had been taken on as one of Hong's dancers. We don't know where she is now. It is possible that she was caught up in events last night.' She ran a hand over her face. 'But that is a private tragedy. What I came to speak with you about was the public repercussions. If you were to investigate, and found that the murders were committed by Chinese, we would all be tarred with the same brush. It is unlikely the general public will distinguish between Hong and his Chinese minions who sought to import opium into Australia, and those of our community who tried to stop them. It will not take much to reignite the flames of bigotry. Therefore, I urge you to let this be, for our sake.'

'I see.' Phryne looked at Camellia with considerable compassion. It must have cost her a great deal to go behind her husband's back in this manner. But her visitor was right. Lin's hands were tied. He could not possibly ask Phryne to connive at concealing two murders. Equally, he did not feel that he could incriminate those who had taken such drastic measures to prevent an outbreak of opium addiction.

She stood up. 'Mrs. Lin, I can't make any promises. But I will do whatever I can to make this right—on one condition. If your people know who committed the murders, I want them punished in some way. I won't have murderers get off scot-free.'

Camellia rose to her feet and fixed Phryne with a steady look. 'I will speak to my husband, Miss Fisher. He knows that I came here. Wives should not keep secrets from their husbands. Shall I tell him that that is your condition for making this all disappear?'

Phryne smiled. 'I don't know if I can make this go away, but I will do my best.'

As if on cue, Mr. Butler materialised in the parlour. 'Will there be anything else, Miss Fisher?' he enquired.

'No, thank you, Mr. B. Mrs. Lin was just leaving.'

Camellia was escorted to the front door, and Phryne watched through the window as a driver in a chauffeur's cap helped her into the front seat of a plain black automobile. The driver turned and, meeting Phryne's gaze through the window, gave her a nod of recognition. It was Li Pen, she realised: the former Shaolin monk who was Lin Chung's bodyguard. Phryne lifted her hand in salute, then sat back in her chair. She now had a great deal of thinking to do.

'Mr. B?' she called. 'Another cup of espresso, if you would.'

It was Dot who brought coffee. 'I'm sorry I had to wake you, Miss Phryne, but Mrs. Lin did say it was urgent. It was very late when you got in last night. Did you enjoy the party?'

Phryne accepted the reviving brew gratefully. 'Well, it certainly was eventful, Dot. Let me fill you in.'

She related the night's doings while Dot sat in her chair, mouth open. When she got to Hugh's arrest of the harbourmaster, Phryne noticed that Dot's eyes were glistening.

'Oh, Miss! I'm so proud of Hugh. I'm sorry I doubted him.'

'And so am I, Dot. With any luck, you'll be seeing more of him from now on.'

Dot left her to finish her coffee in silence, after which Phryne went next door to the study and dialled Jeoffrey's number.

'Hello, Bisset here.'

'Jeoffrey? It's Phryne. Sorry to abandon you last night, but things got a bit hectic.'

'Phryne! I was waiting until a decent hour to call you. What on earth happened last night? You went off with Inspector Robinson, but you never returned.'

'I'd be happy to tell you all about it,' Phryne promised. 'May I come over for lunch?'

'Please do!'

———

Williamstown seemed utterly oblivious to the previous night's excitement. There were more people than ever out and about. Shoppers shopped, hawkers hawked, the sun was shining, and everything was as normal as could be imagined. Phryne made a point of driving past Hong's house. Aside from the fact that the house was shut up, there was nothing whatever to suggest that its owner had been murdered the previous night. The coloured lampions were still hanging, though their illumination was extinguished, which seemed a bit poignant. She turned into Lark Lane, parked the car within sight of Jeoffrey's open front door, and waved. Jeoffrey was sitting out the front on his tiny white-painted veranda in a wicker chair. He wore white trousers with braces, a white shirt, and looked undamaged by the night's traumas. He uncoiled his long, slender body and waved back.

He grinned sheepishly. 'I'm so sorry about last night. I can't believe I…' He left his shame-faced apology in mid-sentence.

Phryne responded crisply. 'Jeoffrey, please don't be embarrassed about fainting. It isn't every day you witness a murder. Even I was shocked, and I'm almost used to it. I hope you are feeling quite all right today?'

'Absolutely,' he assured her. 'And the whole experience seems to have given me an appetite. I've made lunch, as promised.'

Lunch turned out to be small homemade pies and mixed sandwiches, accompanied by a bottle of white wine that Phryne enjoyed far more than she had expected to. The pies—which came in chicken, lamb, and beef—were exceptional. In architectural splendour they lacked a good deal, having that homely asymmetry which spoke of amateur labour, but they tasted wonderful.

'Jeoffrey, if you made these purely for my benefit you may colour me impressed.'

He blushed a pale shade of beetroot. 'I did. And the sandwiches. I couldn't get any cucumber, though.'

'Did you go down twice?'

'Indeed.' Jeoffrey laughed heartily, thus declaring his familiarity with *The Importance of Being Earnest*.

'Now, Jeoffrey, if you could refill my glass I shall tell you some of what eventuated last night after we parted company.'

The story she told him was a heavily abridged one; she had taken Camellia's point about the likely outrage directed against the Chinese community should it reach the public's ears that there was opium abroad. No doubt Jack Robinson would similarly prefer to keep the matter quiet. Instead, she described to Jeoffrey how she had chased the murderer, only to be menaced by a small gang who had covered his retreat. She had taken Inspector Robinson to the spot where the murder weapon had been cast aside, but there had been no sign of it.

'So poor Hong's murderer is still at large?' Jeoffrey asked, wide-eyed.

'I'm afraid so,' Phryne confirmed, though she knew Hong was hardly worth lamenting. 'But I wondered if you might help me to fill in one or two details of the scene after I departed. Did you notice anything out of the ordinary?'

'You mean, out of the ordinary for crime scenes?' Jeoffrey gave a hollow laugh. 'I don't have any prior experience to compare it to. Well, as you know I missed some of the immediate aftermath'—a slight blush stained his cheeks—'but when I came round most of the assembly were milling around like confused sheep.' He mused for a while longer. 'Actually, there was one odd thing. I noticed the dancers.'

'So did I, Jeoffrey. Do go on.'

'Well, a few minutes before the murder, one of the dancers disappeared.'

'Oh, yes? I wonder if she was the one who gave me that note urging me to leave?'

'Perhaps it was. But here's another thing. Another of the dancers disappeared just after the murder. I had admired her, so was looking for her among those waiting to be interviewed by the police. It's possible I just didn't recognise her.' He winced. 'I know it's a terrible thing to say, but…well, the girls did all look rather alike.'

'Indeed,' Phryne murmured, as she was struck by a notion. She rose to her feet. 'I'm very sorry to eat and run, but I've had an idea. It's a long shot, I know, but if I don't follow this up now, the trail will go cold.'

And leaving Jeoffrey open-mouthed in her wake, she strode out to the car.

———

Phryne drove past Hong's house again and wondered who would inherit it. It was more suitable for a substantial family than a single man. What on earth had the man been thinking, selling opium to sustain his opulent lifestyle? Well, he had paid with his life for his folly. Would he be mourned by anyone? It didn't sound like it. Even colleagues such as Jeoffrey, while shocked by the circumstances of the man's death, seemed only to feel a superficial affection for him. As she motored along the Strand, Phryne caught glimpses of children playing skipping games in the side streets. These did not look as affluent as those in the town centre. Dresses, shirts, and trousers were on the shabby side. But the shouts and laughter which wafted through her window were bracing and spoke of resilient optimism. As she headed north alongside the Maribyrnong River the houses grew steadily more shabby. She was passing by the industrial heartland of the inner west now. There were few people about, and those she did see looked spartan and hollow-cheeked. These grim streets were the former home of her adoptive daughters. She found herself shuddering. Well, the girls were safe now.

And speaking of girls, what was she hoping to achieve today? She had told Jeoffrey it was a long shot, and it truly was. Come off it, Phryne! she admonished herself. How likely is it that you'll find the missing dancers wandering around Chinatown? Yet she had to trust her intuition—and her thumbs were pricking. As Lin Chung had told her often enough, *We all look the same to you Westerners.* Jeoffrey had as good as confirmed it. The dancers might have thought that once in Chinatown they would be safe, unrecognisable to Western eyes—such as those of the police. But why would they need to hide? That was indeed the question...

Phryne parked the Hispano-Suiza in an all-but-deserted Swanston Street and entered under the paper lanterns. She stood by a street stall and inhaled. Cooking poultry, frying oil, jasmine, sandalwood, musk, vanilla, ylang-ylang, and other exotic spices. Blue-coated figures bustled about carrying bags of rice, wooden tea chests, and racks of garments. The hubbub of voices, speaking volubly in their own language. For an hour she paced up and down, occasionally turning into alleys before resuming her patrol of Little Bourke Street. She was emerging from one such alley—dodging three small boys who capered past on who knew what mysterious errand—when she saw two women in black jackets and trousers hovering over a barrow of green vegetables. Both were immediately familiar to her. One looked very much like a taller version of Lin's Camellia. And the other—the girl was remarkably beautiful, with a flawless complexion and a look of longing, and fear, in her almond eyes. And Phryne, who had spent considerable time staring at her fewer than twenty-four hours earlier knew her at once. This was the young woman she had seen at Hong's party, sitting apart from the other dancers. Phryne leaned against a lamppost and studied the girl closely. Now, seeing her in trousers, she realised she had seen that girl on three occasions at Hong's party. Once dancing on the low stage with her colleagues; once sitting in a chair, glaring at Hong; and once more, dressed as a man in black with a skullcap covering her hair, plunging a long knife into Hong's chest.

At that moment, the girl looked up from her examination of the barrow, saw Phryne staring at her, and gasped. She whispered urgently to her companion, and then they both turned and fled. Damnation! Phryne tore up the street after them, silently blessing her flat heels and trousers. She was gaining on them. Then, unexpectedly, the tall girl stopped running. She shouted something to her friend, who disappeared down an alley.

The tall girl turned to face Phryne. 'Miss Fisher?' she said. 'My name is Peony. I believe you may be looking for me?'

The resemblance to her sister Camellia really was striking, Phryne thought.

She cast a look down the alley behind the girl. There was no sign of Hong's murderer, and she doubted very much she would be able to find her if the girl didn't want to be found. Peony, on the other hand, might be persuaded to give herself up.

'Your sister is very worried about you,' Phryne told her. 'Is there any chance I could persuade you to accompany me to the Lin house and be reunited with her there?'

The girl's face darkened. 'I won't return to my father's house,' she warned.

Phryne, knowing of the iron rule Chinese fathers exercised over their unmarried daughters, could hardly blame her. 'I expect Mr. Lin will be able to come to an arrangement with your father,' she said, silently vowing that she would make sure of it.

Peony thought this over. 'In that case, I may agree to come with you.' She reached out and took both Phryne's hands in hers, staring Phryne straight in the eye.

Phryne was astonished to realise that she could not move. The girl was as strong as a Mallee bull.

'I think it would be a good idea if you were to let go of my hands. If this demonstration is intended to demonstrate your skill in martial arts, then you may take it that I am impressed. But we cannot have a civilised discussion under such circumstances.'

Peony laughed, and released Phryne. 'I'm sorry. But my friend needs a little time to effect her escape.'

'Peony, your friend killed Hong. I saw her do it. You are asking me to let her get away with murder.'

Peony blinked. 'And what if I told you that Hong got only what he deserved?'

'Is this about the opium smuggling?'

The girl bowed her head. 'Miss Fisher, we never would have worked for him if we'd known about the opium. We were very naïve. It was only just before the party that one of the musicians told us about it.'

'If it had nothing to do with the opium, why did your friend kill him?'

Peony gave a cry of anguish. 'You don't understand!' she burst out. 'Miss Fisher, Carnation and I are lovers. There: I've said it now. And do you know what Hong told her? He was going to hand her over to a Cantonese triad leader after the party! He was giving her to him as a present!'

Phryne inhaled deeply. 'Oh, dear. So may I assume this triad leader was the one who supplied Hong with his opium?'

'So the musician said. It is likely that Hong was in that man's power. He may have threatened Hong. That stupid man had no idea what he was doing. I suppose the triad leader demanded the most beautiful dancer as a concubine, and Hong felt he had no choice. And Carnation, too, had no choice.' Her voice softened. 'Miss Fisher, I will do as you ask and go to my brother-in-law's house...if you will let my lover escape.'

Phryne looked into the girl's pleading eyes. It went against the grain to let murder go unpunished, but Carnation had acted in self-defence. Would Phryne not have done the same in her position? As for punishment: in making her escape, Carnation was to be parted from her lover. That seemed to Phryne like a heavy enough price to pay.

Phryne inclined her head. 'So be it.'

Peony took Phryne's hands in hers again, gently this time. 'Thank you, Silver Lady. I will go to Mr. Lin now, you have my word. And one day, perhaps, Carnation and I will be reunited again in happiness.'

She bent forward to kiss Phryne's cheek, and then she walked away.

———

As Phryne returned to her car on Swanston Street, the bells of St Paul's began to ring out in cascading harmonies down towards the Yarra. Phryne recalled that she had been meaning to pay a call on a friend there. She walked along the footpath, climbed the steps to the cathedral entrance, and stood in the portico admiring the cool sanctity of the interior. There was something majestic about it all right: vast, imposing, and yet somehow not so intimidating as it might have been. Some of the spires looked unfinished. And the sandstone looked…different. Where had she seen that colour before? She tracked down the fugitive memory and realised she had last seen that shade of ochre at Sydney University. Phryne admired the collection of envelopes soliciting funds for various causes, and chose the one she wanted.

The hovering verger paused in his labour of collecting hassocks, and surveyed the young woman with approval. Expensively dressed, he noted, but demure and wearing a proper hat. So many young women came to church wearing hats more suitable for Flemington Racecourse than the House of God. As she passed in front of the distant altar, she inclined her head with the utmost propriety. The verger removed his spectacles, polished them on his handkerchief, and made up his mind to approach this admirably devout and lovely creature.

'Madam, can I help you?' he enquired with solicitude.

Phryne reached into her purse and produced a card. 'Why, you certainly may. Could you present this to Bishop Watkins, if he is at home?'

The verger examined the card and his eyes widened. 'Oh, my goodness! Yes, he is here today. I will take him your card at once. If you would care to wait in the church, we have some splendid stained-glass windows.'

And splendid they were, Phryne agreed. But not as splendid as the Gothic arches, the beautifully inlaid stone flooring, and the studied grandeur of the lofty ceiling. How terribly Anglican all this was, avoiding the excesses of Puritan iconoclasm while simultaneously shunning the taint of Romish idolatry. The statuary seemed to be confined to crucifixes of differing sizes and an enormous eagle holding up the pulpit. She watched as a dark-cassocked middle-aged man emerged from behind the scenes and opened the wooden lid of the mighty organ. Sonorous notes boomed from the enormous pipes. And the verger returned at a bustle, his heavy shoes echoing in the cavernous spaces. He arrived in front of Phryne, breathless, solicitous, and somewhat puzzled. 'Follow me, please.'

He led the way past the organ and off to the right, where there appeared to be a substantial vestry. At the edge of it, the verger opened a heavy wooden door and bowed to her.

A friendly, piping voice sounded from a capacious chair behind a desk of mammoth proportions. 'Why, Phryne! Come right in, there's a girl.'

Lionel Watkins rose from his seat and waved. He was in his forties, but looked older. His purple shirt was surmounted by a clerical collar, and his receding hair was greying. But his bright, piercing blue eyes glowed with warmth as he extended a pastoral hand. 'Do sit down, please. Tea and bikkies?'

Phryne sat in a round-backed chair which would not have dishonoured a prince.

'No, thank you, Lionel,' she said, as her host subsided into his own chair. 'I heard you'd been made a bishop. Congratulations!'

He waved a deprecating right hand, missing three fingers. 'Suffragan only. It means they don't know what to do with me. But I've got my eye on Ballarat, or Bendigo. Looks like I've escaped Sale, which is just as well. Too far from town. But'—his eyes twinkled merrily—'His Grace and his little flock have gone to Shepparton on a state visit for some festival. Don't know why, really. Easter's already been and gone, you know. But this means he's left me in charge for a few days.'

'The cathedral could not be in safer hands, Lionel. Speaking of which, I couldn't help noticing that it appears to be undergoing considerable renovation. In the spire department?'

Lionel waved his hand with becoming languor. 'Oh, we have

a new architect. Butterfield—the original designer—wanted an octagonal central tower. We don't know why, and apparently our predecessors here said no. The fellow actually resigned from the job three times. He was overheard saying he wished he'd never heard of Melbourne.'

'Oh, dear. So you have a new architect now?'

'Oh, yes. Sydney chap named Barr. At least his treble spire won't break the bank. I've always thought the whole story was terribly, terribly Melbourne, you know. Boundless confidence, loss of bottle, redo the whole thing on a less grandiose scale, and leave the whole messy compromise there as a monument to the folly of o'erleaping ambition.'

'Have you ever seen St Albans Cathedral in Hertfordshire?'

Lionel gave a deep, good-natured chuckle. 'Oh, yes. That feller Grimthorpe last century. D'you know, he gave his name to a brand-new verb? To "grimthorpe" an ancient monument means to do it up with far more money than taste.'

'Indeed. Everything there from late Saxon to Victorian Gothic Horror.' Phryne tipped her head back and laughed. 'I'm sorry. It's just that during the war, when I met you covered in Flanders mud, I never thought you'd finish up here in a purple shirt.'

'Indeed not. But there it was, Phryne. I'd had enough of war and soldiering. I'd already seen the fires of hell in Flanders. I thought I may as well try for heaven instead.' His eyes held hers for a lingering moment. 'And an angel did lead me back from the abyss.'

'Oh, Lionel. You do me too much honour.' And it all came back in a rush. The muddy, stinking field hospital. The monstrous anger of the guns. The smell of death and carnage. The frantic orderly. *Oh, Miss, it's Major Watkins. He won't speak. He just lies there, staring at the tent roof. Can't you do something?* Well, she had not been found wanting. She had comforted him with her body and drawn him back to sanity.

'You saved me, Phryne. A ministering angel indeed.' He shook his head. 'Now, what can I do for you? You aren't here just for my company, are you?'

'Well, it is certainly wonderful to see you, Lionel. But I did want to bring to your attention a certain Reverend Winsome of St Kilda.'

Watkins shook his head and sighed. 'That silly boy! He hasn't been picking up tarts again, has he?'

Phryne put her hand to her mouth. 'Well, I'm sure I couldn't say, Lionel. I haven't actually seen him do it with my own eyes—but he did send me some rather disturbing postcards and I found him peering in my bedroom window one night. I wasn't so much alarmed as annoyed, but it really won't do.'

'Indeed it won't. Well, we'd better get him out of there, hadn't we? Leave it with me, my dear.'

'Thank you, Lionel.' Phryne rose, removed her right glove, and extended her hand. Lionel bent over it, kissed it lightly, and bowed.

He beamed at her. 'Thank *you* for dropping by. I'll see you again soon, I hope.'

———

Lin Chung looked up from his desk at the soft knock on the door. 'Li Pen? You have the prisoner? Show him in.'

Li Pen entered, inclined his head, and pushed the prisoner onto his knees in front of the mahogany desk.

Lin stared at the man. 'Ming K'uo, you have many questions to answer. Did you kill the man Wing Loong?'

Hands bound with cords in front of him, Ming glanced briefly at his interrogator then bowed his head. In his black robes, with his black cap and burning eyes, Lin Chung resembled the Black Judge of the Netherworld.

'This person confesses his guilt, honoured sir. It was in self-defence. Wing Loong betrayed us. He had thrown in his lot with the corrupt official. He was going to hand us over to the police! When this person demanded answers, he drew a knife and stabbed me.' Ming K'uo drew aside his jacket to reveal a jagged wound in his chest.

'I see. And you threatened the Silver Lady. Why did you do that?'

'Because she was pursuing Carnation! The girl is innocent. That dog Hong was going to give her to the triads. This person gave orders that she was to be allowed to flee.' Ming took a deep breath. 'Honoured sir, let the others go free. If any must suffer the rope-death, then this person shall. This person's colleagues have done wrong, but they are not to blame for the killing.'

'What happened to Liu and his men that night? What did they do?'

'When the police came, they vanished. No one has seen them since.'

Lin stood up. 'Ming K'uo, I have made no decision as yet. You will remain here, in custody. You will give me the names and whereabouts of the others who worked with you.' He turned to his bodyguard. 'Li Pen? Take the prisoner away. And see to it that his wound is treated.'

Chapter Twenty-Five

Phryne went home utterly spent. She had her dinner on a tray in bed that night and spent a lazy Sunday doing nothing much of substance. On Monday morning, she drove to City South police station. It was a strained interview. Phryne told Jack what she knew about Hong's murder and the justification for it. She left Peony out of her account.

'So all this would be on the basis of more information received, would it?' the inspector enquired in a low voice.

'Well, yes, Jack, it would. I am not going to say any more than that. Because I can't. By the way, has it occurred to you that the way we treat the Chinese is the central problem here? You know what everyone says: "Oh, you can't tell them apart, can you?" Well, it seems to me that if they're not individually distinguishable, then they can't be tried as individuals.'

Jack gave her a long look. 'Yes, but they are distinguishable to some, aren't they?'

'To me, certainly, Jack. But even I would be stretched to identify the'—she paused significantly—'young man I saw stab Hong in the middle of a crowded party. Anyway, if the Commissioner gives you a hard time about this—'

'Which he will.'

'—then you might tell him that we can't have it both ways. We can treat the Chinese as proper citizens the same as everybody else, with the same rights and responsibilities; or we can treat them as inscrutable Orientals who all look the same and can't be positively identified, and cannot therefore be charged with anything.'

'I might try that. By the way, the same argument could be made for the Aboriginals, you know.'

Phryne gave a low whistle. 'That really is a point, isn't it?'

'Well, that's a problem for another day,' Jack suggested. He rose to his feet. 'Glad we've had this little chat, Miss Fisher.'

———

'Hello, Jeoffrey? It's Phryne. Are you free Wednesday night, given that you have Thursdays off and all?'

There was an intake of breath. 'Ouch. I'm sorry, Phryne,' he said regretfully, 'I meant to tell you… You see, term's over, and I'm off tomorrow on sabbatical. They've found a new manuscript of Plautus—the comedy writer, you know—and I really want to have a squiz at it. But I'll be back in July. I'd love to see you then. Really.'

'All right, Jeoffrey. Have fun. I'll see you then.'

Phryne put down the receiver and sighed. There was no question that Jeoffrey Bisset seemed to be in many respects the perfect lover, but scholars were like that. And where could this new Plautus have been discovered? Europe, surely? In that case he was going to fly. A shipboard journey would take far too long. In other circumstances Phryne might have offered to accompany him. But no, she reminded herself, she had responsibilities now—at least until her adopted children were launched from the nest. Besides, she knew very little about Jeoffrey really, beyond her highly favourable first impressions. She gave a dimpled smile, then rang another, more familiar, number.

'Lin? How are you this bright, pleasant day? And how is Camellia?'

'Both of us are very well, Phryne. I was going to call you myself. I wondered if a visit tomorrow might be convenient?'

'Certainly! I would be delighted to see you. Dinner?'

The warm, cultured voice sounded hesitant. 'I fear that won't work. Would lunch be all right? I need to be home by five o'clock.'

Phryne smiled to herself. This would be down to Camellia, whose pregnancy was advancing rapidly. 'Shall I expect you at one o'clock then?'

'That sounds perfect, Silver Lady.'

Lin arrived the next day in a shiny black open-topped Bentley which he had recently acquired. Li Pen, dressed in his usual black trousers and robe, was driving. Lin sat in the back, very much the lord of all he surveyed. As he alighted with easy grace, Phryne was watching from her upstairs window. She smiled. Li would retire to the kitchen to share the company of the kitchen staff, which included Ruth now it was school holidays. Li was very formal with Mr. and Mrs. Butler, but he and Ruth had developed an animated and wildly improbable friendship; and he unbent more with her than with anyone else.

Lin, meanwhile, looked resplendent in Western dress (plain black, with white shirt and a gleaming black top hat, no less), although she wished sometimes that he would appear in his

Chinese silk robes. That would really give her neighbours something exciting to gawp at.

She ran lightly down the stairs to greet Lin formally at the door.

'Why, Lin, how delightful to see you,' she said, offering an ungloved hand. He bent slightly and kissed it. 'Silver Lady,' he said, all Oxford politeness. 'Shall we go in?'

'Let us do that.'

Lunch was quite superb, and perfectly suited to the weather, which had turned a little chilly. A platter piled high with seafood and salad; clear soup, roast chicken, potatoes, and steamed greens, all accompanied by a selection of wines both white (which Phryne accepted) and red (favoured by Lin).

At a certain point in the repast, her guest set down his glass and gave Phryne a meaningful look. 'I gather from Camellia that you are in possession of details concerning our local dilemma.'

Phryne inclined her head.

Lin shook his. 'This has been a most awkward situation for us all.'

'The nerve of that man, Hong!' Phryne cried. 'So far as I'm concerned, he got what was coming to him. Threatening to put you all in peril with his stupid schemes!'

'It was indeed most troubling—not least because when we tried to inform the proper authorities we were ignored. Though I gather the deputy harbourmaster has been arrested?'

Phryne laughed. 'He has indeed. One gathers he decided to help himself to the swag once both Wing and Hong had been eliminated.'

'And someone familiar to this household made the arrest?'

'Indeed so; we are rather proud of Hugh. Now, Lin, please tell me about Peony. What has become of her?'

Lin waited as Mr. Butler cleared their plates, then resumed when he had left the room. 'It has been agreed between the two families that Peony will assist Camellia during her confinement. What could be more natural than that her own sister should be on hand? Thus respectability is maintained at all times. And in due course, perhaps we might persuade her father that Peony should remain under my roof thereafter.'

'I am glad to hear it. She seemed most determined not to return home. And Carnation?'

Lin raised his eyes to the ceiling. 'Now that is indeed an awkward question. All I will say is that Carnation is not under my roof, and I take no responsibility for her.'

And with that Phryne had to be content.

Lin's features relaxed somewhat. 'You have been discreet enough at least to refrain from asking about the men who killed Wing Loong.' He gave her a brief smile. 'I am happy to tell you that all five are undergoing—shall we say—re-education. None of our families sanctioned that operation. We do not arrange murders on our own behalf, whatever the provocation.'

'Re-education?'

'They are digging ditches in a rural setting. It will be very good for their spiritual reawakening.'

Phryne laughed aloud. 'All right. I'm sorry, Lin, but Jack Robinson is a bit miffed at being baulked of his prey. If he asks, I will at least do my best to allay his concerns.' She gave him a quizzical look. 'I would be interested to know how Carnation and Peony met.'

'There is no mystery there. They are third cousins. You know how it is with Chinese families.' Lin sipped from his glass. 'Now, I wondered if I might broach a delicate subject with you?'

Phryne smiled at the idea that the discussion of murderers and their victims did not qualify as delicate. 'Yes, of course. What is it, Lin?'

'Phryne, I know that the newspapers are full of implacable

optimism about the state of the world. Especially in the matter of financial markets, which, despite ructions here and there, do seem'—Lin displayed his palm in a quizzical fashion—'somewhat over-optimistic.'

'You mean we're sitting on a gigantic financial bubble, Lin?'

'Well, it does seem like that, does it not? The market capitalisation of all these companies would seem to indicate that the world is far more wealthy than appearances justify. And so I was wondering if you...' He looked at her with concern.

Phryne stared at this exemplary man with a look of pure love. 'Oh, Lin! You are anxious for me! I am touched, and honoured.' He looked, for a moment, exquisitely discomfited. 'The bond market especially does seem to be overpopulated with bulls, does it not?'

Phryne laughed in honest good humour. 'Lin, the bond market looks like Pamplona during the Festival of St Fermín. I wouldn't touch it with a boathook. That isn't real money, Lin. If I ever want to gamble, I will go to Monte Carlo and try my luck there. Just to set your mind at ease, all my money is invested in a mixture of government securities and companies that manufacture food staples. And beer. If it all goes bang, people will still want to eat and drink.' Her eyes narrowed. 'Are you telling me that it really is going to go bang?'

He shrugged his elegant shoulders. 'What goes up must come down eventually. It depends. If the bulls continue to rampage with their current enthusiasm, it might even be later this year.' He drew a deep breath. 'But I am delighted to hear that you are in firm command of your finances. You do not entrust them to brokers, then?'

'Only on occasion. Of course, they are always telling me to invest in this and that, but I rarely listen to them. And you?'

Lin smiled. 'Phryne, our own prosperity is anchored by wealth that is tangible. We operate in, shall we say, a parallel economy. We have no dealings with Occidental brokers. We do not consider them to be…reliable.'

Mr. Butler arrived at the table bearing a platter with crêpes doused in Grand Marnier. As Lin and Phryne watched, he set them aflame with a long white candle, then served them each a portion. He bowed graciously, then departed with stately grandeur.

'How very apt,' Phryne commented. 'And so, a bonfire of the vanities is coming?'

'It would appear so, Phryne. But this smells wonderful. And armed as we are in caution, let us taste it.'

The crêpes were superb: feather-light, soaked in burned liqueur and topped with heavy cream, the combination was such as to set the tastebuds afire. When both had finished, they exchanged glances. Phryne half closed her eyes, thinking of the honey-coloured limbs which were soon to emerge from Lin's impeccable clothes. He extended a slim hand to her, and she raised it to her lips and kissed it. He smelled of cinnamon, liqueur, and suppressed desire. Lin took her hand in turn and raised it to his delectable mouth. She shivered: a liquid trail of fire cascaded down her spine.

'Well, Lin?' Phryne purred. 'You are not expected at home until evening, I believe?'

He nodded. 'If it pleases the Silver Lady, I would be honoured to share in her company until then.'

They rose, and Phryne offered him her hand. 'Let us ascend the stairs forthwith.'

———

Dear Peony,

I am writing to let you know that I love you, and always will. I should never have dragged you into trouble like this. I am so sorry. I understand you have gone to stay with your sister and help her while she is pregnant. That was very sensible of you. You've done nothing wrong. I feel that neither have I, but the police will no doubt see it otherwise. If you want to write to me, you can give letters to Aunty Ma. She knows where I am, but she speaks no English and she will say nothing to the authorities.

Your devoted
Carnation

———

My darling Carnation,

How splendid of you to arrange a postal service! Now, I want to talk seriously to you, so please pay attention. Yes, I am looking after Camellia until her child is born and a little while afterwards. Mr. Lin knows about Aunty Ma, and he had a long talk with her while you were out. He's been to see my father and they agreed that it would be proper for me to attend on my sister. So that is settled. But Mr. Lin also told me that he understood what you did; and he said that while it was wrong of you, and he couldn't condone it, he doesn't see any point in having you punished.

And here is what I think: I think that after the baby is born, Mr. Lin wouldn't mind if I went to join you. He didn't say as much, but he dropped me some hints. And this way we both get time to think about how we will live together.

When two girls fall in love with each other, everyone seems to expect that it will end badly for them, but I don't see why it should. If you still love me by New Year, then I think we should be together. I've never been to Bendigo, but it sounds interesting. It was one of the great Gold Mountains, and they don't regard us with too much malice. I'd be happy to join you there if you still want me.

Your loving
Peony

PS I'm not supposed to know you're in Bendigo. But I eavesdropped. I'm clever like that. xxoo

Chapter Twenty-Six

The crystal chandelier glittered in the parlour's soft yellow light. The festive sideboard was groaning under the weight of silver dishes which rested on starched damask tablecloths of dazzling whiteness. There were small pies and other pastries. There was an iced fruitcake of gargantuan proportions. There were trays of sandwiches, filled with ham, chicken, smoked salmon, egg and lettuce, and cheese and tomato. There were cheese platters, with slender, almost evanescent biscuits. There were two enormous punchbowls filled with fruit, fruit juices, and soda water, one with champagne added, and one without. Mr. and Mrs. Butler made a stately minuet as they carried in dish after dish. On a separate table they laid bottles of claret, hock, more champagne in an economy-sized ice-bucket, three cocktail shakers labelled *Sidecar*, *Singapore sling*, and *Gin rickey*, and five bottles of beer for what Mr. B described as the Maritime Gentlemen. There were small porcelain plates and dishes, and folded napkins, and glasses of differing sizes for all eventualities. At five minutes to eight Mr. Butler mopped his brow with a handkerchief and exchanged a glance with his wife.

'I believe that is the last of it, my dear,' he observed.

She took his arm and marched him back to the kitchen for a restorative glass of port apiece.

Phryne inspected herself in the parlour mirror and approved. She wore an emerald silk dress, knee-length, cut low front and back and showing off her flawless skin to perfection. Soft leather flat shoes (also emerald), silk stockings, a feathered headdress with a turquoise band, emerald earrings, and a silver-set emerald on a silver chain nestling just above her breasts completed the effect. Thanks to the open fire, the room was warm and she felt no need of additional coverings. She cast a critical eye over the room's layout and approved. There had been a certain degree of rearrangement. The piano had been manhandled to one side. The sofa and most of the available chairs in the house were ranged around the walls, leaving as large an area as possible for gener-alised milling about. She counted the chairs and nodded. 'What do you think, Dot?'

'It looks good, Miss.'

As they waited, Phryne picked up one of the cocktail shakers and poured herself a Singapore sling. As the clock struck eight, Phryne opened the front door in time to see Bert and Cec in their best checked shirts and dungarees. The taxi was parked outside in the street.

'Come in, comrades!' Phryne called.

Bert grinned, Cec touched his hat, and they trooped inside.

'Help yourselves to beer, or anything else you like the look of.'

'Get me one, will ya, mate?' Bert said to his friend. He removed the cigarette from the corner of his mouth and grinned at Phryne. 'Well, I bin down to the Anchor this week. You made quite an impression there, I c'n tell ya.'

Phryne smiled. 'Your friends were extremely helpful, I must say. I left them ten bob to pay for the next round, but it was cheap at the price.'

'Yair, well. They don't mind the Chinks either way, but they really didn't take to the smugglin' racket. Stuff like that gets everyone's backs up and then it's nuthin' but pain and aggravation fer ev'ryone.' Bert accepted the glass Cec proffered and gave the weighted sideboard an admiring stare. 'So what's the deal? We just take what we want and put it on them fancy plates?'

'Yes, Bert dear. In due course. Or now, if you wish.'

The staircase resounded with excited footfalls, and Ruth and Jane made their entrance. They wore the same dresses as they had worn to Frances Reynolds's party, and looked radiant.

'Hello, girls,' said Phryne. 'You both look splendid. Ruth, would you go and knock on Tinker's door? I want him here. And if he's not dressed, tell him to get dressed. He doesn't have to look like a film star. Just vaguely presentable.'

As Ruth departed on her errand, Phryne looked at Jane. 'Did you invite Frances?'

'Yes, I did. Her mother is going via the Blind Institute, as they're going to pick up Jennifer and Miss Thomas on the way. And she'll be returning at midnight to do the return trip.'

'Good. Now, go and talk to Bert and Cec, would you? I need to stand by the front door.'

'Phryne! Thanks for inviting us!' Eliza was the next to arrive, and she presented her cheek for a sisterly kiss. She then drew Alice forward, and Phryne kissed her cheek as well. Phryne noted that Alice was dressed in trousers and a tweed jacket with tie, while Eliza wore a lace-bordered jacket and lacy dress. By sheer coincidence, Phryne had seen a photograph of Beatrice and Sidney Webb in the *London Illustrated News*, dressed exactly thus. Not only did they study the Fabian socialists, they were now even dressing the part. She grinned to herself.

Alice gave her a look of gratitude. 'I hear that one of the

girls from the Institute is playing for us tonight, Phryne. Jolly well done!'

'Jennifer is an exceptional talent,' Phryne answered. 'I hope that her playing will become better known in future. Do come in! Cocktails are on the sideboard.'

The next up the front steps was Lionel Watkins, unexpectedly in plain clothes: tweed jacket, white shirt, and anonymous trousers. 'Lionel! I'm so glad you could come! But...?'

He looked down at his attire and shrugged. 'Do you know, I thought the purple shirt and dog collar might put people off? Besides, I know I'm a bishop. Your other guests don't need to know that.'

'I'm delighted to see you. You were at Balliol, weren't you? There'll be another Balliol man here tonight. Lin Chung. You can swap reminiscences of the dreaming spires if you're so inclined.' Phryne looked beyond Watkins's shoulder to the street. 'How did you get here?'

The bishop's weathered features split into a grin. 'Oh, I made the dean drive me. He was reluctant, but I pulled rank on him.'

'Should I have invited him too?'

Watkins shook his head. 'Dear me, no. The chap's a perfect arse, you know. As well as a bit of an Obadiah Slope. I certainly didn't want him here. Mortification of the flesh will do him good.'

'Do come in and have a cocktail. They're on the sideboard along with everything else.'

Phryne turned towards the front gate, through which Hugh Collins was arriving, dressed in a sombre dark suit. He gave the impression of a violincello tuned well above concert pitch. Phryne waved him into the house. 'Delighted to see you back in circulation, Hugh,' she told him.

Phryne patted him on the shoulder as he passed over the threshold, then extended her hand in greeting as a limousine pulled up out front, with a uniformed Li Pen in the driver's seat. Lin Chung stepped out, in perfect black tie evening dress complete with top hat and monocle on a black cord. He kissed Phryne's hand as Li Pen cruised off into the night. 'Silver Lady,' he murmured.

'Lin. How wonderful to see you. Do come in and mingle.'

When all the company were assembled, Phryne leaned in the doorway for a long moment of pure delight. Snatches of conversation washed past her, making itself heard above the general din.

'No, Jowett was before my time, I'm afraid. But tell me, my dear chap, when were you up?'

'Yair, we druv this bloke home yesterdee an 'e'd 'ad so much plonk 'e couldn't remember where 'e lived. So we went round and round the neighbourhood till 'e recognised the tree 'e'd bin sick on last week.'

'Yes, he's making brushes now. And serves him right.'

'The Thousand Island dressing was a few archipelagos short of the mark, I'm afraid.'

'And can you still get through that hole in the fence just by the punts after curfew?'

'Yair, well, after this year I won't 'ave to go to school no more. Can't wait.'

'When I was presented at court, you know, the King told me that he'd rather be in his library reading a book. And I said: "So would I!"'

Phryne grinned at the lattermost: Eliza's beloved's recollection of her Coming-Out, when she was still Lady Alice Harborough.

Miss Thomas had arrived with Jennifer Barnes, who was sitting at the piano, awaiting her cue. Next to her was Frances Reynolds, in a fashionable party dress, looking at Jennifer with anticipatory enthusiasm.

Everyone was here. Phryne was on the verge of making a little speech—she had some announcements to make—but caught the eye of Jack Robinson, who waved a hand towards her. She waved back, and he motored steadily through the gathering to join her.

'Yes, Jack? Did you have something to tell me?'

He looked at her with a face that appeared to be glowing from within. 'Remember a month or two ago there was talk of promotion? Yesterday the Commissioner called me in and said he'd approved it.'

Phryne clapped lightly. 'And it's very well deserved, Jack.'

'Maybe. I'm a bit gobsmacked, to tell you the truth. It's not like I found either of our murderers.'

'Jack, I am sorry about that, but it really couldn't be helped. And you did find the opium and nail that scoundrel Hammond.'

'Thanks largely to you and Collins.'

Phryne took his hand in hers and held it. 'Jack, something Bert once told me would seem to meet the bill here. He said that life is full of unjust punishments and undeserved rewards. So please, think of your promotion as reward for years of faithful and efficient service.'

'Well, Miss Fisher, you may be right.'

'Do you want this included in the speech I'm about to make?'

Robinson thought about it for a moment, then nodded. 'If you'd like.'

'Oh, but I would like it very much indeed, Jack.'

Jack retreated into the melee, and Phryne signalled to the hovering Mr. Butler for the champagne bottles to be opened and glasses distributed. When this had been accomplished she clapped her hands twice.

'Hello, everybody. First of all, thank you for coming to my party. Now, as you can see, we are fortunate to have Miss Jennifer Barnes here tonight, and she is going to play for us later. But first, I have some announcements to make. Congratulations are in order to my dear friend and colleague Jack Robinson, who is to be promoted very soon to an exalted position well worthy of his mettle. I give you'—Phryne raised her glass of Veuve Clicquot— 'Chief Inspector Robinson!'

When the applause had died away, Phryne gestured to her adoptive children. 'As some of you know, Jane and Ruth have recently undertaken an investigation into the affairs of a well-known charitable institution. Thanks to their work, the wicked have been punished and the deserving rewarded. To Ruth and Jane!' She raised her glass again and drank, a gesture echoed around the room. 'Ruth and Jane!'

Her eye fell on Tinker, who shook his head with emphasis. 'No, Tinker, don't be so modest. Tinker here has also exerted his very considerable detective skills of late in my service, and his cleverness and persistence should be publicly acknowledged. To Tinker!'

'Tinker!'

Phryne was watching Lionel Watkins, whose brow furrowed, then cleared. He gave her a nod of acknowledgement and a beaming smile. They didn't make you a bishop if you couldn't put two and two together; no doubt Watkins had guessed what this was about.

As the murmurs died down, Phryne took a deep breath and said, 'Finally, I would like to call forward Hugh Collins, who has an announcement to make.'

Looking for all the world like a soldier going over the top, Hugh Collins took Dot's hand and led her into the centre of the room.

'Ladies, gentlemen, colleagues, Your Grace…You all know that there has been an Understanding between myself and Miss Dorothy Williams. Well, we are officially engaged, and we would be honoured if you would join us at our marriage, to be celebrated on the fifteenth of June.'

'To Hugh and Dot!' cried Phryne, holding aloft her glass.

'To Hugh and Dot!'

Amid a torrent of backslapping and general congratulation, Lionel Watkins sidled up to Phryne. 'I say, old girl, does he want me to officiate? I'd be happy to.'

Phryne laid her hand on his arm. 'She's a Catholic, Lionel. Sorry.'

'Which means a Catholic wedding, and a promise that their offspring will be brought up as such. Oh, dear. Well, never mind. So long as he knows what he's getting himself into.'

As the bishop hied off to the punchbowl, Lin Chung took his place. 'It's a splendid party,' he observed. Then, lowering his voice, he murmured, 'And you look particularly ravishing tonight.'

Phryne turned towards him and inhaled the glorious scent of his person. 'Perhaps you'd care to stay after the other guests have gone and we can continue the party in private?' she whispered.

Lin looked at her gravely. 'Silver Lady, I would be honoured.'

They exchanged a molten look then both turned to face the room.

The other guests were now watching, enraptured, as Miss Barnes played the piano with astonishing facility. There was just one absentee, Phryne noted, smiling to herself. Tinker was no doubt already back in his shed, playing with Molly. Piano soirées, so far as Tinker was concerned, were something that happened to other people.

Epilogue

Detective Sergeant Fraser boarded the Sunraysia train with a certain level of satisfaction. True, his raid on Chinatown had not ended well. But the Commissioner had told him there was trouble in the orange orchards and he thought Fraser was just the man for the job. And apparently there were Murray cod in the river which would be well worth the pursuit. He had packed his fishing rods in anticipation. With a song on his lips, Fraser stared out the window as the rail yards of North Melbourne hove into view. Life could indeed be a lot worse than this.

AUTHOR'S NOTE

It has long been a curious fact that my novels have been governed by serendipity. In one of this series I was intending to write about Lin Chung being kidnapped by pirates from the South China Sea, but I could not find out anything reliable about them. The internet was very new back then, and I was as yet unacquainted with it. So on my way home from Sunshine Court one day, during my tenure as a Legal Aid solicitor, I dropped in to the local library and resolved to have a brief look. If I could not find anything there and then, I decided, I would drop that plotline. Anything I write needs to have some grounding in historical fact. I entered the building and glanced at the returns trolley. Sitting on top of it was a book titled *Piracy in the South China Seas in the Early Twentieth Century*. I can take a hint.

For this book, I decided it was time to visit Williamstown, where my beloved mother grew up. The best source of contemporary information is always local newspapers. And so I typed 'Williamstown Chronicle March 1929' into the appropriate window on my computer. The first story which came to light was the extraordinary decision by the local council to grant a considerable sum of money to the Royal Victorian Institute for the Blind. Then, as now, governments at state and federal level seemed incapable of meeting the needs of their communities. Back then, the bottom tier of government came to the rescue. And Stanus Hedger really was a bit of a warlord. His father had also been a superintendent of the Institute for the Blind, and Hedger followed in his footsteps. His outburst against the Brushmakers' Union representatives is a verbatim quote from a contemporary account. The man was a law unto himself, but he appears to have been on the side of the angels.

Blind piano tuners and musicians were a priceless asset and source of funds for the Institute. It is absolutely true about Louis Braille being a musician and inventing braille notation for music as well as books. I was also tempted to write Tilly Aston into my story. She was an author who established the Victorian Association of Braille Writers. But my enthusiasm for Jennifer Barnes to represent the inmates instead rather took over that part of my book. Mr. Findlay—so far as we know—was as represented. The plot involving misdeeds at the Institute is entirely my own invention, however. There is not the slightest reason to conclude that any malfeasances would really have occurred there. The villain of that subplot is familiar to me. He is representative of a type whom I met all too often as a young working-class girl in Melbourne University's law faculty. A monstrous sense of entitlement and contempt for others seems to animate their spirits to the exclusion of all else.

Williamstown, now as then, is a singular place, resembling Tinker's hometown of Queenscliff in many ways. And I found out much more about it simply by walking around. The Anchor Hotel (or one very like it) was still there in my father's time, though it has long since vanished. Bill Crowe (the much-feared superintendent of the municipal gardens) I discovered from plaques on the outer wall of the precinct. And you may see the statue of Alfred Clark there. I put his statue in for no other reason than as a symbol of that restless desire to do good which once animated our body politic. Some early Victorian politicians were utter scoundrels, like the aptly named Sir Thomas Bent. He also has a statue, on Nepean Highway. Maybe I shall write about him one day. In an age when statuary has become very much a contested zone, I would like to make the point that at least some of these gentry do merit kindly remembrance.

In my last book, *Death In Daylesford,* I thought it was time that the younger members of Phryne's household were given a chance to do some detecting of their own. Readers seem to have admired that book, and the larger canvas this entails, and so I decided to pursue this further. I hope you enjoyed reading more about Tinker, Ruth ,and Jane.

And on a more personal note…I have had many cats in my life. All were unforgettable, but none more so than my Belladonna, who finally crossed the Rainbow Bridge as this book was nearing completion. Belladonna came into our lives as a replacement for our dear Kári, who used to sit on my lap constantly. I mourned her for a full year before feeling that the time had come for a new cat to be mine. My beloved has cats of his own, of course. Our cats mostly get on well together, but I wanted one who would accompany me on my solitary career as a writer, as Kári had. So off we went in March 2001 to a local veterinary clinic which often had a sign out front reading: kittens for adoption!

They had no young kittens, but three-month-old cats they had—four of them in a furry bundle. I eyed off the three fluffy blond kittens, but no sooner had I put my hand into their cage than a pair of black paws emerged from underneath, and Belladonna grabbed my hand and told her siblings: *Mine!* I took her home with me, mildly astonished at unexpectedly acquiring a black cat, rather than the tabby-and-white cats who had been the staple of my adulthood. If you wish, you may read more about Bella in my beloved's books *Dougal's Diary* and *When We Were Kittens*, but her crucial role in my career came earlier than that.

I discovered that when I was sitting at my Apple Mac writing away, Bella would come and sit beside me on my left. She had tried sitting on the mousepad, but quickly learned that I was not in favour of this. So on my left she would sit, quiet and content, watching me tap away at my strange plastic thing, until an hour had passed. Then she would extend her right paw and gently press the Caps Lock button. Because I don't look at the screen much as I type, there would generally be a whole paragraph of capitals before I realised what was happening. My attention thus secured, Belladonna would tell me it was time for some munchies for the devoted helpmeet—and why not do some of your Human exercises while you're at it?

So I would obey, and when I resumed writing she would settle down again to my left. When another hour had passed, she would repeat the process. After all, why not? It worked for her last time. As time went on, and my health deteriorated, I found myself more and more reliant on my cat in my writing. And when we weren't writing, she would sit on my lap and we would watch TV together. I wrote a great many novels with her invaluable assistance. And while it is good to have a consort who takes care of things like food and paying bills and housework and all that, you really can't write when you're sick without a devoted cat to help you. She lived beyond her twenty-first birthday, until one summer's day she went to sleep in the back garden under the trees and didn't wake up. She is interred beneath her favourite ash tree. I miss her so much, but I thank her for her devoted care of me. Now she lies at her ease in the Field of Reeds, receiving the obeisance due to the Princess of Cats.

Kerry Greenwood

READE ON FOR AN EXCERPT FROM
ANOTHER PHRYNE FISHER ADVENTURE,
DEATH IN DAYLESFORD,

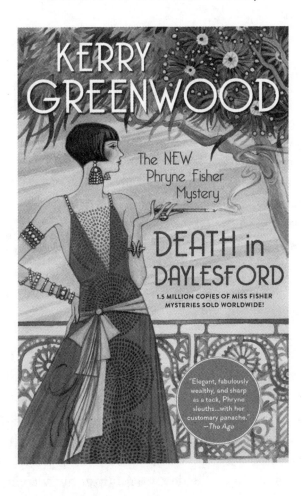

published in the U.S. by

Chapter One

The Sons of Mary seldom bother, for they have
*   inherited that good part;*
But the Sons of Martha favour their Mother of the
*   careful soul and the troubled heart.*
And because she lost her temper once, and because
*   she was rude to the Lord her Guest,*
Her Sons must wait upon Mary's Sons, world
*   without end, reprieve, or rest.*

—Rudyard Kipling, *The Sons of Martha*

It was a lazy, late summer's morning in St Kilda. The early sun was no longer the copper-coloured furnace of January, and instead of beating at the window with bronze gongs and hammers was knocking respectfully at the shutters, asking leave for admittance. Without, the tide was gently turning, lapping over the mid-ochre sands of the beach and promising light refreshment for anyone wanting a matitudinal paddle. Last night's windstorm had blown itself out, and through the open window drifted a cool, damp sensation of overnight rain.

Phryne Fisher rose from her bed, wrapped a turquoise satin dressing-gown around her impossibly elegant person, tied the cord, and tiptoed towards the bathroom, where a malachite bathtub and unlimited hot water awaited her. Pausing at the door, she turned and raked her boudoir with a long, ever so slightly greedy and thoroughly complacent look. She admired the wickedly crimson satin bedsheets. The hand-painted silk bedspread (the Book of Hours of Marie de France, now wantonly disordered, with its scenes of medieval life carelessly strewn over the aquamarine Chinese carpet). The half-empty crystal decanter (with matching balloon glasses, both empty) whose contents had been imported at absurd expense from the sunny vineyards of Armagnac. The outstretched paws and arched back of the sleeping cat Ember, jet-black and sleek with good living. And the jet-black eyebrows and perfect features of Lin Chung, who arched his golden back and burrowed further down between the sheets. She admired his bare, muscular shoulder, smiled with a thrill of retrospective delight, and entered the bathroom.

From her extensive collection of bath salts, Phryne chose the china pot labelled *Gardenia* and emptied a goodly pile into the shaped malachite tub. She opened both brass taps and watched as the twin torrents of water swirled and effervesced. A warm, fragrant aroma of English Country Garden caressed her nostrils. Phryne slipped out of her gown and lowered herself into the water. She surveyed her slender body with a certain level of satisfaction, her imagination still ravished by the previous night's passion. A woman on the brink of thirty always nurtured secret suspicions of fading charms—even someone with Phryne's armour-plated self-esteem. Yet, judging by her lover's awed reactions and responses, it would seem that this was far from being the case. Lin himself was utterly unchanged by marriage. So many businessmen let themselves go; their waistlines expanded along with their incomes.

Lin's copper-coloured body was as smooth and strong as a teen-age boy's. The only sign of change she had observed was a small knot of ebony hair in the centre of his delectable chest, with the merest suggestion of a line of down heading due southwards. Her tongue had given this matter some considerable exploration the previous evening.

Phryne grinned, and began to soap her person. *I'm well and truly on the shelf now, and the world can watch me not care*, she told herself. How fortunate that her idiotic father had shown the fore-sight to dismiss her from his baronial presence some years ago, otherwise she would have been visited with a plague of suitors of varying degrees of loathsomeness. For the English nobility, an unmarried daughter of twenty-nine was a matter of some uneasiness, somewhere on the continuum between Unsuitable Entanglements and Failure to Ride to Hounds. Her father's threat to cut her off with a shilling for gross disobedience had been rendered toothless when, upon obtaining her majority, Phryne had calmly removed her assets from her father's rapacious fingers. To compound his sense of disgrace, his other daughter Eliza had combined the twin horrors of Socialism and Unnatural Vice.

Phryne's opinion of her father had not been improved by this attitude. Socialism was frequently affected in noble families, and lesbianism could easily be forgiven in polite society given that Eliza's Chosen had been of impeccably noble birth. Once you were in Debrett's, unnatural vice was magically transmuted into Passionate Friendship, which had been socially acceptable ever since Lady Eleanor Butler and the Hon. Sarah Ponsonby had set up house together as the Ladies of Llangollen. Even the Duke of Wellington had visited them. Although that said less than it might, since the Iron Duke was renowned for not giving even one hoot for popular prejudice. Nevertheless, Father had broken off all contact with both daughters, and all his attention, such as it was, had been lavished on his son and heir Thos. Of whom the best that could be said was that the future Baron of Richmond-upon-Thames would be a worthy heir to the present one. Neither the present nor future lords would ever visit either Phryne or Eliza. Phryne felt she could moderate her grief.

She sank down deeper into the smooth embrace of the steaming waters. It was so much easier dealing with the Chinese. Lin's wife Camellia was a typical exemplar of Chinese womanhood: small of body and voice, discreet, self-assured, and possessing a will of pure adamant. The greeting she gave Phryne whenever they chanced to meet was gracious, polite, and filled with iron Confucian certainty. *You are my husband's honoured concubine and I trust you implicitly. You may walk through Chinatown in perfect security. Anyone who offers you offence may expect consequences of considerable severity, up to and including a small battleaxe to the back of the head. I, on the other hand, am Lin's First Lady. I have my position, and you have yours. We understand each other perfectly.*

Phryne sat up in the bath and listened. Noises Off appeared to be happening. Since Dot was unlikely to outrage her maidenly modesty by attempting to bring her employer breakfast in bed when Phryne was Entertaining, this must mean that Lin himself was doing the honours, with the assistance of Mr and Mrs Butler. She climbed out of the bath, dried herself off with two towels of spotless white cotton, and wrapped herself anew in her turquoise silk robe. 'Do I smell eggs and bacon, Lin?' she enquired, opening the bedroom door.

Lin Chung pushed a prodigiously laden tea trolley into the centre of the boudoir and gestured to the two cushioned seats. 'Eggs, bacon, and all the accoutrements of an English breakfast,' he announced. 'I believe there are roast tomatoes, sautéed mushrooms, and sausages made from absurdly pampered pigs. There is also toast, Earl Grey tea, marmalade, and strawberry jam. Will the Silver Lady join me at breakfast?'

Phryne lifted the lids of the chafing dishes one by one and inhaled deeply. 'I was scarcely expecting such luxury. How did you manage to get the trolley upstairs? Was Cantonese magic involved at all?'

Lin folded his hands in an imitation of a stage Chinaman. 'Ah! The East is filled with mysteries.'

Phryne gently pushed him down into one of the chairs. 'Well, yes, Lin, otherwise why would it be called the Mysterious East? But how—oh, of course, I forgot: the dumb waiter.'

Mr Butler had of late come down with a serious outburst of Home Handyman and had installed a dumb waiter where one of Phryne's wardrobes had been. Phryne had been about to object in the strongest terms when she recollected that Mr Butler was, it must be admitted, getting on in years and that, moreover, the day would inevitably come when Dot would finally achieve holy matrimony with Hugh Collins and might not be available to attend upon Phryne. Yet refreshments must be conveyed to the lady of the House in her first-floor bedroom. So, the dumb waiter had been installed, skilfully concealed behind a Chinese silk screen when not in use.

For some time, conversation gave place to unbridled gluttony. It was not Phryne's habit to eat breakfast at all, beyond a French roll and a morning coffee, but erotic adventures awoke her hunger for other forms of bodily delights. As Phryne closed the lids on the devastated remains of the hot dishes and looked with devotion at her beautiful lover, he reached out his right hand and closed it around her left. 'Phryne? May I ask you something?'

'Ask me anything, and I shall answer.'

'Yesterday I saw Bert and Cec driving their cab, and as their fare debouched right in front of me, I enquired after their health.'

'As one does.' Phryne buttered herself another piece of toast and smeared it with marmalade. 'And how did they respond?'

'Cec looked inscrutable and muttered something, and Bert gave it as his opinion that he was a menace to shipping. What does this mean?'

Phryne clasped his hand tighter and raised it to her lips. 'It means he is in robust spirits. Your English is perfect Oxford, but I presume Australian argot did not feature in the curriculum at Balliol College.'

'No, it didn't. Is this like a bald man must always be called Curly?'

'And a red-haired man is always Bluey. It's similar, but...not quite the same.' Phryne pondered for a long moment how Lin Chung had got along with the rowdy undergraduates, deciding there were several reasons why he would have flourished there. Balliol was one of the more intellectual seats of learning at Oxford. His imperturbable calm would have unnerved most of the bullies. And the whiff of serious money would have inspired automatic respect.

As she nodded to herself, Phryne became aware that Lin was studying her closely.

'You are perhaps wondering how I fared at Balliol, being so blatantly Oriental?'

'I was,' Phryne confessed.

'It was largely trouble-free. Don't forget I had Li Pen with me. Having one's own servant in college lent a certain cachet. And...' He paused and allowed himself a complacent smile of recollection.

'And Li Pen was also available to chastise the rowdier elements under the influence of excessive alcohol?' Phryne suggested.

'He was. It is his duty and pleasure to serve.'

'I trust no one was seriously injured?'

'He inserted three of them into an ornamental fountain. They suffered nothing worse than bruises, both to the person and personality.'

'Youthful high spirits?'

'That was indeed the official verdict.'

'I see. Lin?' Phryne leaned back seductively. 'How soon must you depart?'

He gazed with appreciation at a glimpse of perfect ivory breast beginning to escape from her robe. 'I have a meeting at noon.'

Phryne glanced at her bedroom clock: a modest walnut arrangement standing on the mantelpiece. 'It's only nine thirty. Plenty of time.' She leaned closer to Lin. 'Tomorrow I am departing for the countryside.'

'And which district will be favoured by your august presence?'

'Daylesford. I have received an unusual request, and I am minded to investigate. Do you know of the place?'

'A little. They are building a new lake there. And, unfortunately, the market gardens of the local Chinese will be submerged by it. There has been a great deal of talk about it in the *Daylesford Advocate*. Everybody wants the lake, but nobody wants a rather expensive road diversion. But no one has spared a thought for the market gardeners.'

'That is very careless of them. Perhaps I should intervene on their behalf. Or perhaps the Lin family...?' She allowed the sentence to hang delicately in the air. Lin leaned back in his chair and retied his crimson dressing gown around his delectable body.

'There is no need, Phryne. Measures have already been taken. The gardeners are being moved to Maldon and elsewhere. The land did not actually belong to our people; it was theirs by grace and favour, and now it is being resumed by the local community. I will send someone around with copies of the newspaper from my files, if you like?'

'That would be most helpful. Lin, do you happen to have files on every town in Victoria?'

He laughed aloud. 'Only those where my people are involved, directly or indirectly—which is perhaps more than you would think. Only thus can we maintain our honoured position here.'

Honoured position! But at least there had been no massacres of the Chinese in Victoria, thanks to Constable Thomas Cooke of the Castlemaine police station, representing in his lonely self the awesome majesty of Queen Victoria and her laws. But fear, loathing, ill-will, and general xenophobia there had most certainly been, and it had not yet abated. Still, divining that Lin would like the subject changed, and quickly, she returned to the subject of her own forthcoming visit to the region.

She stood up, reached into her purse, and unfolded a letter, handing it to him. Lin perused the following with raised eyebrows.

The Spa
Hepburn Springs
23 February 1929

Dear Miss Fisher,

I write to you at the recommendation of Dr Elizabeth MacMillan, who has visited here on occasion. I know that you served with distinction in the war, and you will be aware that all too many of our brave survivors suffer from shell shock. The Army and the Ministry offer them little sympathy, and even less help. They are not shirkers or cowards, but men who have endured more than flesh and blood can manage. At my spa, I am attempting to provide my patients with the rest, recuperation, and care they so badly need. I would like to invite you to see my establishment for yourself, after which I hope you may see your way clear to supporting my endeavours. Would you care to join me for dinner this coming Friday?

Yours sincerely,
Herbert Spencer (Capt., ret'd)

'What do you make of that?'

Lin slipped one hand inside his dressing-gown and ran his hand over his chest. Phryne suppressed the erotic thrill that surged through her body. Any information this admirably well-informed man could supply beforehand might be vital. 'The first thing I should mention is that Hepburn Springs is not Daylesford. While the two communities are contiguous, they have quite different characters. Hepburn Springs is further into the mountain forest.'

'How far away from Daylesford?'

'They are about three miles apart, town centre to town centre. Though there are houses all along the road connecting them.'

'And the spa?'

'It was once a place of secret women's rituals among the local Aboriginal tribes, who were, naturally, comprehensively dispossessed last century. The spa is said to have extraordinary healing properties. And now this Captain Spencer is using it for shell-shock victims? Intriguing. Your Captain sounds like a kind and generous man.'

'Indeed. And how is Daylesford so different?'

'Hepburn Springs is a place of quiet refinement. Daylesford, which is far larger and more spacious, is rather more boisterous. And it possesses a remarkable curiosity.' Phryne raised an eyebrow. Lin matched her by raising both of his own, with matching grin. 'There is a licensed premises called the Temperance Hotel.'

'That does appear to be one of the less successful advertising decisions in history,' Phryne remarked.

'So one would think, at first glance. However, the pub does serve wine, beer, and cider; only spirits are forbidden. This appears to be a compromise widely acceptable in the local community.'

How very Australian! Vociferous arguments in favour of temperance would be made so long as drunken husbands staggered home from the local pub ready to take out their incoherent frustration with the world on their long-suffering wives and children. But while it was possible to get rolling drunk on beer alone, it required a good deal more focus to attain the condition of violent drunkenness; thus, while many Australians had agitated for total prohibition (which had worked so well in America), a substantial body of opinion held that such a compromise was both achievable and prudent.

Phryne smiled at her lover. 'I would be intrigued to visit this place. Perhaps, when I have seen Captain Spencer, I should pay a visit to Daylesford as well. Do any of the other pubs serve spirits?'

Lin chuckled. 'They do. But married patrons are severely discouraged—by their wives—from visiting such places, whereas a few drinks at the Temperance Hotel is something the women of Daylesford can accommodate for their hard-working husbands. Also—' Lin paused, and smiled the smile of a fallen angel '—apparently one of the barmaids is a famous beauty. Her hand in marriage is comprehensively sought.'

'But not yet attained?'

'Not thus far. And I imagine that the rivalry between her suitors sells many a drink on the premises.'

'No doubt. You mentioned wine and cider as well as beer. The wine is because of the Swiss Italians, I expect. Do they make it locally?'

Lin nodded.

'But cider? It is hardly a common drink.'

'This would be the local Cornish influence.'

'Lin, you are a minefield of information.' She squeezed his hand. 'It is now almost ten. You said that you have a meeting at noon?'

'I do, Silver Lady, and I must depart a half hour before.'

'But until then?' She leaned forward, allowing the front of her gown to fall open.

Lin's almond eyes flickered over Phryne's breasts for a moment. 'Until then, I would be pleased to accompany you once more among the chrysanthemums. If it be your will?'

Phryne reached out and took his face between her hands. Her mouth opened, and she traced the tip of her tongue around his lips. 'It is indeed my will.'

Lin's hand closed around her left breast, and Phryne stood up, reaching for the cord of his dressing-gown. She began to chant a poem she had recently discovered. It was called 'Butterflies in Love with Flowers,' and she hoped that Lin might know it, even though it was originally written in Mandarin, and his family spoke Cantonese.

> *'I would rather drink to intoxication.*
> *One should sing when one has wine in hand,*
> *But drinking to escape offers no reprieve.*
> *I do not mind that my clothes are getting looser.*
> *My lover is worthy of desire.'*

Lin's strong arms pulled her body close as their garments fell unregarded onto the carpet. 'Come, little flower, the butterfly is impatient,' he whispered, and he carried her, without effort, back to bed.

BIBLIOGRAPHY

Buckrich, Judith, *A History of the Royal Victorian Institute for the Blind 1866–2004*, Australian Scholarly Publishing, Melbourne, 2004.

A Guide to Charity and to the Philanthropic Work of Victoria, Charity Organisation Society of Melbourne, Melbourne, 1912.

Hanson, Neil, *First Blitz: The Secret German Plan to Raze London to the Ground in 1918*, Transworld, London, 2008.

Van Gulik, Robert, *The Chinese Bell Murders*, Michael Joseph, London, 1958.

Kwan, Choi Wah, *The Right Word In Cantonese*, The Commercial Press, Hong Kong, 1989.

ACKNOWLEDGMENTS

To Tom Lane, prince of scholars; Sally Zixue Yang for her invaluable assistance with all matters Chinese; Susan Tonkin and Ann Solomon for being everlastingly helpful and encouraging; Mrs. Raie Lee for her invaluable reminiscences of growing up in Williamstown; Bernard Muir and Lucy Sussex for general inspiration; my beloved wizard David Greagg; my adored sister Amanda Butcher; and the immortal memory of my much-lamented sister Janet, the first inspiration for my most famous creation. And also to my beloved Belladonna (see Author's Note). My thanks also to the wonderful people at Vision Australia and the City of Hobsons Bay Library, who put up with my constant requests for more information with admirable helpfulness. Above all to Ali Lavau, editor most extraordinary, and all the team at Allen & Unwin. And to Chris and the team at Seddon Deadly Sins cafe for keeping me royally caffeinated and refreshed throughout.

ABOUT THE AUTHOR

Kerry Greenwood is the author of more than fifty novels, a book of short stories, six nonfiction works, and the editor of two collections of crime writing. Her beloved Phryne Fisher series has become a successful television series, *Miss Fisher's Murder Mysteries*, which has been sold around the world. She is also the author of the contemporary crime series featuring Corinna Chapman, baker and reluctant investigator. The most recent Corinna Chapman novel was *The Spotted Dog*. In addition, Kerry is the author of several books for young adults and the Delphic Women series. When not writing, Kerry has been an advocate in magistrates' courts for the Legal Aid Commission and, in the 2020 Australia Day Honours, was awarded the Medal of the Order of Australia (OAM) for services to literature. She is not married, has no children, is the co-warden of a Found Cats' Home and lives with an accredited wizard. In her spare time, she stares blankly out the window.